P9-ELN-880

Sally Quilford has had stories published in most of the major women's magazines. She is a columnist with *Writers' Forum* magazine and has also had articles published in *The New Writer*. Sally lives in Derbyshire with her husband and four West Highland terriers. When the weather is nice enough she writes in her shed, hence her own 'publisher' on her Kindle e-book being labelled 'Tales From the Shed'. Her proudest moment so far, not counting the birth of her children and the day she married, was when the King of Twitter, Stephen Fry, linked to her blog from his Twitter page, describing her as 'pleasantly sane'.

Follow the author on Twitter — @Quillers

THE STEPS OF THE PRIORY

When Becky Wilson and her friend, Jed
Alsop, leave a baby on the steps of the
Harcourt family's home, their actions have
far-reaching ramifications for all concerned. Becky marries Charles Harcourt,
but he is keeping the secret of what
happened to the little boy, who is being
raised as his nephew, Jack Daventry.
Spanning the First and Second World
Wars, *The Steps of the Priory* follows the
Harcourt family, and the people connected to them, through love, loss and
redemption.

Books by Sally Quilford
Published by The House of Ulverscroft:

THE SECRET OF HELENA'S BAY
BELLA'S VINEYARD
A COLLECTOR OF HEARTS
MY TRUE COMPANION
AN IMITATION OF LOVE
SUNLIT SECRETS
MISTLETOE MYSTERY
OUR DAY WILL COME
BONFIRE MEMORIES
MIDNIGHT TRAIN
TAKE MY BREATH AWAY
THE GHOST OF CHRISTMAS PAST

SALLY QUILFORD

THE STEPS OF THE PRIORY

Complete and Unabridged

ULVERSCROFT
Leicester

First published in Great Britain in 2012

First Large Print Edition
published 2014

A catalogue record for this book is available
from the British Library.

ISBN 978–1–4448–2073–7

Published by
F. A. Thorpe (Publishing)
Anstey, Leicestershire

Set by Words & Graphics Ltd.
Anstey, Leicestershire
Printed and bound in Great Britain by
T. J. International Ltd., Padstow, Cornwall

This book is printed on acid-free paper

1

1917

Becky ran through the back streets of Stony Newton holding the bundle in her arms, closely followed by Jed. The pit siren squealed, calling the men to the nightshift. Soon they would start pouring out of the houses and pubs. She knew that many would leave it to the very last minute. That might just give her time to get through the town without being seen.

'What are you going to do with him?' asked Jed, breathlessly.

'I'm going to put him on the Harcourts' doorstep. He'll be looked after at the Priory. They're rich, and happy.'

'Why not take him to the hospital?'

'They'll ask questions at the hospital, stupid! We've got to time it right. I saw Miss Patricia go out in her car earlier. Her mum and dad have gone to London for a Buckingham Palace garden party. Mr. Harcourt is getting a medal for his war work.'

'So if no one's in, how can they help the baby?'

'The servants are there. We just have to make sure they don't see us. Now are you going to help me, or are you going to keep asking daft questions?'

'Of course I'll help you. I'm your boyfriend, ain't I?'

Becky had no answer for a voice so full of hope. She reached the edge of the town. The Priory was at the top of a hill, overseeing them all. As a child she used to dream of living there. She doubted that would ever happen, but she could at least give the baby a chance. She had a fantasy of the Harcourts raising him as their own. He would never want for anything.

'Come on,' she said. 'You can keep a look-out for anyone coming.'

'Becky, I've just thought. What if the servants don't realise he's there?'

'He'll probably cry and they'll hear him.'

'He hasn't cried much so far. Are you sure he's still alive?'

'Yes, he's breathing. I checked.'

'It might have been better to . . . '

Becky spun around, and fixed Jed with a hard gaze. 'Don't say that. Don't you even dare, Jed Alsop, or you can get lost right now.'

'Sorry.' Jed held up his hands. 'I know you're right. Come on, I'll open t'gate.'

They stole through the night, up the

driveway to the Priory steps. Becky lay the child down on the top step. 'Don't worry, little Charlie,' she said. 'Someone will take care of you.' She placed a kiss on his forehead.

'Charlie? In't that the name of Mr. Harcourt's son as went to war?'

'Shut up, Jed.' She wrapped the swathe of bandages more tightly around the baby. There was a burst of light in the distance. It moved across the steps, and towards the end of the building, like a searchlight, seeking out their secrets.

'Becky, come on, there's a car coming from Factory Lane.'

Becky took one last look at the child, swallowing back a lump the size of an apple in her throat. She followed Jed back down the driveway.

They were out of the gate and into Factory Lane when Patricia Harcourt's car nearly hit them.

'Bugger,' said Becky, when they dashed to the other side of the road. 'I hope she didn't see us.'

They ran back towards the town, only slowing down when they met the miners on their way to and from the pit.

'Bit late for you two lovebirds to be out, in't it?' said Len, a miner of about forty. 'Your dad'll not be pleased with you, Becky Wilson.'

'My dad knows I'm out,' said Becky.

He addressed his companion. 'I'd not let my lass run around the streets at night, would you, George?'

'No, I wouldn't. That Sam Jenkins'll have to stay away now your dad's back. Frank'll have his guts for garters if he knows he's been calling on you. Go on, get home.'

It was the last place Becky wanted to go, but she did not want to argue. She and Jed walked in silence to her street. She saw movement in the distance. A young woman walked out of the shadows.

'Oh, no,' said Becky. 'It's Fletcher the Filcher.'

Unperturbed by the insult, Maggie Fletcher held out her hand. 'Have you got any money, Becky?'

'Haven't you, Maggie? Weren't you paid today?'

'Me dad's had it for t'pub. You don't half talk posh. You're not like anyone else here. Jed, have you got any money? I want some chips.'

'Here,' said Jed, taking a few pennies from his pocket.

'You're a nice lad, Jed. Everyone says so,' said Maggie. 'Don't know why you hang around with that stuck-up tart.'

'At least she didn't ask what we'd been doing,' said Becky when Maggie had run away with her gains.

'I don't think Maggie's interested in other people's problems,' said Jed. 'She's got enough of her own. Her dad's brain has gone because of all the booze.'

'Do you feel sorry for her?'

'Sort of.'

'I don't. My mam says there's no excuse for thieving.'

'But it's alright to drop babies on doorsteps, is it?'

Becky slapped him and run away, brushing red-hot tears from her eyes.

When she reached home, all was in darkness. She crept upstairs to the back bedroom. It was furnished with a single mattress and that was covered with a thin blanket and a pile of old coats.

She looked with longing at the adjoining wall. If her father had not come home, she would have been sleeping in with her mother, like she had been for the past three years.

She lay down on the mattress. She had put it next to the wall to be as close to her mam as possible. She could hear her father talking in a low voice.

'Come on, Myra. I've been away for three years.'

Her mother's response was less clear.

'You're not stopping me, woman. I've thought of nowt else for months, out there fighting for this country, then trapped in that hospital.' Becky heard the bed springs start to play out a rhythm, followed by her mother's muffled sobs.

She clamped her eyes shut and said a prayer. 'God bless mam and God bless little Charlie,' she whispered over and over again, to shut out the sounds from next door.

She went to sleep hating her father and wishing he had died in the war.

★　★　★

Patricia Harcourt swore and slammed on the brakes. 'Bloody kids. Why do their parents let them out so late?'

Charles was less interested in the children than the pain to his shoulder, caused by the sudden jolt of the car. With Patricia at the wheel there were lots of those. He wondered how high she was.

'I'm sorry, darling. Does it still hurt?'

'Of course it still hurts, Patty.'

She turned into the entrance to the Priory. 'The gates are open. Do you think Mater and Pater could be back?'

'I can't imagine they've rushed back to see me.'

'Oh come on, darling. You know how proud they are of you. It's just rotten bad luck that this garden party was on the same date as your arrival home.'

'Technically, I've been home for six months. They could have come to see me at the hospital. You did.'

'Well, I had nothing better to do after I left the sanatorium. Besides, your face is not that bad. I think mother and father expected much worse.'

'Thank you.' He picked at the puckered scar on his cheekbone.

'I've heard some airmen had all their faces burned off. Ears and everything.'

'You haven't seen the rest of my body.'

'I don't want to. No offence darling, but you are my twin brother.'

She pulled the car up to the front of the house.

'Where are the servants?' asked Charles, seeing the house in darkness.

'I gave them the night off. I thought perhaps you wouldn't want to see anyone yet. Besides, I'm sure old Stephens spies on me for father. We'll have a blast on our own.'

Patty got out of the car and skipped up the steps of the Priory, almost treading on the

7

bundle that lay there. Charles followed her more slowly.

'Charlie, it's a baby. And look at this. It's wrapped in Harcourt's bandages.' She picked the child up and carried him into the hallway. 'Oh, poor little thing.' She pulled away some of the bandages. 'It's a little boy!'

'Dear God, who can have left him there?'

'I don't know, but . . . ' Patty's eyes filled with tears. 'But I dreamed of this, Charles. Of God leaving me a baby.'

'So you have been taking drugs again? I thought so by your driving.'

'No. Well, some, but that's not it. Charlie, he's the answer to my prayers.'

'That's the drug talking. We need to get the police involved. Or get him to the hospital.'

'No, listen. You don't know what's been happening. We'll take him into the drawing-room first. There's a fire in there. We can warm him up and find some milk.'

A little while later, Patty stood in front of the fire, holding the baby in her arms, gently tipping warm milk into his mouth. 'There you are, sweetheart.'

'Now are you going to tell me why we're not involving the authorities?'

Patty ignored him. 'It's a pity we couldn't get a bottle. He's very quiet, Charlie. I don't like it. Babies should cry.'

'Don't ignore my question.'

Patty sat down on the sofa, and held the baby to her, looking like a wild-eyed Madonna. 'Charlie, listen to me, darling. John and I have been trying for a baby for absolutely ages. I got pregnant the last time he was home on leave, but I lost it after a few weeks. I haven't dared write and tell him. I thought I'd wait till he got home.' Patty paused for a moment. 'The baby would have been due by now. He needs a son and heir otherwise his brother will get the family pile when he dies. You know how much they hate each other.'

'For God's sake, Patty, you're only twenty-five. You've got loads of chances to have a baby without stealing another woman's.' Charlie poured himself a drink from the decanter on the side table, and lit a cigarette. He sat down on the chair opposite his sister.

'No, that's just it, Charlie. I can't. There's something wrong with me. John doesn't know. He's all for trying again when he gets home. If I don't give him a baby, he'll divorce me. There was already that thing with his driver. Why they let women do those jobs I don't know. I have to keep him. He can't leave me for someone else. He will if I don't present him with a son.' Her voice held a note of desperation. 'You're the answer to my prayers, aren't you, my beautiful little baby boy?'

'I'm sorry, darling, really I am. But you're not seriously considering saying that this child is yours?'

'I was due around now. I could say I'd given birth after all. I've heard about it from other women. They say it happens when you're carrying twins and one of them miscarries.'

'This is total madness,' said Charles. 'You can't do it. That child belongs to someone. Whoever it is will need medical attention. They should at least be arrested for just dumping a baby. What is this world coming to?'

'Charlie, you've got to help me.'

'No, I'm not doing that. Don't you think the servants would have noticed if you were in labour tonight? Or even that you weren't expecting. It does show, you know. I'm going to telephone the police.' He went to the telephone and lifted the receiver.

Patty put the baby onto the sofa and ran across the room towards him and grabbed the receiver. 'Charlie, please. I'll take him away from here. To London. I can say he was born there. Then in a week or two I'll write to mother and father telling them the good

10

news. But I won't come back for ages. I hate this place anyway. No one will ever know.'

'For God's sake, Patty. This is just like you. All you ever think about is what you want. What about that child? If he could speak, what do you think he'd want?'

'He wants a mother who loves him.'

'How do you know you'll love him? You've got no reason to bond with him. He's not yours.'

'He is now. I know he was left there to answer my prayers. I'm taking him to London tonight. Now, if you wish to ring the police and set them on me, that's up to you. But I'm leaving.'

'What if his mother comes back for him?'

'We'll deny all knowledge of it. The servants haven't seen him and I was in London. She's hardly going to create a fuss, given that she dumped him there in the first place. She must be evil. He deserves better than a mother like that.'

Charles thought that the child probably deserved a better mother than Patty, but he knew better than to say so. He was tired and his body ached all over. He did not have the energy for one of his sister's tantrums. 'We can't do this, Patty.'

Her eyes shone, and Charles guessed she had taken more than a little cocaine. She was completely loaded. She went across the room and stopped in front of a display cabinet. 'If you don't do this, Charlie, I'll kill myself. I will . . . ' She took out her father's old hunting knife and pressed it against the angry red scars that already marred her wrists.

'Come on, Patty. Let's not do all this again.'

'I will kill myself if you don't let me have this baby.'

Charles knew it was a bluff, like all the other times Patty had threatened to commit suicide. He thought she had learned her lesson when she almost died a few months earlier. Charles realised that was probably as a result of losing the baby, but still did not believe his sister capable of taking her own life. She thought too much of herself. Nevertheless, he could not afford to take chances. Patty might never really commit suicide, but she was capable of leaving everyone a big mess to clean up whilst she languished in a sanatorium, enjoying the extra medication.

She pressed the blade to her wrist. 'I'll do it.'

'Keep your voice down. The servants may be back soon. You really think you can be a mother to this child, do you? When you're threatening to kill yourself every other year?'

'I won't do that if I've got a baby, Charlie. I promise. But I've got to have him. If John leaves me . . . ' She pressed the tip of the knife against her skin. It was enough to draw blood, but without doing any damage.

'You can't go alone,' he said. 'Who'll hold onto him whilst you drive?'

'You're going to help me?' Patty smiled triumphantly, as she always did when she got her own way. She tossed the knife back into the display cabinet and shut the door.

'I must still be suffering from concussion,' he said. 'At least that's what I'll tell the police when they arrest us.'

★   ★   ★

Patty sat in the back seat, with the baby wrapped in a blanket, whilst Charles drove the car. 'I'll call him John,' she said. 'No. That'll be confusing. Jack is a nice name, isn't it, Charlie? Jack Daventry.'

He slowed to pass through the Priory gates. 'Someone's there,' he said. 'On the other side of the road.' Patty put her face to the window.

'Don't let her see you, Patty.'

'Don't worry. That's just Maggie Fletcher, the thieving little minx. Father caught her stealing some money from the office the other day. I would have sacked her, but she gave

13

him some sob story about how her dad always took her money.'

'Father can afford to be magnanimous,' said Charles, bitterly. 'All that money he's made from the war.'

★   ★   ★

Becky bolted out of bed early in the morning and ran down to the privy in the back yard. She reached under the seat and found the wad of cotton dressings her mother always kept hidden there. She was putting one into her blood-soaked drawers when her father opened the door. Instead of closing it, he stood there, looking at her.

'Go away, dad.' She pulled down her dress, feeling the pad lying awkward between her thighs.

'I want you to go to t'factory and get some work, lass. You're old enough now.'

'Mum wants me to carry on with my studies, dad. I got into the high school.'

'High school don't put money on t'table, Becky. Get yourself sorted out lass, and go down to Harcourt's.' He slammed the door of the privy shut. Becky was just about to readjust the bulky dressing when he opened it again. 'I'm off to t'pit to see if they'll take me on. Tell your mother to get out of bed.

14

There's work to be done.'

Becky waited until she was sure her father had left the house, then went back inside and cleaned up the house as best she could. Like all the other houses on South Street, there were only two rooms downstairs. The parlour, which was the best room, and the kitchen, which was where they lived. It still took her well over an hour to clean it all. Her belly ached. Once or twice she had to hold something nearby as the pain gripped and swelled and a thin sheen of sweat covered her brow.

Afterwards she crept upstairs to her mother's room. The room that had been hers too, until her father came home. 'Mam, are you awake? I've made you a cup of tea.'

'Thanks, angel. Put it on the side there. I'll get up in a minute. Your father'll be back soon . . . '

'I've done the cleaning, mam. You rest a bit longer. I'll look out for him and give you a shout when I see him coming up the street.'

'Come here.'

Becky approached the bedside. 'Give your mam a kiss. Are you alright, my baby?'

Becky lay down next to her mother, and was quickly engulfed in comforting arms. In the years that followed, she would try to remember the aroma of that morning. Coal tar soap, underarm sweat and the musky smell of bedding that had not been changed for over a week. It did not put her off snuggling in closer because it was familiar; something she had come to know well in all the years spent sleeping next to her mother. There was a newer scent, which she supposed was her father. She blocked that out. 'I'm bleeding, mam. Lots of it.'

'Did you find the cotton Gamgees, duck? Did you know what to do with them?'

'Yes.'

'Good girl. They're much better than those dirty old rags. My baby's had to grow up quickly, hasn't she?' Her mother kissed her head, stroking her hair back from her face. 'We'll have a good talk about things later.'

'Dad says I can't go the high school anymore, mam.'

'We'll see about that, angel.'

'Why can't I come back and sleep in with you, mam? I don't want him to hurt you again.'

'Shh, it's all done with now, love. Shh . . . '

'Mam?'

'What, baby?'

'Tell me about the time you saw the king outside the chippy.'

'Well, I was going for our supper one Friday. It was the week your nana came up

16

from Wales to visit. Do you remember?'

'Yes.'

'I thought I'd treat us to a fish supper and I let you stay up late. Remember?'

'Yes . . . '

'And you'd had a cold, so hadn't eaten a lot that week.'

'Yes, I remember. Tell me about the king.'

'It was the old king, mind you. King Edward. Standing right outside the chippy, waiting for them to cook some fresh chips. And he says to me, 'Hello, Myra, I haven't seen you since you made your debut in court.''

'What's a debut?' Becky knew because her mother had told her a dozen times. She also knew her important role in the storytelling game. It was to ask the right questions and to believe the answers.

2

July 1919

'The good news,' said Mr. Harcourt, standing on a large wooden crate, 'is that we're officially not at war anymore. The Treaty of Versailles was signed only the other day.'

Everyone cheered, despite the fact that for them the war had been over since the Armistice of the previous year.

'The bad news,' he continued, 'is that we have to let some of you go.'

There was a general murmur of dissent among the assembled workers, most of whom were women. They stood in a crowd on the factory floor, surrounded by the drums holding the Gamgee tissues. Sunlight shone through the windows, throwing up fine sheets of dust. A few of the workers coughed and snuffled, wiping clogged-up noses on the back of their sleeves.

Charles Harcourt stood on another crate, next to his father. The workers averted their eyes, concentrating on Mr. Harcourt the elder. Except Becky. She looked straight at him. 'I know, I know,' Mr. Harcourt said, raising a hand. 'But there won't be as much need for bandages now. We're already seeing a fall in orders from hospitals and the military. The other good news is that my son, Captain Charles Harcourt, whom you all know fought bravely in the war, is coming to join us as a manager. The idea, of course, is that he will eventually take over from me.' This was followed by muted applause.

Not even Charles' own father looks directly at him, thought Becky. She could not understand why. He was still as handsome as ever. Even with the burn marks on his cheek and neck. He caught her eye, and her first instinct was to look away. Instead she smiled shyly, to let him know she was his friend no matter how many scars he had.

'My son has many ideas for the firm, so with any luck, even if we have to let you go this year, we can bring you back in the future.'

Only then did the enormity of the situation hit Becky. She was the last one to join Harcourt Surgical Supplies Ltd. She would be one of the first out.

'So, I hope you'll all welcome my son to the factory and help him as he learns the ropes. Do you have anything to say, Charles?'

Charles Harcourt muttered something to his father, which was lost on everyone else. Whatever it was, it took Mr. Harcourt by surprise. 'Very well, you're all dismissed. Except Rebecca Wilson. Rebecca, will you stay behind please?' Mr. Harcourt spoke kindly enough, but still Becky worried what she might have done wrong.

'Yes, Mr. Harcourt,' she said. She saw Maggie Fletcher hanging back as the others filed away, and mouthed 'get lost' to her. Maggie did not move at first, until Jed Alsop passed her and she followed him out.

'Are you sure you should be here today, Rebecca? Isn't your mother's funeral at two o'clock?'

'Yes, sir, but my dad said I had to come into work this morning as we can't afford to lose too much money.'

'You won't lose money, Rebecca.' It was Charles Harcourt who spoke. 'Go home now, and take the rest of the day off. And tomorrow if you need it.'

'I don't know if . . . ' said Mr. Harcourt.

'I'm sure we can spare her,' said Charles.

'If you say so, Charles. If you say so. Run along, Rebecca. Give your father my best regards and tell him we are all terribly sorry for his loss.'

It was my loss, thought Becky. Not his. 'Yes, sir.'

'We're very sorry for your loss too,' said Charles.

Becky smiled up at him. 'Thank you, sir.'

As she left the factory, she knew that wild horses would not stop her from going into work the next day.

★　★　★

'I just don't see why we need to lay people off, father. You've made enough out of the war to pay their wages for some time.' They sat in George Harcourt's office. The desk was piled high with the account books George Harcourt had been pouring over that day.

'Not when we'll be operating at a loss, Charles,' said George Harcourt. 'And I do wish you'd stop reminding me about the money we made from the war. Someone had to supply surgical dressings. What makes you so bitter about all this?'

'Perhaps it was because when I was in hospital, the only connection I had with you was being wrapped up in Harcourt bandages.' With Harcourt plasters covering his open wounds, and Harcourt cotton wool used to clean them. It brought home to him the reality of the family business. Wealth acquired because people were injured in a brutal and bloody war.

'That isn't fair, Charles. Your mother and I wanted to come but . . . '

21

'You had Buckingham Palace garden parties to go to.'

'Your mother was afraid of what she would see. I'll admit that. It isn't easy to be told that your son has been badly burned in a plane crash. But it's been two years, Charles. Isn't it time we moved on from that?'

That would suit you, Father, thought Charles. Let us pretend it never happened, and if you don't look too closely, you might even forget I'm covered in scars. 'I'm sorry.' He wondered why he was the one apologising. There were other pilots in the hospital, just as badly burned, yet nothing had kept their families away. It was ironic that a family who got rich making surgical dressings had such an abject fear of blood and gore. 'It's just coming here, with everyone looking at me. Or rather, everyone not looking at me.' Apart from the girl with the sad blue eyes, thought Charles. Rebecca Wilson had not averted her gaze like the others.

'I'm sure it will change, son. When they get used to seeing you around the place. And it's not that bad. Your face, I mean. I thought your comment to me about not being fit for public consumption was rather unfair.'

'Let's talk about the accounts, father. There must be some way we can avoid laying workers off. Don't forget many of the women we employ lost their husbands in the war. Or the men like Frank Wilson who didn't have to go but did anyway.'

'Yes, brave man, Wilson. Such a dreadful loss for him after all he's been through.'

'I think we should look at diversifying. Now hear me out, because I know you've resisted it so far. Sanitary products.'

'No. Harcourt's is not that sort of firm, Charles, and we never will be.'

'Why ever not?'

'Because I say so. I realise there may be a need for such . . . things . . . but we are not the ones to supply them. We're a family firm.'

'So what you're saying is that it's perfectly all right to create products that are used in unnatural situations such as war, but not to create a product for something that is a perfectly natural part of life?'

'Don't put words into my mouth, Charles.'

'Father, wars will come and go, and you cannot always guarantee one when you most need it. Women, however, will continue to menstruate and give birth for as long as human beings inhabit this earth.'

'I must say I find your language shocking. Where on earth did you get this idea from?'

Charles laughed. 'You are so Victorian, father. It's a wonder Patty and I were born at all.'

'That's enough of that.'

'Some of the nurses at the hospital talked about it,' said Charles, ignoring his father. 'They're not as shy about such things as most girls. There's a risk of infection and disease for women who re-use sanitary products like rags and knitted pads. It's much better for them if they can use something disposable. Most of the women here use the Gamgee pads for their monthlies. We might as well be making a profit on that.'

'Your grandfather always resisted moving into that area. I'm not sure what he would say if he were here today.'

'Well he isn't here. There are already firms that make them, like the Sanitary Wood Wool Company in London. I could look into their methods and see what we can learn, and then perhaps we could offer the products more cheaply. At the moment few working-class women can afford them, so they're the ones at risk from infection. We have to keep up with the times if we're to survive, father. Better this than hope for another war to keep the finances rosy.'

'I need to think about this, Charles.'

'Very well. We'll leave that discussion for another day. The other idea I've got is packaging. New products are being launched all the time. Perfumes, sweets and medicines.

We could liaise with some manufacturers and offer to create the packaging for them.'

'Yes, I like that better.'

'I thought you might. We'd need new machinery, of course.'

'Ah, now I see what you've done.' George Harcourt's eyes twinkled. 'You started off by suggested something you knew I'd absolutely hate in order to sugar the pill of spending money on the area you really want to move into.'

'Not quite,' said Charles, with a smile. 'I still think moving into sanitary products is a good idea, especially as we already have the machinery in place for the Gamgee tissue and it won't cost us that much more to go into production.'

'I told you I would think about it.'

★ ★ ★

Home was where Becky's father was, so she did not go home. Even if she explained to him about young Mr. Harcourt giving her time off with pay, he would not understand. She wandered around the town for a while, going aimlessly from street to street, before crossing the field and up the hill to the castle ruins.

The castle, or what was left of it, was said

to be from the twelfth century, and was described as an historic monument. Rumour had it Prince John had visited. That, thought Becky uncharitably, was Stony Newton all over. Not quite good enough for Richard the Lionheart, but the perfect stopping-off point for his less popular brother.

Maggie Fletcher called the castle a 'historic wreck'. That was when she and Becky had been close friends in the little school. They used to walk up to the castle together every Sunday afternoon in summer, sometimes taking pop and sandwiches. For Becky it was a time to sit and daydream about being rescued by a handsome knight, who jousted for her favours. For Maggie it was a chance to prattle on about every other girl in school. 'None of them are as pretty as you, Becky,' she would say. It did not take Becky long to realise that Maggie was probably saying exactly the same to Florrie Taylor and Clara Peters.

They would sit there, each with their own agenda, and pretend that they were the best of friends and would be forever, when their friendship was as likely to crumble as the remains of the castle. It took Maggie stealing sweets from the corner shop and slipping them in Becky's pocket to crush the foundations forever.

Becky stood at the outer wall of the castle, looking across the valley towards the Priory. She wondered about little Charlie. Thoughts of him had filled her every waking hour for two years. She did not know if he had lived or died. All she knew was the emptiness she felt, that was now doubled with the loss of her mother.

'Becky,' someone called. 'Becky Wilson? I thought it was you standing up here. What are you doing here?' It was Sam Jenkins, a scrawny-looking boy of about twenty, with a pronounced Adam's apple, and pimpled skin. His aunt, with whom he lived, used to tell Becky's mum that he would be handsome one day. 'He's clearly saving it up to surprise everyone,' Myra had whispered to Becky.

'Just walking. Why are you wearing your uniform? The war is over.'

'My aunty wanted to see me in it one last time.' She suspected that was a lie and that Sam was just showing off. 'You alright, Becky? You look fed up.'

'I'm alright.'

'Thought we could go back to your house. Is your mam in?'

'No. She's dead.'

Sam laughed. 'Very funny.'

'No, it's not funny at all, Sam. She's dead.'

'Honest?'

'Yes. Didn't your sister tell you?'

Sam turned and leaned against the wall, lighting up a cigarette. 'No, not a word. Mind you, she'd been drinking again.' He sucked hard on the filter tip. 'Bloody hell. I'm sorry, duck. When did it happen?'

'Last week.'

'She wasn't that old, was she?'

'She was thirty-eight.' Becky would not be drawn further. She did not want to remember how she found her mother. The sunken cheeks. The glazed eyes. Neither did she want to remember how her mother had been for two years since her father returned. Shuffling around the house, holding in her stomach because Frank kept telling her she was getting fat and ugly.

Becky wanted to remember the pretty woman with a ready smile and bright blue eyes, who made her laugh with her incongruous stories of meeting famous people. That woman, the mother who brightened her life with wild imaginings, disappeared and left a wispy creature.

'I could come to the funeral. When is it?' asked Sam. In trying to recapture her mother, Becky had almost forgotten he was there.

'No. You can't come. If my dad sees you . . . '

'Does he know about me then?'

'Of course he knows. Folk talk, don't they?'

'I'd better get going then. I'm off to London to live. My uncle owns a taxi company down there and he's giving me a job. Perhaps you could come and visit me down there. It's nice in London.'

'I don't think I will,' said Becky.

'Aw, come on, don't be like that . . . I'll ask Clara Peters to go with me instead, then. She's an actress now, you know.'

'That's not what I heard.'

'What have you heard?'

'Never mind. Look, Sam, just go away and drive your taxi. But don't come back here. Ever. Or my dad will kill you.'

★   ★   ★

Her father's arm hung heavy on her shoulder as the coffin was lowered into the ground. She resisted the urge to shrug it off.

'It's just me and thee now, duck,' he whispered to her, loud enough for all to hear.

Mrs. Vickers, a woman of about forty ('Doris Vickers who's all fur coat and no knickers,' Myra used to say) who had lost her husband in the war, muttered 'aw bless'. The slight movement of her father's arm told Becky that he was satisfied to have struck home.

29

'Frank,' said Mrs. Vickers as they all began to troop out of the cemetery, 'if there's anything you need . . . We're both on our own now, aren't we?'

'We are that, duck. We've both lost good 'uns. I wasn't always the best husband to Myra, but I know she's forgiven me.'

'I'm sure there was nothing to forgive, Frank.' That was when Becky gave up all pretence and pulled away from her father's touch. 'Oh, the poor girl. She's right cut up about it, isn't she?'

'Yes, it's hit her hard . . . '

'It hit me hard when I lost my Bert.'

'You never get over it,' said Frank. 'I know I never will.'

'The ache is always there.'

'It is that, duck.'

Their voices faded away as Becky rushed on ahead, and out of the churchyard. She ignored the turn off to her street and headed back towards the castle. She could not face anyone, least of all Mrs. Vickers and her father, who were involved in some sort of macabre flirtation based on who had suffered the most.

She was halfway up the castle field when she heard someone call her. It was Jed and Maggie Fletcher.

'Bloody hell,' she muttered under her

breath. 'Just leave me alone, will you?'

'Becky, where are you going?' Jed caught up with her, out of breath. He had grown in the past two years, and was now taller than Becky. The neighbours said he was a handsome lad, and Myra never argued with that, but to Becky he was still the same gawky boy she had grown up with.

'I'm just going for a walk, on my own.' She emphasised the last words, hoping they would get the message.

'You shouldn't be alone. Not at the moment.'

'She can if she wants to be,' said Maggie, in an insincere show of solidarity. 'Come on, Jed, we'll go down into town. You can buy me an ice cream.'

'Do you ever eat anything but chips and ice cream paid for by other people?' asked Becky.

'No, I had them for dinner on Sunday instead of a roast.' It was no riposte. Maggie said it as though she meant it. As a lie, thought Becky, it was not up there with seeing the king outside the chippy. She did not understand why her mother's fibs had been so charming, whereas Maggie Fletcher's were irritating. She recognised her own inconsistency, but could not reconcile herself to forgiving Maggie as she had forgiven her mother.

'If you say so, Maggie. I'll see you both at work tomorrow.'

'I thought you had another day off,' said Jed.

'I'll be there.'

'Becky . . . ' He left Maggie waiting further down the field. His voice softened. 'Becks, I thought we could go out sometime. For a cream tea. Or a drink. You could pass for old enough now.'

Maggie stood watching them, a deep frown between her eyes.

'Jed . . . I'm not interested in you like that. I'm sorry.'

'Fine. I'll go with Maggie.'

'Sam Jenkins just tried that tack with Clara Peters. If it's supposed to make me feel jealous, it isn't working. Go with Maggie. She's obviously keen on you.'

'I will then.' He turned to walk away, and then turned back. 'Look, I know you're hurt because of your mam, but I'll be there for you if you just say the word.'

Becky wondered why he bothered. She had been turning him down since they left little Charlie on the Priory steps. Jed reminded her too much of that night and she wanted to forget if she could.

'I still think about it, you know.'

'Jed . . . don't.' Becky glanced at Maggie,

wondering how much she could hear.

Jed dropped his voice. 'It's odd, isn't it, that we've never heard owt?'

'I'm not talking about this now. Not today of all days.'

'No, of course not.'

'And you'd better not tell her, Jed,' Becky hissed. 'If you tell the Filcher . . . '

'I've not said owt and I never will. I promise.'

'Right. Go on. Go to Maggie before she starts wondering what we're talking about.'

Jed sighed and turned to walk back down the field, his shoulders slumped in misery.

'Jed . . . '

'What, Becky?'

'Thanks.'

'Anytime. Alright?'

She nodded as she watched her childhood walk away from her. It was hard for her to explain to Jed how far removed she was from him and Maggie. Not that she thought she was any better than them. Only that she had changed. She had nothing in common with Jed, Maggie, or anyone else in Stony Newton.

The workers were good, hard-working people for the most part, but the things they worried about seemed trivial to her. It was all about keeping up appearances, and behaving in a way that would not have the neighbours talking. So there were rituals to observe. She tried to imagine herself in ten years' time, married to Jed, scrubbing the doorstep once a week, church on Sunday, the washing on a Monday, and a Saturday night spent at the working men's club nursing half a glass of stout. No matter how much she told herself there was nothing wrong with that life, the image slipped away and became darkness. On the other hand, she did not fit in with the middle classes either. To them she would always be a girl born in a two-up two-down. She had no one with whom to go to the theatre, and no one with whom she could discuss literature. Her mother had tried to save her from a life of drudgery by sending her to the high school, but her father was even more determined she would fit her designated place in society.

'At least now your mother's gone you won't have any more stupid ideas,' he had said only the day before. 'She indulged you too much, filling your head with books, but you'll not get that with me. We don't have time for all that. We've got a living to earn.' He had illustrated his point by throwing the poetry book she had been reading onto the fire.

What was there for her in a future without her mother to protect her?

She expected the castle to be deserted again. It was the one thing on which she could rely. But not this time. As she grew nearer to the battlements, she noticed smoke rising. Someone was there.

'Hello.' Charles Harcourt leaned over the wall and waved. 'I thought you were going to go off with your friends after all.'

'No. They've gone for ice cream.'

'Are you all right, Rebecca?' He paused. 'Sorry, silly question.'

Becky entered the castle grounds and joined him at the wall. They stood looking out onto Stony Newton together in companionable silence. 'It was nice,' Becky said after a while. 'We sang Bread of Heaven in church.' She searched for something more profound to say, but failed. 'It was mam's favourite.'

'Oh yes, your mother was born in Wales, wasn't she?' He took out his cigarette packet. 'Would you like one?'

'No, I . . . Yes. All right then.'

'You don't have to, just to prove you're grown up, Rebecca.'

'You're the only person in the world who calls me Rebecca.' She silently chastised herself for yet another inane comment. She also noticed with some relief that he put his cigarettes away without giving one to her.

'You're the only person in the world who

35

doesn't turn away when they see my face.'

'Oh, it's not that bad,' she said.

'You should see . . . '

'What?'

'Nothing. Forget I said anything.' Charles blushed.

'Do you come up here a lot?' asked Becky.

'No. I saw some people up here this morning, and thought I don't visit the place nearly enough. We have history on our doorstep and we don't bother to cherish it.'

'You live in a historical place though, don't you? The Priory must be really wonderful.'

'Oh yes, it's wonderful. Terrible plumbing, a roof that costs a fortune to maintain and . . . ' Charles took a drag of his cigarette. 'I'm being ungrateful. I know others live in much worse conditions.'

'Do you have a ghost? At the Priory, I mean. There must be all sorts of stories connected to it. Ghosts, murders, foundling children.'

'What made you say that?'

'What?'

'About foundling children.'

'I don't know. I suppose I'm thinking of Jane Eyre, or was it Oliver Twist? You know . . . foundling children who turn out to be heirs to great fortunes.' She did not like the

36

way his eyes searched her face.

'Sorry, yes. No, nothing like that. Though there is supposed to be the ghost of a drunken old monk. Personally I think it's more likely to be our old butler, Stephens, when he's been on the sauce.' Becky laughed. 'I'm glad I made you laugh, Rebecca. Especially today.'

'Better by far you should forget and smile, than that you should remember and be sad.'

'Christina Rosetti.'

'Yes.' Becky searched for something profound to say about Christina Rosetti and failed again. 'I like her poems.'

'You'd get on well with my sister, Patty. She likes all those old depressing poems. Rosetti and that awful one by one of the Brontës about the cold dreary grave.'

'*Far, far removed, cold in the dreary grave! Have I forgot, my only Love, to love thee . . .*' Too late, Becky remembered her mother. She stopped and turned away slightly so he could not see her tears.

'I'm sorry, Rebecca.'

'It's not your fault, sir. It's hard, isn't it, looking down over Stony Newton, to believe anything comes to an end? This town, it's been here forever.'

'Well, since the twelfth century at least. I suppose to a sixteen-year-old, that's forever.'

'I'm seventeen next week,' said Becky, trying to stand taller. She gazed out over Stony Newton. To her left lay the rows of pit houses. Several fields ran off from the castle, collectively known as 'Castle Field', despite there being more than one. At the bottom was the pit, churning up black dust. Along the roadside to the right, and leading down from the town centre, were the villas of the middle classes — the managers and foremen of the pit and the factory. Behind those on the opposite hill was the Priory, and Factory Lane. A couple of hundred yards from the Priory was the factory itself. 'It's amazing to think this land has been here for millions of years,' she said. 'So has the coal underground. Yet we barely get any time at all. My mam used to tell me stories. She was a real dreamer. Sometimes I didn't know what was true and what she'd made up. But I loved them anyway. If she'd been born in a different class she could have written them down and sold them. Now they're all lost. All that imagination, gone forever and there's no one except me to know how good she was.'

'Not completely gone, surely. Most of the stories we've known all our lives are from the oral tradition of storytelling. Homer's Iliad. Even Robin Hood and rhymes like Baa Baa

Black Sheep. All you have to do is remember them and tell them to your children.'

'I'm not getting married.'

'You're not?'

'No. Marriage is horrible. Husbands are horrible. They make you do things you don't want to do.'

'Like what?'

Becky had no answer to that. Or at least not one she could share with Charles Harcourt. 'Housework,' she said eventually.

Charles laughed. 'Marry a rich man, Rebecca. Then you can have servants to do it for you.'

She doubted servants would fulfil all the duties of a wife, but did not say so. 'Oh well, sir, if you happen to know of anyone going spare.'

'I'll point him in your direction.' He threw his cigarette butt over the wall. 'I'd better get back. I'll see you in a couple of days.'

'Tomorrow,' said Becky. 'I'll come back to work tomorrow.'

A warm tingle in the pit of her tummy told her that she might not be too opposed to doing whatever Charles Harcourt wanted. She had a new dream, and one that did not involve scrubbing doorsteps. It was of Charles Harcourt. He was a real live hero, who had spoken to her as if she were his equal. Even memories of little Charlie began to disappear into the shadows.

* * *

Frank Wilson held court in the parlour, surrounded by neighbours and friends. Doris Vickers sat in Myra's old chair by the fireplace, already having made herself at home.

'I had a good wife, and now she's taken from me,' Frank said to a murmur of approval. He glanced at Doris and wondered what her breasts looked like. 'I'm not one to complain about my lot, as you all know. When that bullet hit me, I'd have got up and carried on fighting if they'd let me. That's what I'm going to do now. I'm going to carry on. It's what Myra would have wanted.'

They waited patiently for him to continue. He wiped his eyes with a large off-white handkerchief. 'When I met Myra, I were sixteen and she were twenty-four and she had that little baby to care for after her first husband died. Our Becky. Always treated that girl like my own, I have. Even gave her my name. Sadly, me and Myra were never blessed with our own kids, but I'd not have treated Becky any different if we had. It's just a pity she couldn't be bothered to be here today, on her mother's sending off.'

'Ay, Frank, you raise them up and they piss on you from a great height,' said Len Peters. 'Like our Clara. Took off to Sheffield and never writes to her poor mother.'

'Daughters are a worry,' said Doris Vickers.

'Let's raise a toast to a decent woman, my Myra,' said Frank. 'God rest her soul.'

'A toast,' the guests agreed, raising glasses of sherry.

'What do you think to the new working arrangements?' asked Albert Taylor, when the necessary silence had been observed. 'I tell you, those . . . ' He stopped, as if remembering he was at a wake. 'Those managers are going to bleed us dry.'

'Ay,' said Len. 'We're doing more work for less money. And they're on about putting the rents up on these hovels.'

'It'll not always be so,' said Frank. 'The Trades Unions are getting stronger now Labour have got more seats and one day we'll have a stranglehold on management. I've a mind to stand as union leader for Stony Newton pit. I'm going to fight to bring in new safety procedures. There's too many accidents happening. Are you all with me?'

A general wave of assent floated around the room. 'You're a good man, Frank. Just the

41

type we need to protect us from the bosses,' said Len.

'Ay, well, if a bullet from the Hun didn't get me, t'management won't.' Frank laughed, and was joined by the others. He looked across at Doris Vickers, to see her looking back with open interest. She was getting on a bit, but her husband had been dead a while. She would be desperate for a man.

3

Jed thought there must be better places to sit than the Castle Fields as the dew started to form on the grass, but Maggie had expressed a reluctance to return home. So they had walked around Stony Newton for hours. He bought her chips, which she ate like someone who had been starved for a week. She finished off his too.

A couple of times he tried to lose her, by saying he was going to the pub, or wanted to meet some mates, but she hung on like a limpet, standing outside the pub whilst he drank a pint of cider. Once or twice he saw Becky in the distance, and longed to shake Maggie off so he could speak to her properly, but it was as if she walked different streets to him nowadays. He had lost her without ever really knowing what it was to possess her.

'I just want to talk to you,' Maggie said when they reached the field, and Jed sat down, defeated. 'Away from Becky. When she's there you only think of her.'

'I love her.' Jed spoke with complete honesty and a total lack of tact. He had some idea of Maggie's feelings for him, but they were as inconsequential as she was; an irksome girl who got under his feet.

'She doesn't love you,' said Maggie.

'I know that.'

'I love you, Jed.'

'Don't be daft.'

'I do. I can make you happier than her. Do things for you.' She moved in closer. 'You can look at my breasts if you want.'

Jed felt a twitch in his groin at odds with his indifference to Maggie. He turned his face to her, and pondered the offer. She was a pretty girl, and she would probably do anything he wanted her to. According to his mates, Maggie was known for that. 'Go on then.'

Maggie grinned in triumph, and started unbuttoning her blouse, whilst Jed watched, excitement building with every undone button. She slipped the strap of her liberty bodice off her shoulder, revealing one plump white breast. Then the other. 'You can touch them if you want.'

Jed reached out a trembling hand and pressed a finger against the dark circle of her nipple, which stood erect in the cool night air.

'You love me, don't you, Jed?' she whispered.

He should have said no. But in that moment, with the promise of something he'd never had, he utterly adored Maggie Fletcher. 'Of course I do.' He leaned forward and kissed her breast, flicking his tongue around the edge of her nipple, just like he'd read about in the books his father kept under the bed.

'Lie back,' she said, taking control of the situation.

'You'll marry me if I have a baby, won't you, Jed?' she asked as she sat astride him.

'Yes, yes.'

'You do love me, don't you, Jed?' Maggie asked after they had made love. She fell against his shoulder like a stone.

He began to love her a little less. Her neediness made the hairs on his neck bristle.

'The other lads I've had . . . They didn't make me happy like you did. You were best ever.'

Jed's face broke into a satisfied smile. For an all-too-brief moment in time he utterly adored Maggie Fletcher.

★　★　★

Charles drove into Sheffield. Every fibre of his being cried out against the idea of going with a prostitute, but too many solitary nights with nothing but his right hand and his imagination were beginning to take their toll.

45

He wanted a real live, warm woman.

Being with Rebecca Wilson had only increased his longing, and he hated himself for that. She was barely seventeen.

The girl he was looking for was not much older. Perhaps eighteen or nineteen, but that to him seemed a safer age. Besides, all the others who frequented that part of Sheffield were much older, or at least looked it, with their drawn-on eyebrows and thin red lips.

He stopped the car next to the girl he sought. She leaned against a lamppost, smoking a rolled-up cigarette, trying to hide the fact that her body, under a thin coat, shivered in the cold night air.

'You looking for something?' she said to Charles, when he wound down his window. She might have been selling fish from a counter in the market.

'Yes. Do you want to get in?'

He took her to a secluded spot just outside the city. Up close she looked even younger. 'Are you old enough for this?' he asked her.

'I'm whatever age you want me to be.' The line was that of an actress who had spoken it every night on stage for ten years and had long since lost the ability to make it sound fresh.

'I don't have sex with children,' he said. 'If

you're under eighteen, you have to get out of the car now.'

'And walk all the way back?'

'I'll give you money for a taxi.'

'Look, do you want it or not? I'm losing money here.' She sighed. 'I'm nineteen, okay?'

'What . . . erm . . . what do you do?'

'Anything you want.'

'I should warn you. I've got scars. It might put you off.'

'Don't worry . . . ' Her voice lost some of its harshness. 'There's lots like you since the war. Burns victims, amputees. They think a normal girl won't want them so they come to us. Is that why you're here?'

'Yes.'

'You're not bad-looking.'

'You don't have to be nice to me,' said Charles. 'I haven't paid you yet.'

'I'm not just saying it to be nice. I mean it. Any girl would be glad to be with someone like you.'

'What's your name? Please don't say it's whatever I want it to be.'

'My name is Annette.'

The pause told him it was a lie, but perhaps she had her reasons. 'Would you like to go somewhere nicer, Annette? A hotel perhaps. You look as if you could do with something to eat.'

47

'They won't let the likes of me into a hotel.'

'They will if you're with me.' Charles started the car. Being in a hotel would help him take the truth away from this situation. He could pretend that she was a girl he had met at a party, and had taken out to dinner then seduced over the coffee. He might convince himself that she wanted to be there as much as he did. She might even enjoy the experience.

'So,' she purred in monotone, as they drove back into the city. 'What do you want in return for a night in a hotel?' She pressed her hand against his upper thigh.

'Everything,' he said, his voice as flat as the dream slipping away from him. 'I want everything.'

★ ★ ★

Becky crept in through the back door just after nine o'clock in the evening. The kitchen table bore the remnants of the wake. She took the cover off some sandwiches and ate one. She lifted a slice of cake from another plate. With any luck her father would be asleep, and she could deal with his anger in the morning, when she was more rested. After Charles Harcourt left her, she had spent an hour or so in the castle grounds, before walking for miles

48

along the river, around the outskirts of Stony Newton, then back to do the same walk all over again.

Still eating her cake, she tiptoed up the stairs and onto the landing when she heard the springs creaking in the familiar rhythmic way. A voice from her mother's bedroom said, 'Do you love me, Frank?' It was Mrs. Vickers.

'Oh, I do, my duck.'

Becky almost ran in, to protest, but her fear of her father was greater than her disgust over his behaviour. Her mother was barely cold in her grave and already he had brought another woman into the house. She let the door close, and went to her own room, dragging the mattress away from the wall and to the window. She lay down and covered her ears.

★　★　★

Sam Jenkins could hear the baby crying when he walked up the narrow staircase to Clara's room, which was in an attic at the top. None of the other residents had bothered to check on the child, and her mother was probably asleep.

He hastened his step and opened Clara's door. The smell hit him immediately, assaulting both his nose and his tastebuds. An unemptied chamber pot, soiled bedding, and mouldy food.

The baby lay screaming in a drawer that hung precariously out of a chest.

'Come on, sweetheart,' he said, lifting her up. It did nothing to stem her bawling. He shook her a little as he had seen Clara doing, albeit not as roughly. 'Now, now, come on.' It only made her worse. He gave her a finger to suck on, and that placated her until she realised it was empty.

'What you doing here, Sam?' Clara burst through the door, kicking off her shoes and hauling herself onto the grimy single bed. There was something different about her, but Sam could not quite put his finger on it. Then it hit him. She smelled clean. 'I thought I told you to get lost.' It was said casually as if what he did was of no real concern to her. She barely acknowledged the child.

'Did you leave Annette alone all night?'

'She's all right. T'other girls always look in on her.'

Sam was just about to open his mouth and tell Clara that no one had paid any attention to the baby's cries, but she was on a high about something. He could not get a word in. 'I got a right good punter, Sam. Charles Harcourt. Can you believe it? I don't think he even knew who I was but I knew him straight away. I told him my name was Annette.'

'For God's sake, Clara! How can you give

your baby's name when you're out there?'

'Oh shut up, Sam. Don't spoil things now. He took me to a hotel and bought me a meal. Treated me like a real lady. And look . . . ' She waved a few notes in the air. 'He gave me ten pounds. Mind you, I had to bloody earn it. He even made me have a bath. He got in and did me. In the bath! You should have seen his body. Right burnt he was. All down one side. Poor thing.'

'I wonder, if the baby paid you by the hour, you'd take more interest in her. She's starving and there's no food in the place.'

'I was going to call at the shop on t'way home but I'm exhausted. Just put her back in t'drawer. She'll cry herself to sleep like she always does.'

'I can't, because once I leave, I'm not coming back.' Sam felt a pang. He could not really leave the baby hungry. 'I'm going to London to work on my uncle's taxis. Just thought I'd let you know I wouldn't be coming around anymore to help you and Annette.'

'He's not your uncle. And your sister's not your sister. You are thick, Sam.'

'No, I just know when to shut my mouth.'

Clara yawned. 'Feed her before you go. Have you got any money? Go and get her some milk from the shop.' She had not heard a word he said.

51

'Come with me. You and Annette. I could take care of you both down there. You wouldn't need to work.' He knew he was being stupid. Clara thought of no one but herself. But he cared about the baby and what happened to her. Annette might not be his, but he had been there on the night Clara gave birth. He had seen the little girl come into the world. If he could not save Clara, perhaps he could save the child.

'London? Yeah, that'd be good. But you're not stopping me working. I like it. There'll be lots of men down there like the one I had last night. With money to spend on extras. I need to sleep a bit first.'

'Clara . . . ' She had already turned over and pulled a filthy sheet over her shoulders. 'Someone I know were buried yesterday. It were a real shock.'

'Well, it happens. I'll give you something on the house since I'm a bit flush and you're an old friend.' She yawned. 'For God's sake feed Annette. Or give her a good shake. She's getting on my nerves.'

★   ★   ★

Charles bathed as soon as he got home, scrubbing at his skin until small globules of blood rose from his pores. What had he been

52

thinking? The girl, despite knowing all the techniques, had been dreadful company. She smirked when he ordered wine, and laughed in his face when he had mentioned poetry. Not only that, but she smelled awful once she took her coat off. Her dress had obviously not been washed for weeks, and her feet were black. So he had suggested the bath, trying to make it sound like part of the seduction. Her naked body aroused him, despite its utter grubbiness, and that bothered him.

The worst of it was imagining it was Rebecca Wilson who moved beneath him. Even that dream was shattered. Annette — if indeed that was her name — had said all the right things, no doubt well-rehearsed, but her language was far too obscene for his tastes. He thought with a wry smile that it would be nice to think he was the biggest she had ever had, but he doubted it very much. He hated himself for being so shallow and fulfilling his baser desires with a woman he would not look at in any other capacity. In the morning he had paid her far more than she was worth, and vowed never go back to that area of Sheffield again. He also hoped and prayed he had not caught anything nasty.

'You were out late last night,' his mother, Veronica, said to him at breakfast. His father hid behind the morning paper.

'I went into Sheffield for a drink, and then decided to stay in a hotel.' Charles took some bacon and scrambled eggs from the dishes on the side table, and went to sit down. Old Stephens was immediately on hand to pour coffee.

'That's very sensible, dear. Isn't it, George?'

His father grunted, and waited until Veronica left the table before starting to talk business. 'I've made up a list of the possible lay-offs. Have a glance and see if you agree.'

Charles took the sheet of paper, and gave the list a cursory glance. He was not going to be able to put his father off, so he did not think it worth arguing. Until he saw the name at the top of the list.

'Rebecca Wilson went to high school, didn't she?' he said.

'Hmm, what? Yes, for a while, I believe.'

'So her arithmetic and grammar would be quite good, I imagine.'

'What are you getting at Charles? It's too early in the morning for riddles.'

'I just thought that perhaps we could use some extra help in the office.'

His father looked at him for a long moment. 'She was the last in, so she must be the first out.'

'It's ridiculous to let someone go who

might be helpful in other areas of the business.'

'You're not going to get silly over this girl, are you, Charles? I got the feeling yesterday you were a bit sweet on her. I don't want a scandal. I've always made it a rule, as you know, that management do not get personally involved with the female workers.'

'Father, I'm just thinking of Harcourt's. You and I will be busy over the next few months, implementing the changes required for the new packaging section. Meanwhile the paperwork will be piling up. I've never understood why you don't use a clerk anyway.'

'Can't we ask Jed Alsop? He didn't go to the grammar school, but he's a clever young man. He reads and writes well enough.'

'I'll agree he's a good foreman, and all the women like working with him. They enjoy having a nice-looking young man on the factory floor. It aids morale. I think Rebecca, Miss Wilson, should work in the office.'

'Very well, but I warn you now Charles, if there's any trouble . . . '

'I assure you my intentions are entirely honourable, father.'

'That sounds as if you plan to marry the girl.'

4

1920

It was Rebecca's eighteenth birthday, so she dressed in her best suit and made sure her hair was neat and tidy. Not that she expected Frank and his new wife to celebrate it with her. Doris sat at the table in the kitchen, holding a cigarette with trembling fingers. A year before she had sparkled vivaciously. Now she looked like a candle that had been left to die out.

'You look very nice, Becky,' she said. Becky smiled and went back to the mirror. She did not hate Doris, but neither did she need another mother.

'I suppose I'd better get some housework done,' said Doris. 'Your father will be back soon. I don't suppose you could . . . '

'I have to be at work soon,' said Becky. Her hackles rose. She would not be responsible for Doris's welfare and hated the fact that Doris turned to her for support when Frank was on the rampage. It was one thing to protect her own mother, but Doris was nothing to her.

'You're doing well in the office, I hear.'

'Yes, the two Mr. Harcourts are really happy with my work.'

'You're a good girl, Becky.'

Becky sighed. The plaintive tone of Doris's voice had hit home, fracturing Becky's resolve. 'I'll do the dishes before I go, shall I?'

'Would you, duck? That's nice. Thank you.'

'But you'll have to sweep the hearth. Do it before he gets back, or he'll be cross.'

'I wish someone had warned me.' Doris looked at her accusingly. 'I mean, before I married him.'

Becky bit back a remark about what happens when you jump into another woman's bed so quickly. 'Would you have believed me? Or anyone else?'

'No. He's a real charmer when he's out, isn't he? Always laughing and joking. Always flirting.'

'That's what he was like when I was little,' said Becky. 'He always used to laugh and joke with me and mam then. He loved me, I think, at first. And I loved him.' She paused, finding that the memory caused her more pain than she would like to admit. She had worked hard at becoming indifferent to her stepfather. 'I don't know. Perhaps the responsibility of bringing up another man's child got too much for him.'

'I imagine being shot didn't help him much,' said Doris.

'He changed before that.' Becky could not have said when or how. It was too gradual, or she suspected her mother had kept a lot from her in the early days.

'He's a good man.' Doris stubbed out her cigarette and lit another one, seemingly forgetting about the ashes in the grate. 'A hero. All the men at t'pit like him. He's really standing up to the bosses. He's a good man.'

Yes, thought Becky, you keep repeating that until the day you find you can't believe it anymore.

'He's coming up the street,' she said. 'We'd better get on.'

'How can you always tell when he's coming?' asked Doris, putting out her part-smoked cigarette and rushing to the grate to clean up the ashes.

'I just can,' said Becky, going to the sink to make a start on the dishes. It was a change in the atmosphere that she could not define. Whatever malevolence Frank carried within him not only travelled on ahead, but also left a trail behind; one to which Becky was tuned. Sure enough, he walked through the back door a minute or two later.

'Have you two only just started?'

Becky ignored him. It was no use arguing.

'I said have you two just started?'

'No,' said Doris. 'We've been busy all morning, haven't we, Becky?'

'It's only eight o'clock,' said Becky.

'There's women on this street as get their housework done by seven-thirty so they can get off to work, whilst you two don't even get started till the middle of the day.'

He was spoiling for a fight, and Becky did not want to be around to see it. She shook the water off her hands, and turned to leave.

'Where are you going?'

'I'm going to work.'

'Finish the dishes.'

'You do them if you're that bothered.'

'You what?' Spittle flew from Frank's mouth, hitting Becky on the cheek. She fought the urge to rub it off, wanting to hold his gaze. 'You're not too old for a slap, my girl.'

'If you ever hit me, I shall call the bobby and have you arrested,' said Becky, pretending more courage than she felt.

'Oh Becky,' murmured Doris. 'Don't, ducky.'

Frank stared Becky in the face, his nose less than an inch from hers. She could see the red mist forming over his eyes. 'You don't speak to me like that, you stuck-up little bitch. Think you're all high and mighty now

59

you're working in t'factory office, do you?'

'No, but you're still not going to hit me. I won't have it. Not from you or any man. You're not my real father, so you've no right to touch me.' All the anger and hatred she had been storing for the past three years came to the fore. 'I will call the bobby . . . ' She left the words in the air, knowing that he would eventually take their full meaning.

Frank's eyes pierced into her for what seemed like an age. She knew she had gone too far, but he had never hit her before and she was determined he would not start now she no longer had her mother's protection.

Time stood still as they stood toe to toe. Becky's neck and shoulders ached from the effort of holding his gaze. Finally he turned away, throwing his newspaper onto the table, and landing heavily in the chair, as though the wind had been taken from him.

'I've never laid a finger on her, Doris. Never. And this is how she repays me. With insolence.' Becky was shocked to see the tears in his eyes. She put it down to his frustration at not being able to take out his anger on her. 'She says I'm not her real father when I brought her up as my own. Loved her like she were my own.'

'You've no love in you,' Becky said. She slammed the back door behind her.

'I ought to be having a baby by now,' said Maggie, sitting up in bed.

'You ought to have had one about six months after we got married. Remember?' Jed stood at the mirror, buttoning up his shirt. Here we go again, he thought. The same old lament. He was getting sick of it.

'It were a false alarm, Jed. I didn't know.'

He turned to look at her. 'Oh, I think you knew. You just trapped me.'

'Let's not go into all that again. I told you, it were a mistake. But everyone's asking me why I'm not having a baby yet.'

'You're a liar, Maggie! That's what you are.' Banging coming up from the ceiling below put a stop to Jed's outburst. 'Forget it. We've upset Mrs. Jenkins again. She said she'd chuck us out if we didn't stop rowing all t'time. And we can't afford anywhere else. Not unless you're willing to go back to work.'

'It's my back, Jed. I pulled it.'

'It's probably just as well you're not having a baby then, isn't it?'

'I think there's something wrong with you.'

'Why me?'

'Because the women in our family never have any trouble getting pregnant.'

Jed nearly remarked about how they died

in pregnancy, like Maggie's mother. He could not be that cruel, no matter how much she annoyed him.

'There's nowt wrong with me.'

'Go to the doctor. Ask for a test.'

'Why don't you go to the doctor and ask for a test? Why does it have to be me?' The thought of approaching old Doctor Latimer with such a problem filled him with dread. It was bad enough when he had to be circumcised. That was nothing compared to admitting he might not be capable of fathering a child.

'Because there's nowt wrong with me. It's got to be you.' She paused, her expression sullen. 'You're not a proper man if you can't get me pregnant.'

Jed flew towards the bed and pinned her arms back, dropping his body on top of her. 'There's nowt wrong with me,' he hissed against her neck. He would not have his manhood questioned. Maggie was liable to go around saying it to everyone. She was that sort of girl. Despite his promise not to mention their night on the Castle Fields, she had told all her friends exactly what they did. Not that Jed minded at first. She built him up to be an incredible lover, when he knew deep down that the sex was mediocre. Until Maggie told him she was pregnant and trapped him for eternity, he had a few trysts with the local girls, thanks to her bragging about his prowess. Then came the awful day she left a letter to him right under her father's nose. It detailed everything they had done together, along with a few things Jed had never heard of, and the news of her supposed pregnancy.

'You don't seem to think there's owt wrong with me when you're waking me up in the middle of the night.'

'You're firing blanks then. Let me go.'

Jed ignored her, keeping his grip tight on her wrists. He had never wanted to be the sort of man to hit a woman, yet he wanted to hit Maggie. She riled him at every opportunity, except in bed, and he hated that despite the animosity between them, she could still arouse him.

'There's nowt wrong with me, Maggie.'

He let her go and stood up, bringing his feelings back under control. He feared that one day he might break and hit her. He knew the darkness was there, inside him, just as it was in his father, but he would not give it free rein.

'I'm sorry, Jed.' Maggie rubbed her wrists. 'Come back to bed. You know I love you.'

'I've got to go to work.'

'Jed, you still love me don't you?'

'I'm here, aren't I?'

* * *

'You look very nice today, Rebecca.' Charles cast an appreciative eye on Becky's blue suit. The effect was not quite elegant. The suit was too cheap and badly cut for that. He guessed she had made it herself. But it was pleasing in the way the skirt clung to her hips, and stopped just above her slender ankles.

Becky looked up from her desk and smiled. It was her smile that made it worth Charles' while to come into work every morning. 'It's my birthday.'

'Is it? I had no idea. Are you off somewhere nice after work?'

'No. I just thought I'd dress up.'

'Aren't your friends taking you to the pub for a legal drink?' He meant boyfriends, but did not want to let her know how much the answer mattered to him.

'No, sir. I don't have many friends. It's a bit hard, working in here.'

'How so?'

'The other girls think I'm stuck-up.' She shook her head as if he had asked her a question. 'I'm not. But I find it hard to know

64

what to talk about with them anymore, unless it's work.'

Before he could stop himself, he blurted out, 'A young man then?'

She glanced down. 'No, no one like that either. I've got the Henderson accounts ready, if you want them.'

'Thank you. I need you to ring Paul Henderson and arrange a meeting with him, about going into production with the, erm . . . '

Becky giggled. He loved the sound of her laughter, yet she did not do it often. She was a sad sort of girl, even a year after her mother's death. 'It helps if you can say it.'

'I can when you're not here. Unfortunately it still shocks my father.'

'I'm not shocked, sir. I know the facts of life.' She blushed and put her hand to her mouth as though she had blurted out something she should not. 'I mean, I've been told them.'

'I knew what you meant. It'll mean a trip to London. I want to try and persuade Henderson to stock them in his shops. I still find it hard to do deals over the telephone. I can't fight the feeling that Mrs. Brown at the exchange is listening in.' The next part was crucial. He did not want to alarm her. 'I wondered if you'd like to go with me. We could see the sights and go to the theatre. In fact, if you can hook up a meeting with him for the next few days we could go down tonight. It would be a birthday treat for you.'

'Go to London? With you?'

'Yes. I don't mean anything untoward,' said Charles, instantly doubting his own honesty. 'My sister, Patricia, has an apartment down there. She could put us up.' That was better. Safer. 'What do you say? You know this business better than I do now. You'd be able to answer any questions that I couldn't. I hope you wouldn't find it too embarrassing, given the subject matter.'

'I'd really enjoy seeing London. I've never been there. You'd have to speak to Frank . . . my father . . . and explain it all to him. I'm not sure he would understand.'

'Of course. I'll go and see him later. I'm sure if I tell him we're staying with my sister, it will be fine.' Charles thought it best not to mention that Patty would not care if he seduced his secretary in her spare bedroom. Before the war, he had often taken girls back to her flat. He told himself it was not the same with Rebecca . . .

*　*　*

Becky flew home at lunchtime; her head filled with images of herself in London, walking at

66

Charles Harcourt's side.

As she tried to pack, she found that nothing in her paltry wardrobe was up to the task of a trip to London or the luncheon that she had arranged with Mr. Henderson. She delved into the bottom of her wardrobe to an old shoebox and found the money she had hidden from Frank's grasping fingers. With it she would buy something better when they got to London. Something elegant and sophisticated. She checked her reflection in the wardrobe mirror. How had she believed the suit was smart? She could see for herself the slightly uneven cut and the clumsy stitching. It was a wonder Charles Harcourt did not laugh at her behind her back.

Perhaps he was making fun of her. She paused as the terrible thought took hold. Perhaps he intended to show her off as a joke to his sister and Mr. Henderson. No, that could not be it. The Henderson account meant everything to Harcourt's. He would not risk it just for the sake of putting Becky in her proper place. Nothing about him suggested such unkindness. Over the previous year he had encouraged her, paying for typewriting and shorthand lessons. Sometimes, she guessed, it went against Mr. Harcourt Senior's wishes. She had often entered the office whilst they were involved in a deep, but whispered, discussion, which invariably stopped the moment she appeared.

She looked at her reflection again. There was no way she could go to London. Not like this. Even if Charles did not intend to embarrass her, she would probably end up embarrassing herself. Her mother had tried to bring her up well by teaching her to speak correctly and instilling good manners, but Becky was intelligent enough to know that even that was not enough for upper-middle-class society.

'Who are you?' she whispered to the mirror. The girl looking back at her was no longer the Becky her mother had loved, or the child who had been happy enough to play with Jed and Maggie. Nor was she the Rebecca who worked and tried so hard in the Harcourt's office. She existed in no-man's land, somewhere in between the Becky she used to be and the Rebecca that she would like to be.

She hoped that someday it would all make sense to her, and she would know exactly where she should be, but at that moment she did not belong anywhere.

★   ★   ★

'She'll be perfectly safe, Mr. Wilson.'
Frank cast a suspicious glance at Becky.

'What have you been up to?'

'Nothing.' She had not had chance to confirm to Charles she would not be going. When she arrived home from her afternoon shift, he was already there, talking to Frank.

'I'll not have any scandal in this house, Mr. Harcourt.'

'There will be no scandal,' said Charles. 'And I must say I resent your implication. Rebecca is a decent girl. You should be very proud of her. She's doing really well in the office, and with her secretarial studies. If she'd been allowed to stay on at high school, she might have gone on to university.' There was something akin to reproach in Charles' voice.

'We couldn't afford it,' said Frank. 'We have to work for a living on this side of town.' He waited, as if to see whether Charles would rise to the bait. He did not. 'If anything happens she'll get my . . . '

'Nothing is going to happen.' Charles stepped a bit closer. Frank was tall, but Charles stood several inches above him. 'And if I find you've hurt her in any way when she gets back, you'll have me to deal with. Do you hear?'

'Of course, Mr. Harcourt. I didn't mean anything by it.' Frank stepped back. 'You're a good, decent man, I know that. I just . . .

well, it's a father's duty to protect his daughter. You must see that. I'm sure she'll be safe with you.'

'Good. I'll come back for you at around seven, Rebecca . . . ' Charles paused and looked from Becky to Frank, then back again. 'Actually no, I think the sooner we go the better.'

'I haven't finished packing,' said Becky. She had given up at lunchtime, too depressed with everything in her wardrobe.

'I can wait. Go on, get ready.' He spoke kindly but there was enough steel behind his voice to let everyone know exactly who had control of the situation. 'We'll be back the day after tomorrow, Mr. Wilson.'

'Yes, of course. Take as long as you want. It'll give me and our Doris a bit of time alone, won't it, duck?'

Doris looked less thrilled by that idea. 'Go on, Becky,' she said. 'Don't keep Mr. Harcourt waiting.'

5

Sam drove across Tower Bridge, heading south of London. The two-cylinder Austin still had to vie with heavily-laden horses and carts for space, so he could never really open the car up until he got out of the city. It made him frustrated. He drove hundreds of miles a week around London, taking fares, but he never really seemed to go anywhere. On the other hand, he could not think of a better job. He had finished a good day shift, earning a few tips along the way. He could earn more if he did nights, but that was out of the question. He had to be back to care for Annette, so Clara could begin her own version of the nightshift.

He shared a two-room flat with Clara in a crumbling mansion south of the Thames. When he got back from his day shift, the room was as chaotic as ever. Clara was asleep in the bed, whilst eighteen-month-old Annette sat in a playpen in the lounge area. She had learned not to make too much noise when alone with her mother. Her little olive- skinned face, with its big dark eyes, lit up when she saw Sam carrying wrapped-up newspaper. She chatted

71

happily in her special baby language. He liked to imagine she was saying, 'Hello daddy, I'm glad you're back'.

He put the newspaper, which was steaming hot, onto the only bit of space on the table.

'Hello, petal,' he said, lifting Annette out. He hugged her close, guessing it was the only human contact she would have had since he went out that morning. She snuggled into him. 'I bet you're ready for your tea, aren't you? Daddy's brought you some chips. Clara. Clara!'

'What!'

'I've brought supper. Have you left Annette in that playpen all day?'

'She's alright. She likes it.' Clara came out, wiping sleep from her eyes. Living in London had not improved her habits. He wondered how the men who paid her found it in them to touch her, before remembering that he also managed to sleep with her from time to time, regardless of what state she was in. They were probably as desperate as he was. Clara crawled out of bed, and went to pull the chamber pot from underneath.

'It's in the bathroom, soaking in cleaning fluid,' said Sam. 'Go along the hall and use the proper toilet.'

'Bossy, aren't we?'

'It's not hygienic for the baby. She's already

pulled it all over her once.' It had taken weeks to get the smell out of the flat. 'Come on, petal,' he said to Annette. 'Let's put you in your chair and get you some chips.'

Clara swore at him and left the room.

He put a few chips and some diced-up sausage into a bowl and placed it in front of Annette, then began tidying the room a little before sitting down to his own supper. 'Is that nice, petal? You look like you're enjoying it.'

Clara came back and sat down, but instead of eating the food Sam had dished up for her, she lit a cigarette and swigged from an open bottle of stout. 'It's gone flat. Go out and get some more, will you?'

'Clara, I've been thinking.' Sam ignored her request. If he let her, she would have him running around half the night for beer and fags. Then he would have no time with Annette.

'That's dangerous, especially for you.'

'My uncle's really pleased with my work. He wants to make me a partner. It means we could buy a nicer place to live in. Somewhere with a garden for Annette.'

'Yeah, that would be nice.'

'But you'd have to give up the game.'

'Why?'

'Because I'm not buying a house in a nice neighbourhood for you to bring your punters back. I thought we could make it really respectable by getting married.'

'Why? We don't love each other.'

'Maybe not, but I love Annette and I want her to have a better life. I'd like her to have my name.'

'You're not turning funny, are you? Fancying little girls.'

'For Christ's sake, Clara. No, of course not.' Sam looked horrified. 'Just because your mind is in the gutter don't tar us all with the same brush. I'd never harm this little girl. Never!'

'I don't want to give up the game. I've told you, I like it.'

'How can you like it? Letting men paw you and do dirty things to you.'

'I don't hear you complain when I'm giving you favours.'

'Apart from moaning that you never give me any bloody change,' he said, trying to make a joke of it. He laughed, thinking it was a strange thing to be arguing about. Such was their life together. 'Think about it. For Annette's sake. Do you really want your daughter to grow up with a prossie for a mother? She's going to be really clever, I can tell. Let's give her a proper life. Otherwise she'll just end up on the game herself. Do you want that?'

'I thought of doing a double act when she got to about twelve.'

Sam almost hurled his plate at her, but he did not want Annette to see him getting angry. 'You really are a sick bitch, you know that.'

'No, I just know how to wind you up. How do you think it makes me feel that you care more about Annette than you do about me?'

'You don't love me. What does it matter?'

'You're right. It doesn't matter. So why bother getting married?'

'Because I don't believe you want to be living this life forever, and I certainly don't.'

Clara sucked on her cigarette, before stubbing it out and lighting another, whilst her food congealed on the plate. 'Yeah, alright then. We'll get married. But I want a really nice house.'

'Great.'

'And you mustn't make me be faithful. I want to go with whoever I want whenever I want. You can as well. I don't care.'

Sam pursed his lips and fingered a scar above his eyebrow from the time a few months before when Clara had heard him talking to a young woman who lived in one of the other flats.

If not for Annette he would get up and walk out, telling Clara to stick it. Because what he would really be doing was giving his tacit agreement for her to keep whoring. It was a compulsion with her and one he realised he was not clever enough to understand. She had told him stories about some uncle who used to give her sweets and money if she did things, but she always spoke about it matter-of-factly, as if it was of no importance, even laughing about how she held out for more when the uncle asked for other favours. 'Then I had all the power,' she told Sam. If she ever thought about what really happened with her uncle, and felt the pain of it, she kept it very much to herself.

'Fine,' he said at last. 'But not in our house, or in the area we live, and definitely not in front of Annette. Deal?'

'Deal.' She reached across the table and they shook hands.

Sam turned to Annette, who was eating but seemed also to be listening intently, her brown eyes wide and interested. He could swear she understood everything they said, which made him feel ashamed. 'We're going to have a nice house, petal, with a garden for you to play in. You're going to grow up big and strong and beautiful and clever. Yes, you are.'

'I think I'm going to be sick,' said Clara, before putting out her second cigarette and tucking into her chips.

6

'Becky, before you go I want to talk to you, in the kitchen.' Frank opened the door from the parlour and waited.

'I'll be waiting here,' said Charles, pointedly. It gave Becky more confidence. She followed her stepfather into the kitchen, and waited for the inevitable lecture.

'We got something for you for your birthday,' said Frank after he shut the door. It was not what Becky had expected to hear. He went into the pantry and took out a brown parcel. 'We were going to give it to you tonight, and take you to the pub for your first legal drink. I suppose that'll not be happening now. The wrapping isn't up to much, but I hope you like what's inside.'

With trembling fingers, Becky opened the package and found a book of poetry, the same edition as the one he had thrown on the fire.

'I know you like poems and all that,' he said. 'Don't go in for them much myself, but I thought you'd like it.'

Why was he doing this to her? She had already decided how she felt about him. She hated him. So why start being kind now just to confuse her? 'Thanks . . . dad.' She almost choked on the last word.

'You be a good girl in London, do you hear?'

'Yes.' That was better. She was on safer ground when he lectured her. Even so there was none of the usual anger in his voice.

'I know we've had our bad times of late, lass, but I do care about you, and I promised your mum I'd always look after you. After the way I treated her, I owe her that much. Now have you got a kiss for your old dad before you go off to London?'

Becky swallowed hard then reached forward and gave him a perfunctory kiss on the cheek, only to be enveloped in his arms.

'I've loved you since you were a baby,' he said. 'And nowt'll change that.'

She fled the kitchen in tears.

★　★　★

'Are you all right now, Rebecca?' Charles had let her cry, before pulling up on a grass verge several miles out of Stony Newton.

'Yes. I'm really sorry,' said Becky, gulping back a sob that threatened to erupt.

'What did he say to you? If he gives you any more grief, I swear, I'll hit him.'

Becky looked up at him wide-eyed. 'Don't

do that. You don't know what he's capable of.'

'With women, maybe, but not with men. You can always tell the sort. I hate to think of you living in that house. Has he ever hurt you?'

'Not physically, no. He seems to think it makes it all right, but it doesn't. I know there were times mam took a beating because of me . . . '

'No, not because of you. Don't ever think that you're to blame. It's his problem, Rebecca, not yours.'

'It's funny, but when I was a little girl, he used to love me. And I loved him. Gradually I began to realise that the happy moments didn't excuse his behaviour the rest of the time. The worst of it is that he doesn't even realise he's done wrong, afterwards. Oh, he talks now about how he treated mam, and how he thinks she's forgiven him, but it hasn't taught him not to treat poor old Doris in the same way.'

'It's a pattern, I think,' said Charles. 'Probably his father did the same to his mother, and his father's father to his mother, and so on. It can be hard to break that pattern. There's a lot more of it going on than you realise.'

'Is there? I've grown up thinking we were

the only ones living like that. It was a secret that we were never allowed to talk about outside the house.'

'You're not as alone as you think.' He reached over and wiped a stray tear from her cheek. 'You poor darling.'

Becky stiffened. 'I don't want you to feel sorry for me.'

'Then I won't,' he said, with mock mortification.

'Besides, I'm already an expert at feeling sorry for myself,' she said, with a wry grin.

'Don't you believe it. I could give you lessons in self-pity.' He started the car. 'Come on. Let's forget about how sorry we feel for ourselves, at least for a day or two. We'll have a great time in London, you and I.'

★　★　★

When Jed returned from work, he found that Maggie had made an effort to tidy their room. The small table was set for two, with a candle in the centre.

'Hello, love,' she said, with a warm smile. It put him immediately on his guard.

'What's all this then?'

'I thought we'd have a nice evening in together. I've bought you some stout, look.' She pointed to the bottles on the table. 'I've

80

got your favourite lamb stew cooking on the stove downstairs. Mrs. Jenkins helped me a bit, and I've said she can share it. But she won't be eating with us.'

'What's it all in aid of? It's not our anniversary, is it?'

'No, silly. Can't a wife treat her husband? I do love you, you know.' She put her arms around his neck. 'Afterwards, I thought we could have a walk up to Castle Fields, and do all the things we did that first night.'

'Including me coming too soon?'

She laughed and nuzzled his neck. 'You don't have that problem any more, do you? You're a real man.'

'Are you going to tell me you're pregnant?' he asked.

'No, but . . . well I had a word with old Doctor Latimer today . . . '

Jed took a step back, out of her embrace. 'I don't think I'm going to like this.'

'He said it's ever so easy to do tests. I've had one, and he says there's nothing wrong with me.'

'There's nothing wrong with me, either.'

'Of course not, love. But it won't hurt to check. I've made an appointment for you.'

'I am not going to see the doctor about this. And if I find out you've been telling all your friends . . . '

'I haven't told anyone anything. Please, Jed, I should be pregnant by now. Florrie Linney has had another baby. A boy. And she says her husband had help.'

'You said you'd not told anyone!'

'I haven't.'

'You must have. Because she wouldn't just give you that information, Maggie.' It didn't ring true. Florrie and Andy Linney had several children. One thing Andy didn't need was help. 'What have you been saying?' He clenched his fists. He turned and struck out at the wall, putting a hole in the plaster. 'There's nothing wrong with me, all right! I've had a kid.'

'What?'

'I said I've had a kid, so there's nothing wrong with me.'

⋆   ⋆   ⋆

Becky and Charles ate a late dinner in a hotel on the outskirts of London. She was acutely aware of the looks given to her by the staff. They probably thought she was his mistress, and she was not so sure herself. He had been charming throughout the meal, telling her stories of his time in the flying corps, and how he had once seen the Red Baron.

'Was he the one who shot you down?' she

asked, but instantly regretted reminding him of his accident.

'No, sadly I don't have that claim to fame. The engine caught fire all on its own. I'm not a hero, despite what people say. I'm just a victim of shoddy machinery.'

'It was pretty brave to go up there in the first place. I don't think I should like to go up in an aeroplane.'

'It's wonderful when you're up there, Rebecca. You see the world from a whole new perspective. It makes you realise how small we all are in the big scheme of things.'

'Do you still fly?'

'I haven't since the accident. Perhaps I could hire an aeroplane. Would you like to fly in one?'

'I don't know . . . '

'I promise you, I'm not in the habit of crashing all the time.'

'That's not what I was thinking. I was thinking that I might disgrace myself.'

'I don't think you could ever do that. You worry too much, you know. About what people think of you.'

'There speaks a man with enough money not to care what others think.'

'Yes, I suppose that might be true. But people like you, you know.'

'Do they? Would you believe that when I

was a little girl, everyone used to call me Smiler? I was always such a happy child. Nowadays I feel adrift from everyone.' She almost told him the reason why, because he looked on her with so much sympathy, but quickly decided against it. His sympathy might just as rapidly wane and she did not want to lose this magical moment with him in the horrible truth. 'It's my own fault, I suppose. I don't make enough effort.'

'There you go again, blaming yourself. Eighteen-year-olds always think the whole world is against them. When I was that age, I was convinced that my parents couldn't possibly be my real family. They were so alien to me, and I to them. I felt sure I must have been adopted or left on the doorstep or something.' The pause that followed the latter statement seemed to Becky to last an eternity. Charles took a sip of brandy, which she copied, almost choking on the heady liqueur. 'We don't treat our young very well in this country,' he said, 'and seldom listen to what they have to say.'

Becky chuckled, relieved that the tension had broken. 'You sound like an old man.'

'I am an old man, compared to you.'

'I don't think you're old. Frank is only a few years older than you are, and yet he could pass for a man of fifty. You don't look 'nearly as old as that.'

'Well, thank you for that. I think. I'd like to carry you around in my pocket, for days when I need a morale boost.'

Becky thought that his pocket would be a very nice place to spend the rest of her life, but did not say so. 'Thank you for tonight, Mr. Harcourt. You've been really kind to me. I was so silly earlier.'

'You weren't silly at all. And it's Charles. Mr. Harcourt makes me feel like your history teacher.' He stopped and listened for a while. Music drifted from the ballroom. The song playing was Apple Blossom Time. 'Let's go and dance.'

'Won't your sister be waiting for us?'

'Patty keeps late hours and she expects everyone else to. It's your birthday, you're young and pretty and therefore you should be dancing.' He put down his napkin and offered her his hand.

★　★　★

'I want to know about it.' Maggie poked Jed in the ribs.

'No. I've said too much already.' He sat up in bed, smoking a cigarette.

'If you've got a kid somewhere, I'm entitled to know about it.' Maggie lay back on the

85

pillow, with the sheet pulled tightly around her and her arms folded. She had never refused Jed sex before, but for the last few hours had resisted all his advances, perhaps guessing that all he really wanted to do was change the subject. 'It's Clara Peters, isn't it? She's got a kid. Did you have to pay her?'

'It's not Clara Peters. I'd be afraid of what I might catch.'

'Florrie Linney? Everyone says her first lad looks more like the milkman's than Andy's.'

'Then how could he be mine, if he looks like the milkman?'

'You know what I mean!' She pursed her lips and exhaled loudly. 'You're lying then. There's no kid. You're just saying it to get out of going to the doctor. You're not a man, that's what it is. A real man would have me barefoot and pregnant by now. You're just nothing.'

Jed spun round and caught her by the throat. 'It was with Becky, alright. We did it loads of times and had a kid. A boy. She had him in secret and we left him on the Priory steps. You even saw us coming back. It were the night her dad came home, remember.'

Maggie nodded, gasping for air, her eyes red with tears and lack of oxygen. Jed had a vision of her going straight to her friends and telling them all about it. Her life was grist for the mill, and nothing could be a secret. 'I'm warning you, Maggie. If you ever tell anyone, I'll go to prison for it. And then I'll kill you. Right?' He pressed harder. 'I said, right?'

'Yes,' she gasped. 'Let me go.' She threw him off and turned on her side, sobbing. 'You don't know what it's like for me, knowing you love her and not me. It's always Becky this and Becky that. Why can't you love me? Why? What's wrong with me?'

'Come here.' Jed put his arms around her, spooning his body against hers. 'There's nothing wrong with you. We'll have a baby soon, I promise.' He cupped her breast in his hand. 'I'll give you a dozen kids before I'm done. But you mustn't tell anyone, Maggie. You mustn't.' He pulled up her nightie. Of course he could have children, and he'd prove it to her.

★ ★ ★

Most of the guests had gone to bed. Charles and Becky carried on dancing, oblivious to the band, who yawned and looked at their watches in between notes. This was what he had dreamed of, holding a pretty girl in his arms, after a good dinner. At first she seemed a little shy in his embrace, standing apart from him, but gradually the music carried her closer, so that he could smell her perfume, laced with the aroma of cheap soap, and feel her soft, supple body against his. Not that he minded the cheap soap. It was a good, clean smell, unlike the girl he had paid a year before.

He never wanted to repeat that experience, though not because it had been unpleasurable. Despite the prostitute's grubbiness there had been something titillating about the whole tawdry experience and that bothered him. He wanted freshness and innocence, and he believed he had found it in Rebecca.

'We should be getting to your sister's,' Becky said.

'Hmm, yes, I suppose.' They stopped dancing, but did not move from the dance floor. Her mouth was only inches away from his, sweet and young. He kissed her, lightly at first, so as not to alarm her, surprised to find she offered her lips to him readily. He pulled her even closer, drunk with the pleasure of finally being able to touch her, kissing her lips, her cheeks, and her neck. 'Rebecca . . . ' he whispered against her ear.

'Yes.'

'I don't want to go to my sister's. I want to take you upstairs and make love to you.' He felt her begin to tremble. 'Sorry.' Charles pulled away. 'That was . . . '

'Yes,' she said, nodding. 'Yes, I want that too.'

'You're not afraid?'

'I'm terrified, but I still want to.'

'If anything happens. If you have a baby . . . '

She put her finger to his lips. 'You don't have to make me any promises. I just want to be with you, even if it's only for one night.'

He booked two rooms. He did not much care what they thought of him, but he would not subject Becky to that sort of disapproval. He waited a while, during which he thought he would go mad with desire, before going to her.

'You haven't changed your mind, have you?' he asked, when she answered her door. 'Just say the word, and I'll go away.' She shook her head and smiled, before letting him in. She wore a clean, but inexpensive white nightgown, which accentuated her youth and inexperience.

They stood at the end of the bed, both suddenly awkward and shy. He found his own fingers were trembling as he reached for her waist and pulled her closer to him. 'You're so lovely,' he murmured, stroking her cheek. She reached up and touched his cheek, the one with the scar.

'So are you.'

He smiled at that, and kissed her in thanks. The kiss became deeper, as he slipped his tongue between her lips. He sensed from her response that she had never been kissed like that, but she soon relaxed and let him explore her mouth, before she understood and mirrored his movements with her own tongue. His hand cupped the soft swell of her breast, and he lowered her onto the bed, gently laying her back. 'I'll stop any time you want me to,' he promised.

'I don't want you to stop. I want you to keep on touching me.'

'I love you, Rebecca.' He spoke the truth.

'You don't have to say that.'

'I mean it. I love you. Do you love me, a little?'

'I've loved you forever,' she said.

He kissed her face, and then her neck, trailing kisses down her body to where his hand caressed her through her underwear, smiling to himself when she responded to the touch of his mouth with a delighted 'oh'.

7

1926

Jack woke up in a cold sweat, with his heart threatening to burst. It was the same nightmare, where something dark and heavy pressed down on his face and chest.

'Mummy,' he croaked. Some noise had woken him from the bad dream, but halfway between sleep and consciousness he could not place it. The noise repeated; breaking glass and his mother screeching at the top of her voice.

He exhaled. They were at it again. Any minute now the call would come, and he would have to gird his nine-year-old loins and try to act brave.

'You won't leave me, you won't! I'll kill you first!' Something else broke. Not glass this time. Porcelain. Jack was becoming attuned to the different noises breaking crockery made. It would be something that his paternal grandparents had given his mother and father as a wedding gift. His mother never broke any of her parents' gifts. He got out of bed and tiptoed to his door, opening it slightly. If she did not hear him, she might leave him out of it. Not that she ever did. They were in the sitting-room, a few doors away.

'For God's sake, Patricia! Keep your voice down. Think of the other residents. Think of Jack.'

'It's a pity you didn't think of the neighbours when you were screwing your secretary. Why do you do it, John?'

'Perhaps because she's easy . . . '

'Oh she is that. From what I hear she's had MPs on both sides of the floor, and half the House of Lords.'

'I meant to say she's easy-going and uncomplicated. Unlike you, where life is always some drama or another. It's over Patty. I cannot be married to you anymore.'

'Oh, you don't think you're going to divorce me, do you? What do you think that will do for your parliamentary prospects? You're not leaving me, John.'

'I am this time.'

'What about Jack? When I think of the hours I was in labour with that child. I almost died, you know.'

'Yes, and you also tried to slit your wrists halfway through your pregnancy. That shows just how much you think of our son.'

'I'd lost his twin!' Patricia's voice rose. 'I

didn't know I was still pregnant.'

Jack heard the story a dozen times. About how his mother had lost one baby, but then he had arrived, like a gift from God. Sometimes he wondered if God had sent him to hell by mistake.

'Don't leave me, John.' Her voice became softer, more seductive. 'You know I love you. I'll forgive you, like I always do. We can go to bed. I'll do all the things you like. You know I can do it better than she can.'

'I don't want you, Patty. I haven't wanted you for a long time. For God's sake, get up off your knees.'

'Don't leave me, John,' she repeated. 'I can't live without you. Oh please.' Her voice broke into a sob. 'I'll die if I can't be with you. I'll kill myself.'

'Don't you dare!' His father's voice became savage. 'You're not going to get me like that again, Patty. I've fallen for it too many times. You've no intentions of dying. If you had, you'd have done it ages ago and saved us all a lot of anguish.'

'You bastard!'

Jack sensed rather than heard movement from the sitting-room. The bedroom door flew open. 'Jack, Jackie, baby, come to mummy. Daddy's being really cruel to me, Jackie. He doesn't love me. He doesn't love you.'

'Jesus Christ, Patricia, don't tell him that.'

'Jack.'

He dutifully, but reluctantly, followed his mother down the hallway. It was not far, but on nights like this it seemed to stretch for miles. He did not want to go to the sitting-room, and see what happened next. It would involve his mother's tears, mixed with blood, or tablets, whilst his father stood by and watched impotently.

'Jack, baby, there you are.' Patricia pulled him into her arms. 'I'll kill myself and him, John. I swear it, if you leave me.'

'Patty!'

'I will. He doesn't want to live, do you, Jackie?'

Jack trembled. Actually he did want to live, but did not want to disappoint his mother either, which he would do if he refused to go with her. How could he answer in a way that would not upset her?

'Jack.' His father held out his arms. 'Come on, son. Come to your old dad. Don't do this to him, Patty. I'll stay. But don't hurt the boy. He's done nothing to deserve this.'

Jack stepped away from his mother, relief washing over him. But he knew one step towards his father would be seen as betrayal by his mother. And he was hers. His father did not love him. Never had. She told him that nearly every day.

Near to the fireplace was a brown vase that they used to hold the fire irons. It did not suit anything else in the room. It was a big ugly old thing that his maternal grandparents, whom he had never met, had bought as an anniversary present. He went to that instead, treading over broken crockery as he did so. 'What are you doing, Jack?' his father asked. 'Jack?'

Jack picked up the vase, and went to the window.

'Jack, what are you doing?'

With a scream that came from the same place as the recurring nightmare, Jack hurled the vase at the large picture window, shattering glass around his bloodied feet.

'Now look what you've done, John,' said Patricia. When Jack turned around to look at her, she was smiling and he was glad to have made her happy.

★   ★   ★

Charles closed the bedroom door and made a play of tiptoeing towards the bed. 'Shh,' he said, putting his fingers to his lips. 'I think they're finally asleep.'

'The move has been too exciting for them,' said Rebecca. They had moved into a three-bedroom apartment above the Priory garages. She sat up in bed, reading. Charles got in beside her, and threw the book out of her hands, before pulling her into his arms. 'Hey!'

'Shh. You'll wake them. What's there to be excited about? We've only moved about a hundred yards.'

'I know, but they've been watching the builders for weeks, dreaming about their room.'

'So have you.'

'Oh yes. It's lovely to have a space of our own at last.'

'And to be away from my parents.'

'Hmm.'

'I'm sorry they've given you a hard time, darling.' Charles kissed her nose.

'They haven't. Well, not much. It's not that they're unkind to me. They've never been that. I think they're both too well-mannered. It's just the feeling that they'd rather I wasn't here. They don't mind you and the twins. I think if they could have you three and not me, they'd be very happy.' Rebecca regretted it the minute she said it, fearing it would lead to one of their rare rows. But Charles was in a good mood.

'That's not true. Father was only saying the other day how hard you worked at the Factory.'

'Your father isn't too bad actually. He tolerates me even if he doesn't like me very much. It's your mother. I still remember her face when you brought me home from London and announced we'd got married.' The memory gave Rebecca a mixture of happiness and immense pain. Until that day, she thought she knew about the divide between the working and middle classes. But in reality she had no idea, until her status was made plain to her by the horrified look on Veronica Harcourt's face.

'Hmm, I remember that night.' Charles bent his head and kissed her breasts through her nightgown.

'You were very naughty, trying to make me scream when your parents were only a few doors away.'

Charles chuckled. 'And now they're all the way across the yard.'

'But the twins are just down the hall. And if they wake up, you can forget any hopes of getting lucky tonight.'

'So . . . '

'So . . . '

'We'll have to be very, very, very quiet.'

'I'm not sure I can make a promise like that,' said Rebecca, wrapping her legs around him and kissing him.

'Are you happy, darling?'

'Yes, happier than I've ever been. I know where I belong now.'

'I know where I belong too.'

'You are filthy.' Rebecca threw back her head and laughed. Regardless of how his parents had behaved, Charles always made life effortless for her, brushing away her fears with light-hearted banter. It was the same when they made love. Any sense of shame she might have felt after the first time was swiftly eradicated by the fact that he encouraged her to enjoy sex rather than treating it as a guilty secret.

'But you like it.'

'I must admit I do.'

'And you the mother of twins. Really, I'm quite shocked.'

'Shall I shock you even more?' She slipped her hand inside his pyjama trousers.

'Oh, please do, Mrs. Harcourt.'

The ringing of the telephone disturbed them. 'Damn!'

'Ignore it, Charles.'

The trilling stopped, and then started again.

'I don't think we're going to be allowed to.' Charles got out of bed and went down the hall to the sitting-room.

Rebecca could hear his low tones, saying, 'Yes', 'No', 'Oh, good gracious', 'I suppose that would be for the best'.

'What is it?' she asked, when he returned to the bedroom.

'It seems young Jack has gone a bit wild. He smashed up Patty and John's apartment.'

'Good God, why did he do that?'

'Probably picked it up off Patty. Mother and father used to have to hide the crockery when she was on the warpath.' Charles climbed back into bed.

'Yes, you've said.' After five years of living with her in-laws, Rebecca could almost sympathise with Patty's frustration. George and Veronica Harcourt lived a sterile life, where any show of emotion was frowned upon. Sometimes, whilst living in the main building, she had touched the walls, half expecting them to feel like Gamgee tissue, sucking the life and emotion out of the atmosphere.

Her first few months of living there had been a humiliating round of saying and doing the wrong thing. Her mother might have brought her up to speak well, but it was not the way real middle-class people spoke. Similarly, she did not know that there could be more than one knife and fork at the dinner table or that one did not go to the kitchen and make one's own cup of tea. She learned quickly and agonisingly under Veronica's disapproving glare.

'The neighbours called the police, but as only Patty and John's own property was damaged, there was nothing they could do. Patty is bringing Jack up here for a while, till the fuss dies down and the neighbours forget.'

'It will be nice to see him at last.'

'That's what mother said.'

'It's odd, that Patty has never brought him here, isn't it? And the way she put us off visiting whenever we're in London. I wonder why that is.'

'Darling, you're seeing intrigue where there is none.' Despite his words, Charles looked concerned, and Rebecca wondered what lay behind it. 'It's just that Patty didn't want mother interfering in his upbringing. You know what she's like with Ricky and Bobby.'

'Oh yes . . . ' Rebecca nodded. 'Do you know the other day they were playing with their cars in the hall, and she actually said they were getting too old for that? They're not even five yet!'

'Mother doesn't much like children. The quicker they grow up the better as far as she's concerned.'

Rebecca secretly believed that Veronica did not much like adults. It took a lot of effort not to criticise Charles' parents to him. Not least because most of the rows they had were about his mother and father. It was a subject best avoided. Besides, she sensed her mother-in-law's coldness was aimed mainly at her. It would be interesting to see how Veronica behaved with Patty.

'Now,' said Charles, putting his arms around her. 'We were just about to christen our new bed, weren't we?'

'God bless her and all who sail in her.'

8

Several months after the end of the General Strike, the miners of Stony Newton clung on to their belief in industrial action. Depression hung over the town as thickly as the smog from the pit. Pickets lined the gates of the mine, jeering and shouting at anyone who tried to pass them. Signs proclaimed: 'Not a penny off the pay, not a second on the day'.

Army trucks stood in the pit yard. Soldiers had been brought in to do the work of the miners.

Frank Wilson arrived at around ten in the morning, driving his new car. He saw Len Peters, Albert Taylor and Albert's son-in-law, Andy Linney at the front of the crowd.

'Scab!' yelled Len.

'Traitor!' called Albert.

The flank of striking miners crossed the gates, barring his path. Frank rolled down his window. 'Come on, lads. Someone's got to keep the pit going. If we don't, it'll flood out and there'll be no jobs to go back to anyway.'

'You used to be on our side, Frank,' said Len.

'I can't strike,' said Frank. 'I'm a manager.'

'Ay, don't we chuffing know it,' said Albert. 'Living in that big house now. You've forgotten your roots, Frank. Forgotten what you started out as. If me and Len hadn't put in a word for you when you got back from t'war, you wouldn't have a job.'

'I haven't forgotten, mate. But a man's got a right to improve himself, hasn't he? Otherwise what are we fighting for?'

'We are not fighting for anything.' Len poked Frank's shoulder through the window, emphasizing the 'we'. 'It's us doing the fighting. You take home a wage every week, and give dinner parties for t'other managers at your house. I hear your grandsons are having a do, too.'

'You don't deny the little ones a birthday party, do you?'

'I do when my grandkids are living off handouts from the benevolent fund,' said Albert.

'Our Florrie's kids got an invite,' said Albert. 'She was all for them going, but I ripped it up.'

'That's nowt to do with me. That's our Becky's doing,' said Frank. 'She's got all high and mighty since she married Charlie Harcourt.'

'She's not the only one,' said Len. He spat on the floor.

'Now step aside and let me pass.' Frank rolled up his window, just in time to deflect a stream of spittle coming from the assembled miners.

He held his head high as he entered his office. Not for the sake of those watching and jeering, but because he still felt a sense of pride in his position. In five years he had risen from the role of face worker to that of manager. He had no guilt about the friends he had trampled over in order to reach his current status. He and Doris had moved into *Bon Chance,* a large house set aside for pit managers, with four bedrooms, a separate dining-room, and about an acre of grounds around it. They even had a maid. In Frank's mind, he had earned it by taking an enemy bullet. He was not particularly concerned about losing his friends. He had never much liked Len and Albert. Frank much preferred the company of women.

'Any messages, Violet?' he asked his secretary.

'Mr. Blake would like to see you.' Blake was the pit owner, and a man with whom Frank enjoyed doing business.

'I didn't realise he was coming in today.'

'He's not. He won't come anywhere near the picket line. He said you have to go to his house tonight. He wants to discuss something with you.'

'Thank you, Violet. How are you this morning?' Frank settled on the edge of her desk. She was a pretty little thing, and only twenty-two years old, yet she showed every sign of adoring him.

'I'm fine thank you, Mr. Wilson. Mum isn't well though. It would be nice if we could buy her some treats, you know . . . '

Frank put his hand in his pocket. 'Here. There's ten bob. Buy her some chocolates and some decent meat.'

'Thank you, Mr. Wilson.'

'I thought we agreed it was Frank.'

'Thank you, Frank.' She fluttered her eyelashes at him. 'I don't know how I'm going to repay you.'

'You don't?'

Violet smiled. 'I've already told you, Mr. Wilson, you're a married man.'

'If you can call it marriage. Doris is ten years older than I am, and as such doesn't want to . . . well, you know. But a man needs that in his life.'

'I don't know. It's very difficult, what with mum being poorly all the time. I could get my aunty to sit with her but she'd want paying . . . '

'Here, take another couple of bob.'

'You're very generous, Mr. Wilson . . . Frank.'

He reached over and stroked her cheek. 'But how generous are you going to be in return, Violet? Will you let me kiss you?'

'Yes.' She stood up and came to him, offering her cheek for a chaste kiss. Instead he took her in his arms, and covered her mouth with his, thrusting his tongue between her lips. He cupped her buttocks in his hands. She struggled slightly, but he put that down to her shyness.

'No, no, we mustn't,' she said, pulling away and wiping her mouth on her arm.

'Will you meet me tonight, after I've been to see Blake? I could take you for a drive in my car.'

'Yes, alright then.'

'I'll want more than a kiss, Violet.'

'I don't know. I've never done it before.' She gazed up at him with innocent eyes.

'Never mind about that, lass. I can teach you everything you need to know.'

★ ★ ★

Violet watched from the door as Frank Wilson went to the pithead. She cringed inwardly. What had she let herself in for? When she was sure no one was in the pit

106

yard, she walked across to the gates on the pretext of going out for a cigarette. Len and Albert detached themselves from the group, and approached the other side of the gates.

'Here,' said Violet, handing him the money Frank had given her. 'Put this in the benevolent fund.'

'You're a good lass, Violet,' said Len.

'If I was a good lass I wouldn't be taking money for kisses.'

'You don't have to take it any further,' said Albert. 'You can get a lot out of Frank Wilson just by keeping him on a promise.'

'What have you got for us?' asked Len.

'Blake has called him in for talks,' said Violet. 'It sounds as if they're cooking something up.'

'Any idea what, lass?'

'No. They don't tell me much.'

'We could do with a fly on that wall at that meeting,' said Len.

'He wants me to see him after,' said Violet, her face glum.

'Are you up for it, lass?'

'No. He wants more than kisses. I can't keep putting him off.'

'Forget it then,' said Albert. 'We're not asking you to prostitute yourself, lass.'

'Aren't you?'

'No. We're not.'

107

'I've got to get back.' Violet looked behind her. There was no one around, but that might change. A few of the soldiers had been underground since the early hours. 'I'll go and meet him, see what I can find out. But I'm not going to go all the way with him.'

'Be careful, lass,' said Len. 'Sometimes it's hard for a fella to take no for an answer once he gets going.'

'I'll deal with him,' she said. 'Speak to you tomorrow.'

She dropped her cigarette on the floor and stamped on it before returning to the office.

* * *

'If things continue,' said George Harcourt, 'we might be forced to sell off some of the housing stock.'

'But if you do that, private landlords will come in and start charging extortionate rents,' said Rebecca.

They were in Charles' office. George hardly ever came in nowadays, so she and Charles knew immediately that his arrival meant something serious.

'Thank you, Rebecca, but I think this will be a decision for the directors. Why don't you go and put the kettle on?' said George.

'Just a minute, father,' said Charles. 'Rebecca may not be a director, but she knows the company and she knows Stony Newton.'

'I'm sure she does.' George looked contrite. 'I apologise, Rebecca. I didn't mean to snap your head off. But things are getting critical. Of course, the cost of converting the garage took a fair bit out of company funds.'

'Which we're repaying out of my salary,' said Charles firmly. 'We didn't know what was going to happen when we drew up the plans, and it wouldn't have been fair on the builders to cancel, given that they'd already bought in materials. There's enough unemployment around here. What do you think would have happened if we'd done them out of a job?'

'Yes, yes, I know that.' George waved his hand as if it were of no matter. 'The truth is that we're struggling. The miners' strike has had a far-reaching effect, particularly on the economy. Our suppliers are buying less because they're selling less, especially in mining areas. It's not just us. It's happening all over the country.

'We're aware of that,' said Charles. 'We're here every day, father.'

'We have a choice, Charles. We either sell off housing stock or we decrease the workforce. I don't have to tell you what that will do locally.'

'At the moment the money women earn is the only income in their household,' said Rebecca.

'Yes, which is why I'm keen to avoid that,' said George. 'I'm not completely unsympathetic to the miners' plight.'

'We should think about scaling down the twins' birthday party.' said Rebecca.

'Certainly not,' said George.

'But you must admit it's in bad taste, given that families in the area are struggling,' said Rebecca. 'Why can't they just have a small party with a few friends?'

'It's out of the question. It's not just about the twins. It's going to be a corporate event.'

'Is it?' It was the first Rebecca had heard. It did explain why George and Veronica had gone to town on the arrangements.

'Yes. Anyway, don't worry. Veronica invited all the local children too. In your name of course. As I said, we're not that unsympathetic to current events.'

Rebecca wanted to suggest they had been tactless, but she bit her tongue. It explained why Florrie Linney had been so cool with her when she arrived at the factory that morning. Usually Florrie spoke to her more than the others did. She did not seem to mind

Rebecca's position as much as the rest of the women.

'Excuse me a minute,' she said, leaving Charles and George discussing their financial situation.

The machinery for making Gamgee tissue was placed in the centre of the factory floor, with rolls of gauze piled high nearby. The women worked at individual tables, set in rows alongside the windows, putting the Gamgee tissue into individual envelopes. Rebecca found Florrie's table. Florrie was pregnant again, her fifth child since she had married at the age of sixteen. Despite only being twenty-four, she had the look of a much older woman.

'Florrie?'

'What is it, Mrs. Harcourt? I'm a bit busy, and I can't afford to stop.'

'That's all right, Florrie, keep on working. I just want to talk to you. I wanted to say that I hope you weren't offended by receiving an invitation to Ricky and Bobby's party. I know things are difficult at the moment, what with the strike.'

'Me dad were there when it came. He ripped it up.'

'I see.'

'We don't need charity.'

'It wasn't charity. It was a party invitation.'

111

The back of Rebecca's neck bristled. She did not like the way the rest of the women looked at her, as if she were guilty of some crime. Her in-laws had got her into this situation and now she had to face the repercussions. 'My in-laws . . . ' She stopped herself. She would not pass the buck. 'It was tactless to send them, given how difficult everything is for everyone in Stony Newton at the moment.'

'It's a bad idea to be spending money on a huge party when the rest of us are struggling,' said Florrie.

Rebecca was not going to be blamed for that. 'Actually that was Mr. Harcourt senior's idea. He's meeting with some customers, which will be good for everyone here if it works out as he hopes.' She took a deep breath, feeling her face getting hotter and hotter under the scrutiny of the workers. 'Anyway, I apologise if it was the wrong thing to do.' She started to walk away.

'Mrs. Harcourt,' said Florrie. 'It wasn't the wrong thing to do. Not really. My boys were really excited till their granddad ripped up the invite. It's all right for the men, they've got all these high ideals. We're the ones left feeding kids on thin air.'

'So bring them to the party. I'll make sure there's plenty of food for them. There's going to be a Punch and Judy show, and clowns.'

Florrie glanced at the other women. From the expressions on their faces, Rebecca guessed that Florrie was breaking ranks. 'We can't afford to turn down treats,' Florrie said, more to them than to Rebecca. 'Let's give our kids a good day out. Lord knows they've had very little else lately.

Len Peters' wife spoke up. She was a buxom woman in her fifties, with silver grey hair piled on her head, and a Victorian manner. As a child, Rebecca had been terrified of Edna Peters, and she couldn't say the forthright miner's wife didn't still strike fear in her heart. 'The men'll be angry, Florrie. You know what they've said about sucking up to the management.'

'Yes,' said another woman, 'but they think food arrives out of nowhere. They don't know that we've all had to sell things off. I had to pawn my wedding ring the other day, and I daren't tell my bloke. I've had to pretend I've taken it to be cleaned. I'm sick of struggling whilst they sit in the pub spouting their rhetoric. They can all manage a pint whilst we scrimp and save. I say we let the kids of this town have a bit of a treat. I'll be there, Mrs. Harcourt, with my two.'

'Thing is,' said Florrie, 'we can't afford presents.'

'Oh.' Rebecca felt giddy with relief. 'That doesn't matter. In fact ... ' she stopped. She'd been about to offer the women some of the boys' old toys and clothes for their own children, but decided to save that for another day. One wrong word and she could lose their support. 'You'll all be welcome. We'll make a day of it. Bring your husbands too.'

'They'll not come if your dad is there,' said Edna Peters. 'I won't be there, and neither will any of mine. I knew you when you were nothing, Becky Wilson, so don't start coming the big I Am with us. You lot ought to be ashamed of yourself, letting her buy you all like this.'

The other women murmured amongst themselves, terrified of crossing Edna. She had been there the longest, so tended to have the final word in everything.

'I'll leave you all to decide,' Rebecca said. 'The offer is there. It's up to you if you take it.'

★ ★ ★

'We're here, Jackie.' Patricia pointed up at the Priory. 'You'll be seeing your grandparents at last.'

Jack sat sullenly in the corner of the back seat. He did not see why he had to be

114

dragged out of school to come to this miserable town. 'It's the dirtiest place I've ever seen,' he said to his mother.

'What? The Priory? No, grandmother keeps it very clean.'

'I meant this town. It's horrid.'

'Well, yes, it is rather. That's why I don't come here a lot.'

The chauffeur pulled up at the front door, which opened as soon as they got out of the car. A woman Jack supposed was his grandmother came rushing down the steps, followed by an old man.

'Patty, dearest,' said Veronica. 'It's been too long.'

'Hello, mother. Father. This is Jack.' His mother seemed nervous. He wondered why. 'Jack, these are your grandparents.'

'Well, isn't he a handsome boy? Jack, come and give your grandmother a kiss.'

He allowed himself to be kissed. His grandfather held out his hand, and Jack took it. 'Is Uncle Charles here?' asked Jack. 'I want to see his scars.'

'Jack!' Patricia laughed. Her nervousness was catching. He did not know what to say to these two very serious-looking people. He was used to his mother's fun-loving friends, who fussed over him and gave him money for sweets.

'Charles and Rebecca are living over the garage,' said George. 'We wanted to be the first to greet you. Did you know you have two cousins, Jack? They'll be along in a short while.'

Jack shrugged. He had been told something about it but he did not much like other children.

'Come on in,' said Veronica. 'We've got tea and cakes for you, Jack. Patricia, you've kept him from us too long.'

*   *   *

Charles stood at the window, watching as Patty and Jack arrived. He was as eager to see Jack as his parents, albeit for different reasons. He wanted to see how the scrawny child Patty had picked up on the doorstep had turned out. From what he had been told, the child was over-indulged and had picked up some of his sister's worst habits.

'Are they here?' asked Rebecca, carrying a tea tray in from the kitchen.

'Yes, they've just arrived now.'

'You sound almost as excited as your mother.'

'I am, I suppose. After all, he is my nephew.'

'What does he look like?'

'It's hard to tell from this distance. I just hope he isn't going to start smashing the Priory up.'

'I've wondered that too. Did Patty ever say why he did it?'

'No, but she's only spoken to mother. If she knows, she's keeping it to herself.'

'Do you want a cup of tea?'

'Thank you, darling. Where are the boys?'

'They're playing with their new train set. Or should I say your train set?'

'I didn't buy it for myself.' Charles turned and smiled sheepishly.

'No?' She raised a sardonic eyebrow.

'Well, I must admit to feeling a certain amount of childish delight when I saw it in the shop.'

Rebecca sat back on the sofa, sighing.

'What's wrong? Are you nervous about meeting Patty, darling? Don't be. She'll probably be very rude to you, but Patty is that way with everyone. It won't be anything personal.' He sat next to her and put his arm around her shoulder.

'It's not that. It's the boys' party. I feel a bit like Nero.'

'Fiddling whilst Rome burns?'

'Yes.'

'Life has to go on, sweetheart. We can't put everything on hold because of the strike.'

'No, but we could be a little more tactful.'

'Do you think Florrie and the others will come?'

'I don't know. Edna Peters is quite formidable. She used to scare me to death when I was a child. I still wouldn't want to meet her on a dark night.'

'No . . . ' Charles was about to say more, but someone rang the doorbell.

'Sorry, darling,' said Patricia, when he answered the door, 'but Jack would not be put off meeting you.'

'Oh, bring him through. Hello Jack.'

Charles had stopped feeling so self-conscious about his looks, but Jack's blatant stare and questions made him want to look away.

'Do they hurt?'

'No.'

'Are they all over your body?'

'Some of it.'

'Can I see?'

'No, I don't think so.'

'Who is it, darling?' Rebecca came into the hallway. 'Oh, you must be Patricia. And Jack. It's nice to meet you both.' Rebecca held out her hand. 'I'm Rebecca.'

Patty took it, but let go just as quickly. Jack, continuing to stare at Charles, said, 'Oh, you're the gold-digging whore that Uncle Charles married.'

Charles saw Rebecca turn pale. 'Now, just a minute, young man . . . '

'I don't know where he got that from,' said Patricia. At least she has the grace to look embarrassed, thought Charles.

'You don't?'

'No. Of course not.'

'Well, perhaps you ought to teach him some manners then.' Charles glared at Jack. 'I don't care for you speaking to my wife like that, so I suggest you apologise.'

Jack looked around at his mother, as if seeking confirmation. Patty was studiously looking at a print on the wall, and clearly trying not to laugh.

'I'll smash your house up,' said Jack. 'I do that all the time. Just ask mother.'

'Then I'll put you over my knee and spank you,' said Charles. 'I don't care what your mother does.' He glared at Patricia then back at Jack. 'I don't let young boys behave like that in my home. And I certainly don't let them insult my wife. Do you understand?'

Jack nodded, his demeanour less arrogant than it had been. 'I'm sorry, Uncle Charles.'

'I'm not the one who needs an apology.'

'I'm sorry,' he whispered to Rebecca.

'That's all right, Jack,' said Rebecca. 'Let's forget it and start again, shall we?' She smiled, but Charles could see her lower lip

119

trembling and knew that she was struggling to contain her tears. 'I've just made some tea,' she said to Patricia. 'I'm sure you're ready for a cup after your trip. Come on through.'

As they walked to the sitting-room, Jack smiled up at Charles and took his hand.

9

Five-year-old Lizzie Alsop did a clumsy spin in her party dress.

'Oh, you do look pretty,' said Maggie, sweeping her daughter up into her arms. 'Isn't she pretty, daddy?'

'She is that,' said Jed. He sat at the kitchen table, reading the paper. He smiled at Lizzie, his heart swelling. How they had managed to create such a happy little child from the deep dark pit of their marriage mystified him. 'She's the prettiest girl in Stony Newton. What's the dress in aid of?'

'She's going to Ricky and Bobby Harcourt's birthday party, aren't you sweetheart?'

'I don't think we should go.'

'Why not, Jed?'

'Because there's folks struggling at the moment.'

'That's nowt to do with us. Is it, Lizzie? You tell daddy. Those silly miners are not our problem.'

'They're not silly,' said Jed. 'Besides, your father is one of those silly miners.'

'Like I said, it's not our problem.' Maggie fiddled with Lizzie's dress. 'The Harcourts don't seem to mind.'

'I must admit, I'm surprised at Becky. She used to care more.'

'No she didn't. She's always thought she were a cut above us. Anyway, she's not Becky anymore. She's Rebecca.'

'She's not like that.'

'Oh yes, I forgot about how much you love her.'

'Don't start, Maggie. Not in front of Lizzie.' Jed was relieved to see that worked. Whatever her other faults, Maggie was a good mother, shielding their daughter from unpleasantness. It was a reason that Jed tried to have Lizzie there whenever he and Maggie spoke. Evening was harder, when he had no choice but to be alone with her.

'What are you reading?' asked Maggie, her mouth full of pins, as she adjusted Lizzie's dress.

'The paper.'

'Yes, I can see that. But you read it this morning. Nowt will have changed.'

'I'm looking at lettings.'

'Lettings? Why? We're alright here, aren't we? Bloody hell, Jed, we've moved five times in as many years.'

'Yes, well, if you paid the rent when you should . . . '

'Not in front of Lizzie.'

'Harcourt's are talking about selling off housing stock. If they sell this house, we might have to move out. Especially if a new landlord comes in and ups the rent.'

'I like this house. It's the sort of house Lizzie should live in. She's going to be a famous actress, aren't you, darling?'

The house, on Factory Lane, had been the residence of a Harcourt director who had died the year before. It was detached, with three bedrooms. Charles Harcourt had let Jed take it the last time they received an eviction notice. Even with a subsidy on the rent, it took most of Jed's wages. Maggie had gone back to Harcourt's to work part-time since Lizzie started school, but even then they struggled. Or Jed did. Maggie had a knack of pulling treats out of a hat. Or, his conscience told him before he could quieten it, off the shelves without shopkeepers noticing.

'Sing your song for daddy, darling? The one I taught you.' Maggie put Lizzie down in the centre of the carpet.

'She'd be better sticking to her education,' said Jed, hating that he sounded like his own father.

'She won't need that when she's a big star.'

'Actresses need to be able to read scripts.'

'Her reading is already coming along nicely, isn't it, sweetheart?'

Lizzie sang her song, before she spun around and fell over.

* * *

Violet Chambers waited under the gaslight. It only accentuated her shame of behaving like a prostitute. The idea of Frank Wilson touching her made her nauseous, but she believed in the cause and would not run away. Too many men in her family had lost their lives in the pit.

Her stomach tightened into a knot when she heard Frank's car approaching.

'Hello, my sweet,' he said, when he pulled up. 'You look as pretty as a picture, standing there.'

The smile she had been practicing all day jumped to attention, and she imagined her face to look as if struck by rictus.

Within a few minutes they were heading out of Stony Newton and into the Peak District. 'I can't be too late,' she told him, hoping he would stop before they got too far out of town. 'Mum is still poorly and Aunty Ada can't stay for long.'

'Don't you worry about that, my sweet,' he said, pressing his hand on her knee. He slid her dress up, stroking the stockings beneath.

'No. Don't do that. I'm not ready for that.'

Frank pulled his hand back but kept it on his knee. 'You will be by the time I'm finished with you.'

'How . . . ' Violet coughed a little, to clear her throat. 'How did the meeting with Mr. Blake go?'

'I don't want to talk pit business. Not tonight.' Frank pulled up onto a roadside verge. Violet glanced around but could not see any houses nearby. 'Come here, give me a kiss.'

Violet allowed him to kiss her, clamping her hand over his when he tried to cup her breast. 'I said no.'

'But you're here alone with me, sweetheart, so you must mean yes.'

'I just wanted to see you and speak to you, that's all.' Her own inexperience hung over her head. It was one thing to flirt in the relative safety of the pit office, where someone might walk in at any time. It was another to be alone with him in a secluded place. 'Because I like being with you so much and we never get a chance for a proper talk.'

His hand reached up and stroked her face, before slipping back down to her neck. His dangerously gentle touch put her on alert.

'Let's get into the back seat,' he whispered against her hair.

'I don't think we should.'

'But you promised me I could have more than a kiss. Remember? Little girls shouldn't make promises they can't keep.'

Violet thought back to what Len and Albert had said. About how men were unable to stop once a girl had led them too far. She did not want Frank to hurt her. 'Okay.' She opened her door, fighting the compulsion to run off into the darkness.

Once they were in the back seat, he pulled her into his arms and kissed her roughly, scraping her face with the bristles on his moustache. 'Don't be afraid, I won't hurt you,' he said.

Despite his promise, he was less than gentle with her. Afterwards, she felt sore, sticky and dirty. Was the cause really worth this sacrifice?

She expected him to hold her, but he lit a cigarette and stared out of the window into the nothingness. Sitting up, Violet adjusted her clothes, trying to recover some semblance of respectability, but inside she was already dying.

'So,' she said, once she had composed herself. 'What was the big meeting about?'

'Wouldn't you like to know?' Frank turned to her, with a big smile on his face.

'I'm . . . I'm just trying to make conversation,' she said.

'Of course you are, sweetheart. Just like Len and Albert told you to. Did you think I was really that stupid? Well, perhaps I was. It was Mr. Blake who tipped me off. Do you know what we talked about?'

'No,' said Violet in a horrified whisper. What else could she say? She had let him do it to her.

'Whether I should have you more than once before telling you you're dismissed.' He looked her up and down, accentuating her feelings of disgust, with herself and with him. 'Given you've put so little effort into it, once will do.'

10

Sam Jenkins heard his wife get out of bed as he peeled the potatoes for their tea. Annette was due home from school within the next hour, and he knew that if he did not prepare anything, Clara would forget to feed her.

'What time is it?' Clara sat down at the kitchen table and lit her first cigarette of the day. Despite her persistent laziness, she had cleaned herself up a lot since they moved from their first flat. She no longer exuded grubbiness from every pore.

Their house was in an up and coming area, full of professional families, and Clara had enough sense of pride to want to look as good as the young wives who walked in the park with their babies. She had even made an effort to keep the house tidy, just in case anyone popped around. No one ever did. Clara's inbred toxicity was such that she seldom made friends.

'Nearly three.'

'Annette back yet?'

'No.' Sam turned around to face her. 'I thought we could go out tonight. Me and you?'

'Why?'

'Because I'm your husband and you're my wife. It's what married people do.'

'We've never done what married people do. Why start now?'

'For Annette's sake. One day she's going to realise exactly how you spend your evenings.'

'I don't care.'

'Well I do!'

'You should have thought of that when you married me.'

Sam sighed. 'I suppose I hoped you'd want to change eventually, once you were in a nice house. I even thought you might start to love me.'

'That was stupid of you.'

He turned back to the bowlful of potatoes, stabbing at them with the knife. 'Come on, Clara, let's go out. We'll have a nice dinner. We could come back after and make love. You know, like a proper couple.'

'Ooh, *make love*! You've been reading those books again, haven't you?'

'I might not be a clever man. If I were I'd have married a lass who enjoyed being in bed with me, and loved me as much as I loved her. I do know that what you think is control over men is nothing of the sort. They're not thinking you're powerful for taking money off them. They're just wondering if they can knock you down a few bob.'

Clara scoffed. 'You think too much, Sam, that's your trouble. I learned a long time ago that thinking gets you nowhere.'

Sam sat down on the chair opposite her, and lit a cigarette for himself. 'I don't know why I bother.'

'You bother because of Annette. She's all that's ever mattered to you. Me, I'm on the outside, whilst you two are reading your books and having your discussions.'

'You could be a part of it, if you tried. What is it that hurt you, Clara? I know you said about your uncle . . . '

'I don't want to talk about that.' She got up and took a bottle of stout from under the sink, snapping the lid off with the tin opener, and gulping down half in just a few seconds. 'At least not whilst I'm sober.'

'If you don't want to come out with me tonight, let's take Annette to the zoo at the weekend. You'll be involved then.'

'You seem to think I care, Sam. But I don't.'

'You must do, otherwise you wouldn't have mentioned being left out.'

'What's that? Psychology?'

'No, it's common sense based on what you said a little while ago.'

'All right,' she said, swigging back more stout. 'We'll go out tonight. And we'll come back and make love.' She drawled the last two words. 'No charge. I can play at being the perfect little wife for a while if it's what you want.'

'I'd like it to be what you want.'

'I don't care either way. I'm easy.'

Sam bit back the obvious reply. It would not be fair to remind her of her promiscuity given that she was making an effort.

A little while later, Annette came bounding through the back door, a frenzy of olive skin, a toothy grin and waist-length, jet-black hair. She chucked her satchel onto the table and went straight to Sam for a hug. She plonked herself on his knee.

'Hello, petal. How have you done at school today?'

'I got a gold star for my spelling, and I wrote a story which Mrs. Palmer said is as good as any Agatha Christie.'

'Good girl. Isn't she clever, mum?'

'Hmm.' Clara got up from her seat and went to the sink. She picked up an onion from the pile and started chopping it up.

'I've already put the onions in,' said Sam.

'You never put in enough.'

'Do you want to see my gold star, mum?' asked Annette.

'Later. Go and wash your hands, ready for your tea.'

'Are you crying, mum?'
'No, stupid. I'm peeling onions.'

★   ★   ★

The ache in Rebecca's gut reminded her of when Frank was due home from work; a sense of malevolence building with each passing moment. Her feeling of impending doom was not helped by the news that Violet Chambers had taken her own life. The town was a powder keg, waiting to explode.

'We should cancel,' she said to Charles and her father-in-law. They were sitting in the drawing-room of the Priory. Patricia flicked lazily through a fashion magazine, dropping cigarette ash on the floor. Jack took up what had become his regular place right next to his uncle Charles, scowling if Ricky or Bobby came to speak to their father.

The twins played quietly on the floor, having learned the rules of the Priory very early in their lives. Patricia and Jack seemed able to follow a different set of rules.

Rebecca knew that when she got her boys back to the flat, there would be half an hour of madness as Ricky ran around the flat letting off steam. Bobby would sit in quiet contemplation, as if he took every slight on his little shoulders.

'There are people coming all the way up from London, Rebecca,' said George. 'They'll be arriving tonight. We can't just turn them around. What happened to this young woman is very sad, God rest her soul, but it's nothing to do with us.'

'Can't we have a party, mummy?' asked Bobby. The question took everyone by surprise. Bobby seldom spoke.

'Of course you can, darling.' Rebecca held out her arms, and he came to her. 'I just thought it doesn't have to be such a big party, that's all.'

'I've always wanted a big party,' said Ricky. 'With lots of cake and clowns and things. I'm going to eat and eat and eat until I'm sick.'

'I certainly hope not,' said Rebecca. 'Charles? What do you think?'

Jack scowled at Rebecca for daring to address Charles.

Charles grinned. 'No, Ricky, you can't eat until you're sick.'

'I meant about the party.'

'I think it's too late to change anything now, darling. It cost us money to book everything, and they'll still want to be paid. Don't worry everything will be all right. No one is going to want to do anything to spoil a child's birthday party.'

Despite his words, Rebecca's unease

continued, to the point that she actively started when Stephens entered the room.

'Mr. Wilson is here to see you, Mrs. Harcourt.'

'Grampy!' said Ricky, jumping up and running to the hall. Bobby followed behind, more cautiously. By the time Rebecca got to the hall, they had both been lifted high into Frank's arms. She struggled with her usual feeling of sickness when she saw him embrace her sons. For reasons she could not fathom, they loved Frank. He fed that love with a bag of sweets and a sense of fun that she had not witnessed since she was a child.

'How are my favourite lads? Growing nice and strong, eh?'

'I'm five tomorrow,' said Ricky.

'So am I,' said Bobby.

'Five. Well, you'll soon be able to come down t'pit with your grampy.'

'Digging coal?' said Ricky, his eyes wide.

'Yes, digging coal.'

'It's what I've always wanted.'

'What can I do for you . . . dad?' asked Rebecca.

'I just thought I'd call and see my boys before it all got too busy tomorrow. I hear you've got a new train set.' He played with his cap. Despite being cock of the walk around Stony Newton, Frank shrank when he

134

entered the door of the Priory.

'We have. It's huge.' Ricky made a sweeping gesture with his arms that took in the whole of the hallway. 'It's what I've always wanted.'

'So these from your grampy won't be much fun then?' Frank put them down and took two bags of marbles out of his pockets.

'Cor, marbles,' said Ricky. 'They're what I've always wanted.'

'Thank you,' said Bobby, more quietly.

'Are they what you've always wanted, Bobby?' asked Frank, winking at Rebecca.

'They're very nice, thank you,' said Bobby. Rebecca wanted to take him in her arms and hug him tight, but she knew as the mother of boys to save expressions of maternal affection for when there were no witnesses.

'Would you like a cup of tea?' asked Rebecca, remembering her manners.

'No, I'm not stopping. I know you've got visitors coming. I just wanted to see the lads before the big rush. Me and Doris will be here tomorrow.'

'That's good.' It was not, but what else could she say? 'Oh, and I'm really sorry to hear about your secretary. Violet.'

'Ay, that were a dreadful shock. They reckon the lass had got in with a bad lot.'

'I always thought Violet was a nice girl.'

'They all start that way,' said Frank, in mysterious tones. 'I'd better get off.'

Rebecca waved to him as he drove back down the driveway, and out into Factory Lane. As he reached the corner, several men appeared at the junction, having walked down the hill from the castle. They were wearing beige tartan caps. From a distance, it was hard for Rebecca to say whether she knew them or not. Frank stopped the car near at the junction, and she saw him lean over in his seat and say something. There was a conversation lasting several minutes, before Frank drove on up the hill towards the house he shared with Doris.

'It's time we went back to the flat,' she said when she went back to the drawing-room. 'Come on, boys. It's nearly time for bed.'

'Daddy.' Ricky went to his father, earning another scowl from Jack. 'You said you'd play with us before bed.'

'I certainly did.'

'I want to come,' said Jack.

Charles looked up to Rebecca who shook her head imperceptibly. Jack had spent every day at the flat since his arrival, and was not averse to pushing his cousins out in order to claim all Charles' attention.

'Not tonight, sport,' said Charles. 'I

promised the twins I'd play on the train set with them. After that your Aunt Rebecca and I want a bit of time alone.' He ruffled Jack's hair.

'Oh, take him with you, Charles,' said Patty, looking up from her magazine for the first time. 'He's a pain when he can't be with you.'

'Not tonight,' said Charles, firmly. 'I'd like to be with my family. We'll see you in the morning, sport. Meanwhile, show your grandfather how you win at chess.'

Jack stood up. 'I'll break something if you don't take me.'

'I seem to remember we've had this talk, Jack,' said Charles. 'Remember what I said?'

'Yes.'

'So are you going to grow up a hero or a zero?'

'A hero.'

'Good boy. Now be heroic and share me with Aunt Rebecca and the twins for a bit, eh?'

Rebecca bristled. Why should Charles have to negotiate with a child to spend time with her and his own sons?

Jack sat up, his chin held high. 'Okay. I know you'd rather be with me.'

'If you say so.'

Charles put his arm around Rebecca, and beckoned the twins to come with them.

London Zoo bustled with visitors. The Winnipeg bear transfixed Annette. Winnie was a small black bear, who had been smuggled into England by Lieutenant Harry Colebourn. She was the star of London Zoo, and Annette adored her.

'Can I have one, daddy?' asked Annette.

'Yes, we'll keep it in the shed,' said Sam, smiling. He and Clara walked hand in hand through the zoo, whilst Annette ran on ahead, determined to be the first to see everything. 'You all right, love?' he said to Clara, when her hand wriggled in his momentarily.

'Yes, I'm fine. It's a nice day, isn't it?'

'Lovely. Especially being here with you and Annette. It's good to be out, isn't it?' Sam was beginning to feel a part of everything. He could smile at the other families as they wandered through the zoo because he had his own family with him. The sun was shining and everyone smiled back at them.

'It's better than being stuck in the house,' said Clara.

'I'm really grateful you came today,' said Sam. 'It makes me happy. Does it make you happy?'

'Hmm, yes.'

'Honestly?'

'Oh, I don't know, Sam. I don't do these things very well. You know that. My family was never happy. My father only thinks of the pit and his beer and my mother is as cold and heartless as they come. But I'm trying, aren't I?' The hopeful look in her eyes made his heart swell.

'You've been great these last few days. We've got a beautiful daughter and a good life together. What more could we ever want?'

Clara pulled away from him. 'I'll go and get us some ice cream,' she said. 'My treat.'

'That's great. Hey, Annette, mummy's bringing us ice cream. We'll come with you, shall we?' He was almost afraid to lose sight of her.

'No, it's okay. I can manage. You sit down and let Annette look at the bear. I'll be back soon.'

Sam counted the minutes till she returned. Despite her efforts over the previous days, he could not shake off the sense that Clara was like one of the caged animals in London Zoo, always looking for a means of escape.

He breathed a sigh of relief when she returned with three ice creams. 'Bet you thought I'd run away,' she said with a grin, as if she knew what he was thinking. 'Annette, here's your ice cream.' Annette ran to the bench, then straight back to Winnie the bear.

'Why would you run away when there's people here who love you?' Sam asked.

'Do you, Sam?' She sat down next to him. 'I sometimes think you only stay because of Annette.'

'If I were only interested in Annette, I could have taken her when she was little, and you'd have probably let me.'

'Yes. Perhaps. I don't know. It would have made life easier for me.'

'She's not a bad kid.'

'That's thanks to you. I was a mess, wasn't I? I remember the night you came to see me in Sheffield and suggest we move down to London.'

'You were a bit of a mess. But you're not now.'

'Not on the outside perhaps.'

'Why are you a mess on the inside, Clara? What is it that you want?'

'I don't know. There's no love in me, Sam. You must know that by now.'

'I think you tell yourself that, but it's not true. Just as easily as I could have taken Annette away from you, you could have walked out and left us. But you haven't.'

'That's because I like having a roof over my head. If not for you, I'd be sleeping under the Embankment by now.'

'You'd have survived.'

'Don't, Sam. Don't try and fool yourself into thinking there's something special deep inside me. This is not me; the happy little mummy, walking through the zoo. Inside I'm completely empty.'

'You know your trouble, Clara?'

'I'm sure you're about to tell me.'

'Things are only an effort because you make them that way. Really, life is simple. You wake up in the morning, you try and do well at whatever it is you do, you love and care for your family, and then at the end of the day you go to sleep ready to start all over again the next day. That's all there is to it. And yes, there are some hard bits, like being short of money, or getting sick, or losing someone you love.' He paused for a moment and swallowed hard. 'But if you can cherish the simple things and keep returning to them, then the harder times aren't so difficult to cope with.'

'What a philosopher, you are, Sam.' Clara chuckled, and he was pleased that it was not one of her usual sarcastic laughs at his expense. She slipped her hand in his as they sat eating their ice cream and watching Annette fall in love with Winnie.

11

George Harcourt had arranged for a mini fairground to be set up in the Priory grounds, with children's rides and sideshows for the adults. The workers had arrived with all their equipment at six in the morning, setting it up in time for the late afternoon event. Sad-looking donkeys stood at the outskirts of it all, ready to give the children rides later in the day.

Ricky and Bobby sat near the donkeys, watching the workers, having been ordered by Charles not to go any closer. When a worker passed by, Ricky would jump up and ask questions, whilst Bobby listened to the answers. Rebecca sometimes wondered if Bobby transmitted the questions he wanted to ask by telepathy to his brother. Not that Ricky was incapable of coming up with his own questions. They often had to say, 'No more questions tonight, Ricky. Go to sleep.' Then he would beg to ask just one more. And all the time, Bobby would be listening, as if his life depended on the answer to that final question.

Jack wandered exactly where he wanted,

despite having been told several times not to get in the way. Not that Patricia said anything. It was always George or Charles who had to tell him.

'I think he's fallen out with me,' said Charles, standing on the steps of the Priory with Rebecca, watching the preparations.

'Why? Because you spent time with us?'

'Yes. I don't think John pays him much attention. He wants a father figure.'

'He's a strange boy. I want to feel sorry for him, because he's so out of sorts with the world, but I can't.' Rebecca lowered her voice. 'Patricia has indulged him far too much. It's sad, because it makes him unlikeable. No child should have to cope with the idea of people not wanting them around.'

'If you knew . . . ' Charles stopped, as if he had said too much.

'If I knew what?'

'Oh, the problems she had when she was pregnant. She lost one, you know, and thought that was it. Then Jack arrived. I think that's why she spoils him. He was her last chance of motherhood.'

'Talking of which,' said Rebecca, smiling secretively.

'What?'

'I was going to wait until after the party to tell you, but I got a call from Doctor Latimer yesterday afternoon, and he told me I'm having another baby.'

'What? Really? Oh darling, that's wonderful.' Charles enveloped her in his arms and kissed her. 'Is it twins again?'

'We don't know that yet.'

'What am I thinking? You should be sitting down, resting.'

'I'm fine, Charles. Never felt better.'

'Still . . . Come on into the house and take the weight off your feet.'

'What's all this?' George came out of the house. 'Couldn't you two have a bit more decorum?' It was not said unkindly.

'Can I tell him?' Charles asked Rebecca.

'Yes.'

'You're going to be a grandfather again. Rebecca just got the news the other day.'

'Oh, splendid. Even more reason to celebrate today!' George kissed Rebecca on the cheek, which surprised her. 'Wait till I tell your mother.'

'I'll go and tell her,' said Charles. 'You persuade Rebecca to sit down and rest. She might listen to you.' Charles went into the house.

She always felt awkward when alone with her father-in-law, so they just stood and watched the fairground being erected.

'You really do love Charles, don't you?' said

144

George, eventually.

'Yes, of course I do.'

'I can see that now. I wasn't sure at first. I thought you'd give up work and just live off us, but you've proved you're a hard worker at the factory. It doesn't go unnoticed.'

'Thank you.'

'And I've seen you and Charles together. He's happier than he's ever been. More at peace with himself, I think and less angry with me and his mother. We let him down, when he had his accident. We did the wrong thing. There's no excuse, other than that we feared the unknown. You've two fine boys there. That's why I wanted to give them a good day today, Rebecca. It isn't just about corporate back-scratching. It's about letting the world know how important they are to us.'

'That's lovely, thank you, George.'

'I love Jack because he's my grandson, but ... well ... there's something about him, isn't there? Of course we had all that with Patricia, when she was growing up. I just hope he hasn't inherited her more extreme tendencies.'

'If you don't mind me saying,' said Rebecca, 'I think Jack's behaviour is very well-thought-out. He can stop it just as quickly as he started it. Real fury isn't like that. It knows no boundaries.' She was thinking of her stepfather's worst behaviour, including the time her mother threatened to leave him and he took an axe to all their furniture. They had fled the house, convinced he would strike them next.

'Attention-seeking, perhaps?'

'Yes, that's part of it. But I think he also believes it makes his mother happy. I'm afraid he may not be wrong.' Rebecca waited for George to correct her, or at least stamp on her criticism of his daughter. He did not.

'I tried to work out the other day who he looks like,' said George. 'As far as I could see he hasn't inherited any Harcourt or Daventry characteristics. Then, I saw him with the twins, and they all have very similar eyes. But the twins have got your eyes.'

'Really?' Rebecca frowned. She had not really thought about it. Whenever she looked at Ricky and Bobby, she saw miniature versions of Charles.

'Yes. It's odd, isn't it?'

'Perhaps our families were related somewhere way back in time.'

Rebecca thought he would scoff at the idea. Instead he said, 'That's more than possible in a small town like Stony Newton. My grandfather was a coalminer, you know.'

'I think I heard something about it.'

'It's a deep, dark family secret.'

She was so unused to her father-in-law displaying humour, it took her a moment to realise he was joking.

'We all have those,' she said, lightly. A cloud passed across the sun, blocking out the heat momentarily. For the first time since the night the twins were born and had been passed to her wrapped in tight blankets, she thought of little Charlie.

★ ★ ★

Despite Rebecca's fears, the party got off to a good start. The fairground was a buzz of activity and laughter. Children ran from ride to ride, carrying 'golden tickets' which they had been given as they arrived. The children took them very seriously, despite the fact that no one was going to refuse a ride to any child who had lost theirs. As the tickets were handed in, they were recycled and put back onto the pile at the entrance, ready to hand out again. Ricky and Bobby dashed through the crowds, with Ricky dressed as a cowboy and Bobby dressed as a pirate, complete with black eye patch.

'Aye aye, cap'n,' Bobby said, running up to Rebecca after he'd climbed down from the carousel.

'Aye aye, yourself. Are you having fun?'

'Yes. I'm going to join the fair when I grow up.'

'Are you now? Is that so you can chat up all the pretty girls?'

'Ugh, no. It's so I can build rides. I'm going to go to my room and draw one now.' That was Bobby all over. He would have an idea to draw something then have to retreat to his room.

'Why don't you do that later, darling? You can't really leave all your guests.'

'Mummy.' His voice dropped to a whisper and he beckoned her to him.

'What?' She crouched down next to him.

'I don't really like it when there are lots of people.'

'Why not darling?'

'Because I like it best when it's just me, you, daddy and Ricky. Not Jack though. I don't like it when he's there.'

'What if I had another baby?'

'That would be okay, because he'd be ours. Anyone who's ours is alright.'

'I see. What if it was a girl?'

'Would she be ours?'

'Well, yes.'

'I suppose she'd be alright then.'

Rebecca's heart swelled with love. She sometimes worried how Bobby would make his way in the world. Ricky was the outgoing one, and she had no fears about him surviving, whereas Bobby retreated into himself. He needed his family with him at all times, or else he became fretful. Any kind of cruelty from a stranger might make him close off completely. 'Can I give you a cuddle, birthday boy?'

'Okay, but do it quickly so no one sees.'

★ ★ ★

A marquee had been set up in the gardens behind the house, where the adults sat drinking beer and wine, and eating from the expansive buffet. Jed and Maggie Alsop were there, looking a bit out of things. Rebecca went to join them for a chat.

'Hello. How are you both?'

'We're fine, thanks, Becky ... Mrs. Harcourt,' said Jed.

'It's still Becky to my old friends.'

'It's a nice enough party,' said Maggie, sniffing. 'A bit overdone if you ask me, especially now.'

Jed glared at his wife. Rebecca wondered what the story was behind his annoyance.

'Yes, I agree, Maggie,' she said. 'I did ask for it to be toned down, but everything had been arranged. I didn't realise myself how big

149

it would be.' She wondered why she felt the need to explain herself to them. After all, they were not so disapproving that they stayed away, like many of the locals who had been invited. 'Lizzie is growing into a lovely little girl,' she said, eager to change the subject.

'She's very clever,' said Maggie. 'Isn't she, Jed?'

'Yes. She's already reading the newspaper.'

'I bet your boys can't read the newspaper,' said Maggie.

'I'm not sure they'd want to,' said Rebecca. 'They're only just starting on their ABCs. Ricky likes his toys, and Bobby likes drawing things.'

'Boys are always less developed than girls,' said Maggie. 'Of course, nurture is everything. I spend a lot of time helping Lizzie with her sums.' Maggie's statement was followed by another puzzled look from Jed. 'I don't suppose you do any of that with the boys, being at the factory full-time. I always think it's important for a mother to be with their children in the day.'

'We weren't brought up like that, Maggie,' said Rebecca. 'Our mothers worked, and our fathers. Yet we managed to learn to read and write.'

'I suppose you'll be sending the boys to boarding school, to get them out of the way.'

'You suppose wrong. They're going to attend day school. I couldn't bear to be parted from them.'

Rebecca was almost relieved when Patty entered the marquee and made a sudden beeline for them. She held a gin and tonic. Rebecca could have done with one herself, but had decided not to drink now she knew she was having a baby.

'Well,' said Patty, 'if it isn't Jed Alsop. My, how you've grown.' She sat down in the spare seat.

'Hello, Miss Patricia. This is my wife, Margaret.'

'Hello.' Patty waved a dismissive hand in Maggie's direction. 'Honestly Jed, have they been standing you in compost? You used to be a scrawny little kid. Now you're all tall and handsome.'

'We have a daughter,' said Maggie, her eyes narrowing. 'She's five, and as I was just telling Becky, she's already reading and doing her sums.'

'Oh, that's wonderful. I'm sure she'll be teaching you very soon.'

Rebecca stifled a giggle. She did not much like her sister-in-law, but in that moment she could have hugged her.

The party had been going for an hour when Rebecca went around the front of the house and saw Florrie Linney standing hesitantly at the gate with her four boys.

'Come on in,' called Rebecca, walking down to meet them. 'I'll get the children some tickets.'

'I didn't realise they had to have any,' said Florrie.

'They don't. It's just part of the fun. Charles' idea. Hello boys, you're all looking very smart today.' Florrie's lads, aged from six down to two years, wore their Sunday best, with their hair slicked down. 'There's candy floss if you want it.' She pointed to the stall, where several children already waited to be served. 'Come on, Florrie, we've got drinks in the marquee. Take the weight off your feet.'

'Thank you.' Florrie walked alongside Rebecca. 'I don't know if anyone else is coming. Edna Peters . . . well, I don't want to speak ill of her. She means well, does Edna.'

'Yes, I'm sure she does. The town is going through a bad time at the moment, and feelings are running high.'

'They are that. But none of us wish you any harm, Mrs. Harcourt.'

Rebecca looked sharply at Florrie. It was something in the way she had said it, emphasising the 'you' as though the townspeople did mean harm to someone. 'I wish you'd call me Becky again. It feels odd being Mrs. Harcourt to you, to say we were in the same class at school.'

'You've heard about Violet Chambers, I suppose, Becky,' said Florrie.

'Yes, it's awful. She was a year or two below us at school, wasn't she?'

'Yes. It's just . . . never mind. It don't matter.'

'Go on, tell me.'

'She were seeing your dad.'

'Frank? You mean they were having an affair.' A cold hand clutched Rebecca's chest.

'Yes. And they say he treated her rotten.'

Frank was at that moment holding court in the marquee, trying to show Harcourt's business associates that he was every bit as good as they were, whilst Doris sat in her best suit, casting beatific smiles at everyone.

'That doesn't surprise me, Florrie. He never treated my mam all that well.'

'No, he didn't. She were a lovely woman, your mam. Always smiling.'

'Yes, she was.'

'Oh. Look, Becky, I'm sorry, I forgot.'

'What?'

'About your mam and how she died. I shouldn't have mentioned Violet.'

'Yes, you should. I'd rather know the truth than wonder why people are whispering as I go past. Promise me, Florrie, that you'll always be honest with me.'

'I will. You're alright, you know.'

'Everyone thinks I'm a stuck-up cow, don't they?'

'No one thinks that. Well, perhaps a couple of people do but they don't matter. You've more friends in Stony Newton than you realise.'

'Thank you. That means a lot.'

'It's just that after your mam died, you shut us all off. No, it were a bit before that, I think. But it was like you closed the door on us, and wouldn't let us in. You happen had your own reasons.'

Rebecca knew it started the night little Charlie was born. The secret was so enormous, that she was afraid that if she got close to anyone she would blurt it out. There were times early in her marriage that she wanted to tell Charles. She had not been secure enough in his love. Now she felt that it was best to leave the past in the past.

They walked to the marquee in silence, having deposited the boys at the fairground. Rebecca asked a couple of the servants to keep an eye on the smaller boys. She settled Florrie down and got her a glass of lemonade.

Across the way, Patricia still flirted outrageously with Jed. Maggie had a face like thunder. Jed did not seem to mind at all, despite his face being beetroot red. Rebecca could imagine the effect of someone like Patricia making a beeline for him. She was a very sensual woman.

'Have you picked any names for the baby yet?' Rebecca sat opposite Florrie.

'I'm running out of boys' names, and kings — Arthur, Henry, Edward and James — so I'm hoping it's a girl. I thought I'd call her Esther, after my grandma. It means star.'

'Esther Linney. That's a fine name.'

'Yes, that's what I thought.'

'I'm having another baby too.'

'Congratulations! When?'

'I'm not sure of the exact date, but it'll be sometime in the New Year.'

'Will it be — ?'

'Twins?' Rebecca laughed. 'Everyone's asked that. Who knows? They certainly run in the Harcourt family. Charles' father was one of twins. His twin brother died as a young man.' Rebecca shivered, and for a moment it felt as though the sun had gone in. She could not imagine a life without either one of her sons.

'Are you okay?'

'Someone just walked over my grave.'

'Rebecca?' She turned and saw Paul Henderson standing nearby with his new

155

wife, Clementine. She was a vibrant girl of around Rebecca's age. Paul Henderson was in his fifties, and still very handsome.

'Excuse me,' she said to Florrie, leaving her to go to the Hendersons. 'Sorry, Paul and Clementine, have I been neglecting you?'

'No, not at all,' said Paul. 'We've just heard the good news and wanted to congratulate you.' They both kissed her. 'Clementine, did I tell you about the first time I met this lovely girl? I was going to run off and marry her, but as you know Charles beat me too it.'

'That was fortunate for me then, wasn't it?' said Clementine. 'And lucky I don't bear a grudge. Rebecca, we'd love for you, Charles and the boys to come and stay with us at our holiday home in France next summer.' It was clear that the current financial situation had not affected the Hendersons' outlook on life.

'That would be wonderful, if we can get away.'

'We'll have lots to talk about,' said Clementine, patting her stomach.

'Really?'

'Yes!'

'Must be something in the water in Stony End,' Rebecca quipped. 'Florrie there is due at any moment.'

'She looks to me as if she was ready to have that baby several weeks ago,' said Paul. 'Will she be all right, do you think?'

'I think so. I'm keeping an eye on her,' said Rebecca.

'Good girl. Tell her to try Henderson's Salts. I've heard they're pretty good for getting things going.'

'Really?' Rebecca raised an eyebrow.

'Of course. My mother swore by them.'

'That or sex,' said Clementine, winking. 'So they say.'

'I think you'll find men came up with that idea,' said Rebecca, laughing.

'It certainly wasn't my mother,' said Paul. 'To the day she died, she was still convinced the stork brought me.'

'Did your father put her to sleep with Henderson's sleeping draught?' asked Clementine.

'That's how I got you pregnant.'

Perhaps, Rebecca thought, things were not going to be so bad today. Everyone was on good form, happy to be there, apart from Maggie, who sat alone. Jed was at the bar, getting drinks, and it looked as if Patricia was helping him.

Doris seemed a bit lonely, whilst Frank chatted to other pit managers, so Rebecca started walking towards her. As she did, Charles entered the marquee and beckoned to her and his father.

'I think we've got problems,' he said, taking them around to the front of the house. He pointed across to Castle Hill. 'Look.'

At first it looked like a black cloud, moving down the hill. Then Rebecca realised they were the pit workers.

'They won't be heading here, surely?' said George.

'I think we should lock the gates just in case,' said Charles. 'And get the children away from the fairground. I didn't know they were marching today, did you?' He looked at Rebecca and his father, who both shook their heads. 'I'll get Stephens to lock the gates, and you two fetch the parents so they can help round up the children. If the march passes by, all well and good, but if it doesn't, we need everyone safe.' Charles went in search of Stephens.

'You think this is because of the party, don't you?' George ran his fingers through his hair.

Rebecca reached out and patted her father-in-law's arm. 'You meant well, George.' She nodded towards the marchers. 'But sadly, I don't think they see it that way. Come on, let's get everyone away from the front of the house.'

12

Patricia stood next to Jed at the bar, oblivious to the ensuing drama. After several weeks of living at the Priory she was desperate for some fun. 'Come for a walk with me, Jed,' she said.

He looked at her astounded. 'Why?'

'Why do you think?'

'I'm a married man, Miss Patricia.'

'Oh, for God's sake, stop calling me Miss Patricia. It makes you sound like a southern slave.'

'Nope, I'm a northern slave.'

'Oh, witty. I like that. We don't treat you that badly though, do we?'

'No, not really. Mr. George and Mr. Charles are very fair with us.'

'That wife of yours looks as if she chews wasps for breakfast every morning.'

'She's alright. She's a good mother.'

'Well, that's something then, isn't it?' Patricia yawned, and put her hand in front of her pretty mouth. 'What's happening here?' She looked around to see everyone starting to trail out of the marquee. 'You know, we could escape in this crowd.' She took his hand and led him out through one of the flaps at the back of the marquee, whilst everyone else trooped towards the front.

'Where are we going?' Jed asked, grinning.

'There's a place in the copse at the back of the grounds, where Charles and I used to hide as kids. Come on, before they notice us.'

They ran across the field, and climbed over a fence, where he followed her to a clearing in the centre of the copse. 'This was our den,' she told him, sitting down on the grass. She held her hand up to him. 'You want me, don't you, Jed?'

'Yes, but this is mad. If anyone found out . . . ' He ignored her hand, but sat next to her.

'They won't. Is it the first time you've cheated on your wife?'

'Yes. No. There've been others.'

'Why?'

'She's not let me touch her since she had Lizzie.'

'Please don't give me that sort of line, Jed. My husband could probably give you pointers.'

'Well, she hasn't let me touch her much.'

'You're going to tell me next that you don't love her and that you never have.'

'Sometimes that's the truth. I've only ever loved one woman.'

'Let me guess. Ah yes, I saw the way you looked at her. That saintly gold-digger, Rebecca. Aw, that's so sweet, Jed. Young love unrequited.'

He started to stand up, but she pulled him back down. 'Rebecca is no gold-digger.'

'Sorry.' Patricia gave a mocking laugh. 'I'm feeling generous today, Jed, so I'm going to let you do everything to me that you'd do to Rebecca if you could.' She pulled his face around to hers and kissed him. 'I'm not like your average woman. There's nothing I won't do.'

'I don't even know if I like you,' said Jed, as he pushed her back onto the velvety grass.

'You obviously don't like your wife very much, but that never stopped you. Now shut up and kiss me.'

★   ★   ★

They watched from the front steps of the Priory as the flank of miners marched down Castle Hill. As they reached the bottom of the hill, shouts could be heard, like a sergeant marshalling the troops.

'Are the children safe?' Rebecca asked.

'Yes, they're watching the puppet show in the ballroom,' said Charles. 'It should keep them out of the way.'

'I haven't seen Jack for a while. Where is he?'

'I don't know.' Charles looked around as if expecting Jack to appear from somewhere. 'Last time I saw him he was heading for the marquee.'

'Someone should find him and bring him into the house. I'll go.'

'No, darling. I don't want you going out there at all. I'll send Stephens.'

The marchers had reached the junction. If all were well, they would carry on down the hill and into the pit. When they turned and started walking up the hill to the Priory, Rebecca knew that all was not well.

'We ought to telephone the authorities and ask them to send the troops in,' said Frank Wilson. He had a gleam in his eye that Rebecca did not much like. It was as if he had been expecting it.

'I don't think we need to exacerbate the situation,' said George Harcourt. 'These are our friends and neighbours. We don't mean them any harm. I'll go down and talk to them.'

'Be careful, father,' said Charles.

Rebecca did not think George truly understood the situation. He believed that because he was one of the better employers in the area it meant he had the undying loyalty

162

of the townspeople.

'I'll go with him,' Charles said. Rebecca watched them walk down the path, and then decided to follow. She was not going to be kept inside just because she was a woman.

Charles put his hand under her elbow, and tried to turn her around. 'You should stay back, darling, in case there's trouble.'

'I want to know what they say. I know them all, Charles. I might be able to help.'

'What seems to be the problem, lads?' George spoke in familiar tones, suggesting they were all friends together.

'We've no beef with you, Mr. Harcourt, nor Mr. Charles and his wife there,' said Len Peters. 'We want Frank Wilson to come out.'

'Why?' asked Rebecca. She scanned the crowd, and saw the men in beige caps. She knew everyone in Stony Newton and they were not locals. The sense of foreboding that had haunted her for several days increased. Something was not right about the situation. The men of Stony Newton were not troublemakers, regardless of their dispute with the government. All they wanted was to be able to put food on the table for their families, and have a few hours of the day when they were not lying on their bellies deep within the mine.

'There's nowt for you to worry about,

163

Becky. You're a nice lass, you always have been. It's that no good stepfather of yours we're wanting.'

'Len . . . Mr. Peters. It's my sons' birthday party today. Couldn't this wait?'

'Kill the bastard,' said a voice from the crowd. Rebecca suspected without really knowing for certain that it had come from one of the men in beige caps.

'Now, now,' said Albert Taylor, 'we'll have none of that. We just want him to explain himself, about young Violet Chambers.'

'I'm sorry for what happened to her,' said Rebecca, 'but if they were having an affair, surely . . . '

'There's more to it than that,' said Albert. 'Stuff a nice young lass like you didn't ought to know about. He used her, he did.'

'Which is no more than you did.' Frank had joined them without anyone realising. 'You sent her to spy on me. And on t'management. It were you who prostituted the lass.'

'We never told her she had to do that,' said Len, his ears turning pink under the rim of his cap.

'Get back to the house, Becky,' said Frank. 'This is not women's business.'

Rebecca stood her ground. 'This is our home,' she said in quiet but firm tones, 'not yours. You can't order me around here.'

'Darling . . . ' Charles put his hand on her shoulder. 'Your father is right. You shouldn't have to listen to all this.'

'I'm not made of porcelain, Charles. Believe me when I say there's nothing they can tell me about Frank that will shock me.'

'I don't like that tone, young woman,' said Frank. 'Get back up to the house now.'

'And I don't like yours,' said Charles. 'So I'll thank you not to speak to my wife like that. This is her home, and she doesn't have to do anything you say.' He moved in closer to Rebecca, and kissed her head. 'Please, darling. Go back to the house and take care of the boys. For my sake.'

'Rebecca!' It was Clementine, calling from the Priory steps. 'Rebecca, it's Florrie.'

'What?' Andy Linney came from amongst the crowd. 'What about Florrie?'

'She's going into labour.'

The crowd moved towards the gate, so that it bowed inward. 'Let me in,' said Andy.

'We can't,' said George. 'If we open these gates, Andy, then everyone is going to surge in.'

'She's my wife and I want to see her!'

Rebecca did not hear any more of the argument. She was already heading back to the house.

'Where's Florrie, Clementine?'

'She's in the drawing-room. Veronica is taking care of her.'

Outside became a cacophony of noise, with the miners yelling, wanting to be let in.

She went to the drawing-room, where Florrie lay on the sofa, her face contracted in pain. Veronica held her hand, but looked uncertain as to what she should be doing.

'How far apart are the contractions?' asked Rebecca.

'I've no idea,' said Veronica. 'I did not realise I should be counting.'

Rebecca had no answer for that. It would not surprise Rebecca if she had totally forgotten her own pregnancy, as something too unpleasant to remember. 'I'll sit with her. Veronica, ask the servants to boil water and bring clean towels.' Her mother-in-law scowled, not used to being bossed around, but she left the room anyway. 'Florrie, can you hear me?'

Florrie nodded. 'Yes. Oh God, Becky, I've never known pain like it. My last four were nothing like this.' She followed the statement with a scream.

'I'm going to have a look,' said Rebecca, lifting Florrie's skirt. Her underwear was awash with blood. 'I need to take these off, is that all right?' Florrie nodded.

When Rebecca took off Florrie's underwear she gasped in horror. 'It looks as though the baby is a breech, Florrie. Clementine?'

'Yes, I'm here. What can I do to help?'

Rebecca blessed her. At least someone was not too squeamish to help. 'We need to get a doctor. I've no idea how to do this and if we're not careful they might both be harmed. Telephone Doctor Latimer. His number is on the pad next to the telephone in the hall.'

'I don't know how he's going to get in, Rebecca. Have you seen it out there?'

'There's a back road, through the copse. Tell him to take that.' Rebecca quickly outlined the route.

'Okay. Got it.'

Rebecca heard the front door slam, and the bolts shut. Charles, George and Frank came into the drawing-room.

'What's happening, Charles?'

'They've nearly broken the gate off its hinges. How is Florrie?'

Rebecca explained the situation. 'We need someone on the back road, to guide the doctor in. If he doesn't get here soon, I'm afraid . . . '

Florrie interrupted Rebecca's comment with a high-pitched scream as another contraction rocked her body. Charles and George, realising that Florrie was not decently dressed, started to mumble about going out of the room.

'I'll go and find the doctor,' said Frank. 'Just tell me again where this back road is.'

Rebecca gave him instructions. As Frank left the room they heard a scrape of metal against concrete that set their teeth on edge. The miners had broken the gate down. Charles dashed to the window.

'Dear God,' he said, 'they're in and they're smashing the fairground up. Andy Linney is heading this way.'

'Someone should let him in,' said Rebecca.

'If we open the door,' said George, 'they're all going to get in.'

'Andy needs to be here. Perhaps if we'd let him in to begin with, this wouldn't have happened.'

'Very well. I'll see if we can let him in without alerting the others. We need guards on all the doors and windows. And someone is going to have to find a way to get the doctor in. Charles?'

'Yes, I'm coming.'

The next hour was a nightmare for all concerned. The miners, infuriated, and egged on by the men in beige caps, ran through the Priory grounds, smashing up the fairground and pulling down the marquee.

There was no sign of the doctor. Whilst the

chaos reigned outside, Florrie writhed and moaned in agony, losing a lot of blood in the process. Somehow, Charles and George managed to get Andy Linney into the house through one of the side windows.

'I'm sorry, about all this,' Andy Linney said as he sat at his wife's side holding her hand. 'I didn't tell them to knock the gates down. Someone suggested it, and they all went mad. I didn't want this, honestly, Mrs. Harcourt.'

'I know, Andy. This was orchestrated, I'm sure of it. And now I think Frank has taken off and avoided it all. I should never have trusted him to bring the doctor to us.'

'Even if the doctor came, there's no way he'd get through the riot,' said Clementine, who was helping Rebecca tend to Florrie.

'Are the children all right?' asked Rebecca. 'They must be terrified.' She felt that she was neglecting her duty as a mother but Florrie's need was greater.

'Don't worry, they're fine,' said Charles. 'I think the puppeteers deserve a really good tip for working above and beyond the call of duty.'

'Remind me when this is all over and I'll see they get it.'

Florrie's daughter was born just as the police arrived and began to round up the rioters. Rebecca put her into Florrie's arms, but Andy had to help his wife hold the baby. She was very weak through blood loss.

'Oh, she's beautiful,' said Florrie, crying.

'She is that,' said Andy, kissing his wife.

'Hello, Esther.' Florrie hugged the baby closer to her but the effort cost her dearly. She lay back, exhausted. Andy took Esther from Florrie, gently rocking the baby in his arms. 'Mrs. Harcourt . . . Becky . . . '

'What is it, Florrie?'

'Andy won't be able to cope on his own. Not with the boys as well. Will you take care of her for me?'

'You'll be able to look after her yourself,' said Rebecca. 'But I'll be glad to help until you're back on your feet.'

'No,' said Florrie, as a tear rolled down her cheek. 'I won't be doing that.' She kissed the tip of her finger, and pressed against her daughter's head. And then she died.

Rebecca stumbled into the hallway, where Charles stood watch by the front door. 'What is it?' he said. 'What's happened?'

She fell into his arms, sobbing.

★   ★   ★

Jack stood amongst the trees, watching the miners create havoc through the Priory grounds. He was not afraid, only envious that he dare not join them in their wrecking crusade.

He could do one thing and everyone would think the miners had done it. He crept along the edge of the grounds, and moved toward the garages. The miners had not shown any interest in them so far, perhaps because they were some way off from the main house. He found the keys under a plant pot and let himself into the entrance to Rebecca and Charles' flat, climbing the stairs to the front door.

The twins' train set was in the centre of their bedroom, between their single beds. Jack approached it, and brought his foot up, smashing it down onto the first engine, and then the next, till it was completely destroyed. That would teach Uncle Charles for loving the twins more than him.

He heard a sound, as if the miners were drawing nearer, so ran out of the flat and back to the copse, running further into the centre. This was where he found his mother sitting astride a strange man, with her breasts uncovered.

'You bitch!' he screamed, wondering how many more times he would be betrayed by his family.

Patricia looked up, and her mouth formed into an o, whilst her eyes filled with horror.

171

'Jack, darling. Jackie . . . it's nothing. Mummy is only playing.'

But he had already started running away, back towards the Priory, where he joined the miners in smashing up what was left of the marquee, until the police came and arrested them all, including him.

★ ★ ★

'Darling, are you sure you can manage?' asked Charles. 'You'll be giving birth soon, and now you're talking about bringing up Florrie's daughter? She'll only be about six months old when our baby is born. It's too much for you.'

They were walking back to their flat with the boys. Florrie had been taken away, and Andy had gone with Esther to the hospital so she could be checked out. Rebecca had wanted to go too, but Charles would not hear of it, telling her, not unreasonably, that Ricky and Bobby needed her. One of the local women was taking care of Andy's boys.

'I promised, Charles.' It was not strictly true. Florrie had died before Rebecca had a chance to agree, but she felt she was bound by a promise despite that. 'Anyway, we managed with the twins, didn't we?'

'Yes, but they're ours. It's different.'

'Andy won't cope. I don't know how he's going to manage with the boys. The poor little darlings.'

'Well, we certainly can't acquire five extra children!'

'No, of course not. I understand that. Darling, try to understand. I grew up with Florrie. Despite me pushing her aside for years, she trusted me enough to ask me to take care of Esther. It means a lot to me. But, I don't want to take Esther in if you're going to resent her. No child should be brought up in that atmosphere.'

'I can't promise to love her as much as I love Ricky and Bobby. Surely you can understand that.'

'Of course I do.'

'I would never be unkind to a child. I hope you know that too.'

'I do, and that's why I love you and why I know you'll help me with her.'

'Did I ever have any say in this?'

'Not really.'

'I didn't think so, but it was nice of you to pretend I did.'

'Do I tell you enough that I love you?'

'Yes, but I'll be expecting a lot of extra credit for this.'

'And you'll get it!'

The boys, who had been dawdling behind,

caught up with them. 'Mummy?'

'What Ricky?'

'Are we having a sister?'

'Yes, Esther Linney is going to come and live with us.'

'Is she ours?' asked Bobby.

Rebecca hesitated. She did not want to lie to him, but she also remembered what he had told her earlier. 'She will be when she lives with us.'

'I've always wanted a sister,' said Ricky.

'By next year you might have two,' said Charles.

'I've always wanted two sisters.' He ran on towards the garages, and burst open the lower door.

'That's odd,' said Charles, 'I thought I'd locked that. Ricky, come back, son! Damn it, if the miners have got in . . . '

They rushed up to the flat. 'Everything seems to be in order,' said Charles. The hallway was as neat and tidy as ever, and all the doors were closed, except for Ricky and Bobby's bedroom. 'I can't imagine the rioters would have bothered closing them all,' he said. He looked in all the rooms with closed doors, and told Rebecca that all was in order.

'Daddy . . . ' Ricky stood at the entrance to the twin's room. 'Daddy, the miners have broken my train set.' He started to sob.

Bobby joined him at the door, his little face breaking into a grimace.

'It's broken, mummy.'

'I can't imagine the miners broke in just to smash up a child's train set, can you?' she said to Charles. He put his finger to his mouth. Rebecca shook her head vehemently. 'We're not going to protect him if he's done this, Charles.'

'No, but they don't have to know, do they? Besides, he's in enough trouble with the police. Father is sorting it out, putting it down to the miners being a bad influence on him.'

'He doesn't need the miners. He's got Patricia. Wherever she is at the moment.'

'Jack did it, didn't he?' said Bobby.

'We don't know that,' said Charles.

Ricky nodded, but in agreement with his brother. 'Yes, it was Jack. I hate him and don't want him to ever come here again.' Ricky took Bobby's hand. They went into the bedroom and slammed the door shut.

13

1927

'It's only for a fortnight, Charles, whilst Patricia has the baby.' His mother's eyes were stern across the coffee table. So this was why he alone had been summoned to his parents' house early in the morning. Jack was a four-letter word where Becky and the twins were concerned.

'I remember the last time Jack was here,' said Charles. 'The twins were heartbroken over their train set. And then he joined the miners in smashing up the place.'

'They set a bad example,' said Veronica. 'I'm sure Jack would have done nothing of the sort.'

'Mother, you're forgetting why Jack came here in the first place. He smashed up Patricia and John's flat. How many chances is he going to get?'

'Patricia says that he's settled down since she sent him to boarding school. He's doing well at his studies. He's a very bright child.'

'Look,' Charles put down his cup. 'It's really not my decision. It is, of course, up to you and father if he stays here at the Priory, but I don't want him at our flat. I'm not having my children upset.'

'Rebecca and the children will be away in France. What harm can Jack do? He's never hurt a person.'

'Of course he's hurt them, mother. Perhaps not physically, but emotionally.'

'I don't hold with all that psychological nonsense.'

'You ought to, after all the money you've spent on Patricia's frequent breakdowns.'

'Now, Charles, that isn't fair. Patricia is happy now. She and John are over the moon about the baby.'

'A baby she wasn't supposed to be able to have,' muttered Charles.

'Pardon?'

'Nothing. It's just that when Jack arrived Patricia told me she couldn't have any more children.'

'Perhaps she thought she couldn't.'

No, thought Charles, Patty knew she was lying. She was just willing to say anything to get her own way that night. He wished to God they had never found Jack. The boy was nothing but trouble.

'George, dear, don't you have anything to say?'

'It all seems to have been decided,' said

George from behind his newspaper. Just as Charles thought his father had said all he was going to say, he spoke again. 'Give the boy a chance, Charles. How is baby Charlotte getting on?'

'Charlotte is doing very well. I worry that Rebecca has taken on too much, what with caring for the boys and Esther too.'

'Yes, it's a bit silly to be taking in waifs and strays,' said Veronica. 'Personally I think the child, Esther, should be brought up amongst her own kind.'

Despite his own misgivings about having an extra child foisted onto the family, Charles felt duty-bound to defend Esther. He had become very fond of the little girl. 'She's a sweet child, with a lovely smile. It would be nice for Rebecca if you could try and treat Esther like another grandchild.'

'But she isn't ours,' said Veronica. 'It was Rebecca's decision to take her on. I don't see why we should be burdened with the child.'

'She's hardly a burden to us,' said George from behind his paper. 'We'll make a bit more effort, Charles, I promise.'

'Honestly, George . . . '

'We'll make a bit more effort.' George folded his paper and put it on the arm of the chair, fixing his wife with a firm stare. 'Remember, Veronica, that the little girl was born in this very room. So she's practically a Harcourt.'

'Yes, I remember. It cost us a new settee,' said Veronica. 'You do what you like, George, but I will not be bullied into accepting a child that has been foisted upon us.'

If only you knew, thought Charles. *If only you knew.*

He left his parents and went back to the flat. 'Sorry to leave you to it, darling,' he said to Rebecca. She was in the sitting-room, breastfeeding two-month-old Charlotte, whilst eight-month-old Esther lay on her belly in a playpen, chewing on a rattle. The twins were in the kitchen, eating breakfast. Charles could hear Ricky chattering away, and Bobby's monosyllabic answers.

Charles picked Esther up and smiled at her, feeling more protective towards her because of his mother's indifference. 'Hello, Esther. Are you being a good girl for Aunt Rebecca?' Charles sat down and bounced her on his knee, whilst she chatted away happily in baby language. 'I was summoned to hear the news that the ghastly Jack is going to be coming to visit.'

'When?' Rebecca's tired eyes became wary.

'Whilst you're away.'

'That's something at least.'

'Are you sure you're going to manage a trip

to France with them all on your own? If you waited till next year, I could take time off and come with you.'

'Don't worry, Paul and Clementine promise wall-to-wall nannies. They'll be travelling with us. I'd really like to go, darling. I need the break. It would be nice if you could come.'

'I can't. We're only just getting back on our feet after the miners' strike.'

'It's grim out there still,' said Rebecca. 'I feel bad that some of the men were sacked due to what happened here. We ought to speak up for them, Charles. Tell the management about those provocateurs.'

'I've a feeling the management already know. You said that you saw Frank talking to them. My guess is that it was a set-up. If the management took the miners back they'd have to admit that.'

'Meanwhile, Frank's promoted to Mr. Blake's right-hand man, and given a pay rise, whilst others still struggle. It isn't fair.'

'Have you spoken to him since?'

'No . . . ' Rebecca paused and looked towards the kitchen. 'I don't want any more to do with him and I don't want the boys to either. They keep asking about him. It's strange that they should love him so much, when I know the truth about him.' Her eyes became haunted. It was something Charles had noticed whenever she spoke of Frank. He knew that her life with him had been unhappy, but he could not shake the feeling that there was something else behind it all.

'What truth?'

'You know, about Violet Chambers, and the provocateurs. And the way he treated my mother, of course.'

'They're children. They've yet to see the true darkness in others.'

'They managed it with Jack.'

'Yes, but Jack did something specific to hurt them. Frank hasn't done anything to them directly, so they judge him as they see him. He's a loving grandfather who brings them sweets and treats.'

'Not any more if I can help it.'

Charles put Esther back in the playpen, and knelt down by Rebecca's chair. 'What did he do to you, darling? Tell me.'

'Isn't what he has done enough?'

'No, this goes back to before then. Before we even married.'

'You saw what he was like when you asked him if you could take me to London.'

'I saw a father, protective of his daughter. I'm not so sure if, in eighteen years' time, a man comes and asks to take Charlotte to London overnight, I won't just knock the blighter out.'

'You like Frank!'

'No, not at all. Not many people do.'

'That's strange. He always thought he had a lot of respect from people, being a war hero and all that.'

'One mention of 'when the Hun shot me' is impressive, but when it turns up in every conversation, it starts to look like overstating the case. Some of the men think Frank shot himself in the leg.'

Rebecca rolled her eyes heavenward. 'That wouldn't surprise me at all.'

Ricky and Bobby came bursting into the room. Ricky hovered around his baby sister whilst she was being fed. Bobby went to the playpen and gazed down at Esther.

'Do you like Esther now?' Rebecca asked him.

'She's alright. But she doesn't look like us. You said she was ours.'

'Esther is ours.' Rebecca looked at Charles, her eyes full of meaning. 'But she's also Andy Linney's. That's why she's got all that auburn hair.'

'I've always wanted two sisters,' said Ricky. 'So I don't mind her.'

'She needs our love,' said Rebecca. 'Because she lost her own mummy.'

Bobby looked up with serious eyes. 'Grandmother says we don't have to love her.'

'Did she now?' said Charles. 'Your grandmother is right, I suppose. We don't have to love anyone. But we should be kind to her. We've always taught you both to be kind, haven't we?'

Bobby nodded. 'Okay, I'll be kind to her.' He picked up Esther's rattle and shook it in front of her face in a studiously kind sort of way.

14

Rebecca was unused to relinquishing her children to anyone apart from Charles, but Paul and Clementine's staff made it very easy for her from the moment she got onto the train bound for Dover. Two young nannies took care of Esther and Charlotte, whilst an older nanny occupied the twins with board games. All Rebecca had to do was sit back and relax. It took some getting used to.

'You're to shake off the shackles of earth motherhood,' Clementine told her, as she reclined in the seat next to Rebecca, drinking a gin and tonic. 'And relax. You do far too much.'

'You sound like Charles. In fact it's as if I haven't even left home.'

'Then I'll shut up.'

'Where is little Verity?'

'She's already in France with Paul. He won't let her out of his sight! Fatherhood at such a late stage in life does something to a man, I'm sure of it. Turns him into a soppy wreck. He dotes on her, even has her lying in her cot next to him whilst he's in his study.'

'Don't you mind? Being apart from her, I mean.'

'I'm not the maternal type. Oh, don't get me wrong, darling. I do love her and I make sure she knows it when I see her. I just don't feel that wrench that most mothers feel when they're apart from their child. Perhaps having nannies is something to do with it.'

'I hope Bobby is okay with them. He's very particular about who he likes.'

'He'll be fine. He's such a sweet little man. They both are. But Bobby seems like something from another age. A Victorian gentleman in miniature.'

'He's very much family-orientated, and doesn't always take to new people. My mother-in-law is the same, and it worries me. She's not always a very warm person. The temperature in a room can go down by several degrees when she enters it. I don't want Bobby to grow up like that.'

'He won't. Not with you as his mother. Ricky is a little dynamo, isn't he?'

'He never stops from morning till night. He exhausts us with his quest for knowledge.'

'Now we've exhausted the subject of children, let's go on to more interesting things. What did you think of the late lamented Rudolph Valentino?'

'Mmm, have him scrubbed and sent to my tent.'

'Poor man would have to be now, but I concur anyway. Douglas Fairbanks.'

'Divine.'

'Charlie Chaplin?'

'Oh, too strange-looking.'

'I agree. So now I know we're perfectly in sync, I can tell this is going to be a fantastic holiday.'

They clinked glasses and spent the rest of the journey discussing handsome film stars.

Rebecca had not realised she was missing someone like Clementine in her life until the trip to France. It brought back the sense of fun her mother used to have, before life became so much darker. With Clementine she could forget the darkness, and laugh again. Laughter with Charles was different to that with a girlfriend with whom she could share all her secrets. Well, nearly all her secrets. little Charlie was locked so tightly in Rebecca's heart that even she had lost the key.

★ ★ ★

Jack would not have admitted he felt nervous about seeing his Uncle Charles again, but he did. When he arrived at the Priory his throat felt constricted.

'Come on in, Master Jack,' said Stephens. 'Your grandmother is in the drawing-room.'

His first thought was that she had not rushed to the door to meet him, as she had on his first visit. The injustice of it angered him. He was supposed to be loved. That was what his mother had told him when he expressed his reluctance to leave her. 'Everyone loves you, Jackie,' she had said. But clearly everyone did not, otherwise they would have made more fuss about his visit.

'Ah, there you are, Jack. Your grandfather and Uncle Charles are at the factory today. Would you like some tea and cake?'

Jack nodded sullenly and sat down. 'Where are Aunt Rebecca and the twins?'

'They've gone to France for a fortnight. So you have us all to yourself.' She poured him a cup of tea and put a slice of cake onto a plate.

That cheered Jack up. With the twins gone, he would have his Uncle Charles' undivided attention.

'Now, Jack, how are you enjoying boarding school?'

'Not much.' That was a lie. Jack had been surprised to find he enjoyed being away from his mother and father. It was true that some of the other boys had not liked the way he behaved, so had sent him to Coventry after the first time he had a tantrum.

He quickly learned that children were far less forgiving than adults. So he had to behave before they invited him to join in a little more. He was good at his lessons, notwithstanding a few pranks that got him detention. They were only done occasionally so the other boys would not think he had gone soft, but not so often that they interfered with his learning. More importantly for Jack, he could put his head on the pillow at night and not fear the crashing of porcelain or the needy entreaties by his mother to come and save her from his hateful father. With his grandmother, he fell back on his customary nihilism. 'I hate everything about it.'

The conversation that followed was stilted. His grandmother clearly did not know much about boys or their interests, and he could feign no interest in her pursuits with flower arranging. A few times he yawned and looked at the clock, willing five o'clock to arrive so his grandfather and Uncle Charles would return.

'Could I go for a walk?' he asked, at around four-thirty. He thought he might go and meet them.

'No, Jack, I don't think so. I've been told not to let you out of my sight.'

'Why?'

'I don't have to remind you what happened last year. I'm not happy about this either. I do have other things I could be doing, but your grandfather insisted upon it. Now, you're to stay there until your grandfather and Charles return. Then we'll have dinner, and then you can go to bed.'

Jack saw a fortnight of sitting drinking tea with his grandmother stretching ahead of him. He thought about it for a while, wondering how he might get around her. He thought of screaming and shouting, but decided against it. They would only be more determined to keep him in.

'Grandmother?'

'What is it, Jack?'

'If you have other things to be doing, and I would rather be out fishing and playing football — which I am sure you should hate — why don't you just let me out when grandfather and Uncle Charles aren't here? I'll be sure to return before five o'clock every evening. They'll never know.'

'Hmm.' Veronica considered it for a moment. 'We'll see. If you are a good boy tonight, and tomorrow, then I may let you out the next day. But you must not tell your grandfather or Uncle Charles, and neither must you do anything to get into trouble. Is that clear?'

Jack smiled. It was close enough.

George and Charles arrived home soon afterwards. Jack jumped up and ran to Charles, ready for a hug.

'Hello, Jack,' said Charles, patting his head, before moving away to the tea tray. 'How was the trip?'

His grandfather said, 'Hello,' and went to pour out his own tea.

Jack came to a very painful realisation. No one in his family liked him.

15

Annette could not understand what had gone wrong. They had been happy, all three of them. Her mother had started asking her about her school work, and even came to watch her perform in the Christmas play.

True Clara still slept in late, and sometimes she drank too much, but not as often as she used to do.

Despite her father's efforts to keep it secret, Annette had always known about the other men. Her mother did not care if she knew or not. But all that had stopped too. Until tonight.

Her mother had started drinking at breakfast time.

'Clara, what's troubling you?' Sam asked before going out to work.

'Nothing.'

'What have I done?'

'If you don't know, I'm not going to tell you.'

'How the hell am I supposed to work it out from that? It doesn't even make any sense.'

'Mrs. Overton, down the road.'

'What about her?'

'I saw you talking to her at the gate.'

'I always talk to her at the gate.'

'Really?'

There had followed an argument, the gist of which Annette did not follow clearly. Only that her mother did not like her father talking to nice Mrs. Overton and would rather he did not do it anymore. Then her father had made a comment about her mother not being in a position to judge, before leaving in his taxi.

'Go to your room, Annette,' her mother had said. 'I don't want to see you all day.'

That had not happened for a long time either. Her mother had started to enjoy spending time with her, and Annette had not had to sit quietly in her room until her father came home. She did as she was told. It did not do to ignore her mother. Soon after the front door slammed and Annette realised she was once again alone in the house.

She crept downstairs to make herself a sandwich at lunchtime, furtively looking over her shoulder, in case her mother returned and caught her. She took the sandwich back to her room and chewed at it miserably, wondering why they were not happy anymore.

She had just started eating the second half of the sandwich when the front door opened and she heard voices. It was her mother and a strange man. Annette picked up the book she had been reading and tried to get into it. Normally she liked reading *Winnie-the-Pooh*, but the words jumbled on the page, resembling ants running riot through a picnic. She remembered her trip to the zoo and the sound the animals made when they fed. That was what it sounded like in her mother's bedroom. She went back to her book, willing the ants to keep still and finally losing herself in the Hundred Acre Wood.

She had reached the part where Tigger bounced in when her bedroom door opened. 'What have we here?' A man stood at the threshold, stark naked. Annette gasped and averted her eyes.

'Mummy . . . '

The man moved further into the room. Annette did not want to look at him but her eyes betrayed her, casting a glance at his face just as he licked his lips.

'What the hell are you doing in here?' Clara came in, wearing just her bathrobe.

'Is she still a virgin?'

Annette did not know what he was talking about. She had only ever heard that word in church, with regard to Jesus' mother.

'I want you to leave now,' said Clara. Her voice became shrill. Annette slumped back into the corner of her bed, not liking the way things were going. 'Go on, get out.'

'I'll pay you more. Fifty quid. Go on.'

'Leave now.' Her mother's body trembled from head to toe.

'I don't think I will. I think you'll go downstairs and make me a drink whilst I play with this little girl here.'

To Annette's horror, her mother turned around and left. She heard her walking down the stairs, whilst the man moved towards her.

'Mummy . . . ' she sobbed, as the man's hands reached out to touch her. She heard her mother running back up the stairs, and was vaguely aware of the glint of the bread knife as her mother entered the bedroom.

'I told you to leave her alone.'

Annette's life quickly descended into fear and chaos and blood.

⋆ ⋆ ⋆

Sam and Annette sat in the waiting room of the sanatorium, a cold, dank place, where the screams of other patients filled the air.

'You can see her now.' The police woman from the Women's Auxiliary Service spoke in clipped and disapproving tones.

Sam took Annette's hand, and led her into the ward. He wished he had left Annette with a neighbour. A policewoman stood guard in the corner.

Clara lay strapped to a bed, her eyes bloodshot and underlined with dark shadows. Annette's hand tightened in Sam's.

'Clara . . . '

She turned her head to look at them. 'I'm sorry.'

'There's no need to be sorry, love. You were protecting Annette.'

'I tried, Sam, but I wasn't meant for happiness. I could feel it smothering me.'

'Hush now. We'll get you a good solicitor, say it was self-defence.'

'No. I did it. I killed him.'

Sam glanced around at the policewoman. 'Shh, be careful what you say.'

'Oh we know she's guilty,' said the policewoman. 'So you've no need to hide anything. This is the result of her promiscuity, and the law will take her in hand.'

Sam turned on the woman. 'Have you no sympathy for a stricken woman?'

'Not one who has strayed from the path of righteousness.'

'And what about the man? The one who was going to rape my daughter?'

'Men would not behave in such a way if women did not let them.'

He looked at her for a long moment. 'I'd

like you to leave us,' he said. 'I want to be alone with my wife. Go on, get out!'

The policewoman thought about it for a minute, then sniffed and said, 'I'll be right outside the door.'

Sam sat next to the bed, with Annette perched on his knee, and took Clara's hand in his. 'We'll get through this, love.'

'Don't you see?' Clara screeched. 'I don't want to get through it. I want this. I want them to lock me away where I can't hurt you and Annette.'

'And you can't hurt yourself either?'

'Yes, that too. I saw him, Sam. The man who hurt me. I saw him in that room with Annette. Oh he had a different face but they're all the same. I knew I had to destroy him for good.' She squeezed his hand. 'I'm a bad lot, Sam. I always have been. Take Annette away from me, where I can't damage her anymore. My parents are up in Stony Newton. They're good people. They'll take care of her.'

'Like they took care of you.'

'It weren't their fault. He said he'd kill them if I ever told.'

'And this was the man you say you controlled?'

She let out a sob. 'I had to tell myself something to get through it.'

'I know, love. I know.'

'You think I love you and Annette, don't you?' she said, her voice becoming calmer and more controlled. 'But you're wrong. I don't want either of you here. Just let them lock me up and forget about me.'

'Clara . . . '

'I said go. I hate you both. Her . . . ' She pointed to Annette as best she could with her hands restrained. 'She's been a burden since the moment she were born. And you! You're pathetic. Not a real man at all. A real man would have given me a good hiding and told me not to go out. You're pathetic, Sam.'

Annette put her head in Sam's shoulder and started to cry quietly. He shushed her gently. 'Okay, Clara, I'll go, but we'll be coming to see you every week. Every Sunday, me and Annette will be at that gate.'

'I don't want you to. I told you, take Annette to my parents.'

'I'm not losing her as well. She's staying with me and whether you like it or not, we're staying with you. Aren't we, petal?' He stroked Annette's hair. She nodded, miserably.

He stood up and leaned over to kiss Clara's cheek but she turned her head away. 'It doesn't matter if you don't love us. We love you and always will.'

16

It was all Mrs. Parker's fault. If she had not told daddy about Lizzie taking the bar of chocolate, then Lizzie would not be in so much trouble.

Lizzie could not understand why her daddy was so angry with her.

'Lizzie, don't you learn in Sunday School that it's wrong to steal?' Jed asked her.

'Mummy does it.'

'Oh that's a lie. I never do,' said Maggie. She sat next to the fire, darning socks. Lizzie opened her mouth to protest, but no sound came out.

'You're a bad influence on her, Maggie,' said Jed. 'I don't care what you do, because you're too old to change, but you shouldn't drag Lizzie down with you!'

'It's only a bar of chocolate,' said Maggie.

'See? That's the problem. You say it's just a bar of chocolate, but it's Mrs. Parker's livelihood. Lizzie . . . ' Jed took his daughter by the shoulders. 'I'm very disappointed in you.' He looked back over his shoulder towards Maggie. 'Promise me you'll never steal again.'

'I promise,' said Lizzie, furious with the injustice of it all.

'And you.' Jed turned to face Maggie. 'You stop doing it as well. You should set a good example.'

'Don't you tell me what to do, you sanctimonious git.' Maggie stood up, throwing the socks at Jed.

Lizzie slipped out of the back door while they were arguing.

* * *

Jack sat on the riverbank, idly watching the fish swim to the surface. Whenever one did, he had a stone ready to throw at its head. He wished he were back at boarding school. At least there he had someone to talk to or to play with. His grandmother had given him a packed lunch with orders not to return until four o'clock.

Uncle Charles had let him down the most. He only spoke to Jack fleetingly, to ask about his day, or if he had slept well. But he had not invited Jack to visit him at the flat over the garage, or suggested they spend any other time together. Jack's first idea had been to go and smash the flat up, but even he had to admit that game was getting boring. The outcome was always the same. Grown-ups one — Jack nil. He needed another way to get their attention.

As he tried to knock out fish with pebbles, he considered his options. One boy at boarding school was always setting fire to things. Whenever he did, his mother would come and take him off to their home in France for a few days. Jack did not know anyone who had a home in France. The twins did, which was why they were off having more fun than him. With that thought he picked up a bigger stone and threw it at a carp which had just popped up for some air.

Another boy at school stole things. His father always beat him black and blue when he was caught. Jack doubted any of the Harcourts would do that. The problem was that they would probably end up liking him even less. Did he care about being liked? He had to admit that he did. His mother loved him, but whether she liked him was a different matter. Sometimes he would catch her looking at him, as if she were wondering how he could possibly be hers. As for his father, John Daventry had tried, but Patricia had made it clear to Jack from an early age that his loyalties had to be with her, not his father.

It was whilst he was pondering all these options, his head full of things he could do to get the grown-ups' attention, that he heard the splash. It was followed by a scream.

Jack stood up and turned to his left. Ten yards away a small wooden bridge crossed the river. Flailing about in the water beneath it was a girl. 'Help,' she sobbed. Jack threw off his shoes and ran along the bank.

'Hang on, I'll get you.' He walked into the river, until it came up to his waist. The girl was about a foot away, and still flailing about. 'It's not that deep,' he said. He took a few steps further forward, and felt the ground give way beneath him. The river was much deeper in the centre. Jack swam to her, and unceremoniously grabbed her by the hair, the only part of her body that was above the water. He was able to get her head out, and wrapped his arm around her neck. He pulled her back to the bank.

'How are you feeling?' he asked a few minutes later, when the girl had coughed up all the water.

'Alright.' She coughed again, spitting up water.

'It was a bit stupid, falling in.'

'I slipped.'

'Well, it was still stupid. What's your name?'

'My name is Lizzie Alsop and I live at number five West Street.'

'I didn't ask for your life story.' That was

something he had heard his mother say to someone once, and he had been waiting for a chance to repeat it.

'You'd better get home, Lizzie.'

At that the girl began to sob. 'I don't want to. Daddy will tell me off again.'

'Did you smash something up?'

'No, I took a bar of chocolate from the shop. Mummy does it all the time.'

'Grown-ups are always allowed to do things we're not. When my mother smashes things, father buys her new jewellery. When I smash things I have it taken out of my pocket money.'

'You shouldn't smash things,' said Lizzie. 'It's naughty.'

'So is stealing.'

'I didn't steal. I just took it. Like mummy does.'

'It's called stealing. Your mother is a thief.'

'She isn't!'

'If she takes things without paying, she's a thief and a liar.'

Lizzie stood up, then walked over and smacked Jack across the face. He raised his hand, but quickly changed his mind. It was not done to hit girls, because they were weak and stupid and did not know any better. That was not quite how his Uncle Charles had put it. He had said something about women being right. Or was it 'having rights'? But Jack had known what his uncle really meant. He rubbed his cheek. 'Don't hit me again.'

'Then don't call my mummy a thief.'

'Alright. I won't. But she . . . ' When Jack saw the murderous gleam in Lizzie's eye, he shut up. Perhaps Uncle Charles knew of other reasons for not hitting girls. Perhaps it was because they were better at hitting back. 'What time is it?'

'Don't know.'

'I've got to get back. Come with me and I'll ask grandmother if you can have tea.' Jack stood up and held out his hand. Lizzie hesitated, then put her small hand in his.

★ ★ ★

'I've telephoned Elizabeth's mother and told her what's happened and that she's staying for tea,' said Veronica. 'We'd better find her some clean clothes. She'll have to wear some of Ricky's or Bobby's for now. Not that I like to see girls in shorts. I can't understand this fashion for wearing slacks that some young women have nowadays.'

'That was a fine thing you did, Jack,' said Charles, pouring out lemonade for the children. 'Pulling Lizzie out of the river. You probably saved her life. So we'll forget that

you shouldn't have been out there, shall we?'
Charles winked.

'Can Lizzie come for tea tomorrow as
well?' asked Jack.

'I'll ask her mother if she can come over
every day whilst you're here,' said Veronica.
'Would you like that?'

'I'd have thought she was a bit young to
play with Jack,' said Charles.

'I don't mind,' said Jack. Her presence
would be a constant reminder to his family of
the good thing he had done. Then they would
have to like him.

17

The twins followed Mackenzie Henderson everywhere that summer. Paul Henderson's fifteen-year-old son, from his second marriage, had borne their presence with good grace. Mack had taken the boys to a rock pool on the beach, where they eagerly collected shells and shiny pebbles. Mack was twice their size, almost a grown man, but with enough clumsiness left to show he was still a boy.

'He's a good boy,' Rebecca said to Clementine as they relaxed on deck chairs, further up the beach. The three baby girls, Esther, Charlotte and Clementine's daughter, Verity, were back at the gîte, being taken care of by nannies. Rebecca told herself it would only be for a couple of weeks. Clementine did not seem to mind at all.

'He's going to be gorgeous in a few years.'

'Yes, he's okay.' Clementine lowered her voice. 'I thought he'd hate me, but his mother's an absolute monster. So he spends as much time with us as possible.'

'Bobby adores him. I don't think I've ever seen him take to someone outside of the family so much. Ricky adores everyone.'

'Hey, wicked stepmother,' said Mack, running back towards them, with Ricky and Bobby following closely behind. 'If you were half a decent woman, you'd buy us all ice cream.'

'Sadly I'm not even that, oh evil-barrier-to-my-getting-all-your-father's-wealth,' said Clementine. She put her hands to her mouth in mock horror. 'Oh, did I just say that out loud? Here, take some money. Buy as many ice creams as you like. Have gold flakes on them if you want, but forget I said anything.'

Rebecca threw her head back and laughed. She had been doing a lot of that with Clementine. Everything was a joke, but she supposed that was the way life was when one had a lot of money. 'I wonder how Charles is getting on with Jack being there,' she said out loud. Mack and the boys were already on their way to the ice cream parlour on the promenade.

'Not your problem, darling. Forget the little monster.'

'I can't. He haunts me. I hate him, yet I feel bad about hating him. After all he is only a child, and children aren't always responsible for how they turn out. Patricia is a bit like Mack's mother. A total nightmare. Yet Mack is growing into a charming, easy-going boy and Jack is dangerous and will become more dangerous if he isn't checked.'

'A master criminal, perhaps?'

'No, a murderer.' Rebecca felt a sudden chill, yet the sun overhead still shone as brightly.

'You don't think so. Not really?'

'Yes. I do, actually. Unless something happens to change him.'

'I've seen the most awful kids grow up to be okay. Anyway, he's not your problem, darling.'

'That I'm not so sure about, Clem,' said Rebecca, remembering Jack's hatred of the twins. 'Since the first day I met him, I've had the feeling that it is within him to bring our world crashing down around us.'

'That's it,' said Clementine, clapping her hands together. 'You are far too pessimistic, so this conversation is going to end now.'

'I'm sorry. It's because I'm so happy. I've got a husband who loves me, and four beautiful children. I'm having a great time here with you. But I've always had this idea that moments of happiness have to be paid for. To balance the universe.'

Clementine laughed. 'Utter nonsense. And besides, from what you've told me of your early life, it seems to me you've already paid for all your happy moments, so enjoy them.'

'I haven't told you everything,' said Rebecca. And once again it felt as though a cloud shifted in the sky, turning her life into a shadow.

'Well, that's not fair, darling. I want to know everything.'

Rebecca thought about it for a moment. Did she dare trust Clementine with the truth? 'It was the night my father came home from the war,' she began. 'No, it started before that.' It all seemed a million miles away, from that cold evening to the golden beach in the south of France. It was almost as if she were telling someone else's story. This helped as it meant she did not cry, as she normally did whenever she thought about the events of that awful night. She did not finish speaking until Clementine knew everything.

'You can't tell anyone ever,' she said afterwards. 'Not even Paul. And especially not Charles. I don't know what he would think if he knew the truth.'

'He'd say you did the only thing you could do, darling, I'm sure of it,' said Clementine.

'Please, Clementine. I can't take that risk. You should hear him when reads about babies being abandoned.'

'Of course I shan't say anything.' Clementine reached out and squeezed Rebecca's arm. 'I'm glad you've told me. It explains a lot. You always have that sadness behind your eyes, even when you're happy. But do be happy darling, because you deserve to be.'

'Thank you.' Rebecca felt lighter than she had for a long time. Part of that was down to Clementine's reaction. She had not recoiled in horror, as Rebecca thought she would. She had always assumed that the reaction to her story would be disgust.

★ ★ ★

With Rebecca and the children away, Charles decided to work in the evenings. It helped fill the gap left by their absence. He missed seeing her face every morning, and hearing the cheerful chatter of the twins or the quiet cooing of Charlotte in her crib. He even missed Esther. It was odd how children grew on one when they lived in the same house. He was a lucky man.

He liked the factory when it was quiet. In the daytime there was always some call on his time. Problems with machinery, spats between workers, or telephone calls that lasted ages, meaning he had lost his place in the accounts ledger by the time the conversation ended.

When he got to the factory floor, he could

see a light on up in his office. When he opened the door, he found Maggie Alsop, with her hands in the petty cash box.

'What on earth are you doing?'

'Oh, Mr. Harcourt, I'm sorry. It's just that . . . '

Charles held out his hand. 'No, don't give me excuses, Maggie. This isn't the first time you've done this. My father caught you several years ago. Why we let you return, I don't know. Get your things and leave. You're dismissed.'

'Mr. Harcourt, you can't. If my husband finds out . . . ' Maggie looked flustered, but then her face cleared. 'I don't think you really want to fire me, Mr. Harcourt.'

'Why not?'

'I know something, you see. About your wife and about your sister.'

'Don't play games, Maggie. Nothing you say is going to get you out of trouble.'

'Oh, I think this will. You see, I saw you, that night at the Priory, when your sister was supposed to be in London having a baby. I didn't know for certain till I saw your nephew but I know now.'

Charles froze. 'What are you saying?'

'Jed told me that he had a baby with Becky and that they dumped it on the Priory doorstep. A boy. I remember the night, because I saw them coming back. Then I saw you and your sister get into a car with a bundle. I didn't realise at first, not till I saw Jack Daventry last year. I'm surprised you haven't seen it yourself. You see him more than I do. He's got Becky's eyes, don't you think?'

'You're talking rubbish, Maggie. None of this is true.' Charles felt the world begin to spin out of control. He recalled Rebecca asking him, on the day of her mother's funeral, about whether they'd had any foundlings on the doorstep. Is that why she asked? To find out what happened to the child she abandoned?

Rebecca had never given him any cause to doubt her love for him. She was a good wife and a good mother. The idea of her leaving a child on a doorstep disgusted him. It rendered everything in their lives a lie.

'Ask her when she gets back from France. No, you won't do that because you know it's true. I can see it in your face. You know about the baby. Perhaps not about Becky, but you know your sister's been bringing up some other woman's brat. I wonder if Mr. Daventry knows . . . '

'You're to say nothing, Maggie. Keep your job, but don't let me catch you with your hands in the petty cash again.'

'Oh no, I want more than that. I want Jed

to be made a manager, with more pay, and I want us to live in a better house.'

'That's blackmail.' It would be almost impossible. They were already in the process of selling off some of their housing stock.

'How much is your wife and sister's reputation worth to you, Mr. Harcourt?' Maggie had a gleam of triumph in her eyes. Charles suspected that she had been saving up the information for a long time in order to gain some advantage from it.

He drove back home, his head in a daze. He parked outside the garage and was about to make his way up to the flat, when Jack came bounding across from the Priory.

'Uncle Charles, Uncle Charles. I helped an old lady across the road today.'

'Good for you, Jack,' said Charles, with more bitterness than he intended. After all, it was not the boy's fault. He had known all along Jack was not really his sister's. He had even helped her to cover up the truth. That Jack might be Rebecca's and Jed's changed everything.

'I thought you'd like to know. I'm trying to be good, Uncle Charles. So that people will like me better.'

'Jack, I haven't got the time or inclination to listen to your many acts of heroism. Leave me alone please.'

He felt the boy's eyes staring into his back. He could see the pain of rejection in them. He was behaving badly towards the boy. How could he be any different now he knew the truth?

18

September 1939

Every Sunday Annette and Sam travelled to the sanatorium for two hours of not knowing what to say. It did not help that any news had already been passed between them. They still had to find conversation to share with Clara. She had increasingly become a passive participant in the discussion.

'I'm joining the police force, mum,' said Annette. Her words left her mouth and hung in the air, before popping like a soap bubble. Clara glanced at her briefly, as if she might say something, but appeared to think better of it. A woman visiting an equally reticent relation smiled sympathetically at Annette.

With Germany invading Poland only two days earlier, and children having been evacuated from London in Operation Pied Piper on the same day, that temptation to speak to other visitors instead of the silent patients was strong. It was something that had failed to touch the patients' lives. They were all too locked up in their own nightmares to worry about the nightmare facing the whole of Europe. Annette envied them their ignorance.

'Yes, I was against it at first,' said Sam, in an overly jocular manner that belied the furious argument he and Annette had really had when she made the announcement to him. 'Because of the way they treated you, Clara. Those bloody women's auxiliary service women, looking down on you and treating that bloke like he was some saint.'

'But I'm not joining them,' said Annette, afraid that Sam's mention of that fateful night might cause one of Clara's furies. 'Like I said to Dad, the W.A.S. doesn't have much to do nowadays. Because of the way they were with . . . ' She almost said *prostitutes*. 'I'm joining the new Women's Service. I want to be able to help women like . . . ' She paused again. 'Well, I just want to be able to speak up for women in trouble, that's all. And if we're going to go to war, there won't be many men around, so they'll need to look to women to sort things out. Dad agrees now, don't you dad?'

'Yes, I can see now she's doing a good thing. I'm proud of her. She's a clever girl, Clara. We raised an intelligent young woman here. Me and you.'

Clara looked at him. Her mouth opened, and then slammed shut again.

'Yes, you both did,' said Annette. 'I remember that. You both looked after me until . . . until . . . it happened. And even though dad and I have been on our own at home, we know you're here, caring about us.'

'We went to see Winnie at the zoo yesterday, didn't we, Annette?' Sam wiped his brow with his handkerchief.

'Yes, we did. Me, dad and . . . ' Annette stopped and looked at her dad, panic-stricken. That was a bit of news they did not want Clara to know.

'And we had ice cream,' said Sam. 'Like we always used to when Annette was little.' Annette very nearly contradicted him. Clara and the zoo had only happened the once, but Sam always looked back at that time through rose-coloured spectacles.

Clara glanced at them both, then back to the window. 'I don't want you to come again,' she said. It was the first time she had spoken to them in more than a monosyllable for years. 'You're to get on with your lives. Don't come back.'

'Mum . . . '

'I mean it this time.'

'Clara, love.'

'Don't 'love' me, Sam Jenkins. I know there's someone else. I've seen it in your face the last few weeks. You're happy. As you

216

should be. I never gave you any happiness, perhaps she will.'

'Even if you don't want to see me,' said Sam, 'I can understand that. But don't send Annette away.'

Annette thought differently. How she wished she could get out of this painful duty. This weekly round of lies about how happy they had all been. Annette remembered far more than she ever pretended. She remembered her mother's indifference, until that last year. One year of her mother playing happy families did not undo the pain of neglect Annette had to live with daily. She had not known real happiness until her mother had been locked up, leaving Annette and Sam alone. Only then did she have a proper childhood, with Sunday mornings as the only cloud in an otherwise sunny week.

'Annette wants to stop coming,' said Clara. 'So let her. She owes me nowt. What I did . . . well, that was to make up for all the times I failed. We're even.'

'Mum, I don't want to stop coming to see you,' Annette lied.

'Stop coming for a year,' said Clara. 'If after that time you decide you want to come back, then come back, but only if you really want to. I mean it. I'll tell the nurses not to let you in for a year. I want to go back to my room now. Nurse! Nurse!' Clara stood up unsteadily. The nurse approached. 'I want to go back to my room. You're not to let them in again for a year, do you hear?'

'She doesn't mean it,' said Sam.

'Yes, I do. Take me back now. I'm sick of visitors. Sick of listening to them go on about life outside, when they know I'll never see it again.'

Later, Sam and Annette sat in a café, drinking tea and nibbling at buttered toast. Outside the street was a hive of activity, as the nation prepared for war. Air raid wardens watched the skies, waiting for the first attack. Inside the café a wireless played swing music in the background. People sat around it, eager for the news. Sam and Annette were deep in conversation. Clara had been their world for twelve years, and now she had set them free. Odd that it did not feel that way. They had accepted her command far too readily.

'She knows about Marian,' said Sam. 'I don't know how she knows, but she does.'

'Don't let it upset you, dad.' Annette reached over and took his hand. 'You've done nothing wrong. No one could expect you to be alone for the rest of your life. Mrs. Overton . . . Marian . . . is good for you. She's been good to me too. Now her husband is dead, it's only right you two should be together.'

'But your mother's not dead, Annette, and I'm still married to her. I can't ask Marian to live in sin.'

'You and mum did. At first.'

'That's because your mother wouldn't get married and it was the only way I could stay and help look after you. Marian is a nice woman . . . not that I'm saying your mother isn't . . . I mean . . . '

'Dad, I'm not an idiot. I know what mum was.'

'Do you?' Sam's eyes widened with shock.

'Kids see a lot more than you think.'

'I wish you hadn't. I don't want you remembering your mother like that. I want you to remember her as someone who loved you enough to protect you.'

'Did she? Sometimes I wonder whether she was killing him to protect me or to purge herself of something. I remember her that night, with the knife. She just couldn't stop.' Annette closed her eyes.

'Don't upset yourself about it, sweetheart.'

'I'm not upset. Not anymore. I used to have nightmares about it, but I haven't for a while.'

'That'll be Terry I suppose.'

Annette smiled dreamily. 'Yes.'

'So are you two getting married?'

'Not yet. We can't afford it.'

'I've got some money put by . . . '

'That's for you and Marian. Take her on holiday or something. Have a good life, dad. You've given up so much for me, you deserve it.'

'I wouldn't do anything differently, love. You might not be my blood, but I still think of you as mine.'

'And you're mine too. If mum did one good thing in her life, it was letting you into it.'

'She didn't exactly let me into it. We grew up together, you know, in Stony Newton. So I've always been in it in some way or another. That's another thing. About your grandparents . . . '

'I don't want to know them any more than they want to know me.' Annette held up her hand to prevent him saying anything else. 'They're ashamed of me.'

'They wouldn't be. Not if they knew you.'

'But they've never wanted to.' She looked down at her olive-toned hands. That was another reason her grandparents might not want to know her.

Clara had once told Annette that Len Peters had said, 'Don't bring that half-breed here.' Clara might only have said it to hurt Annette during one of her many rages, but it was not a chance she was willing to take.

'I worry about you, Annette. I'm all you've got, whilst your mother is in that place. If anything ever happened to me . . .'

'Nothing's going to happen to you. You're only forty.'

'They might call me up.'

'Nobody knows what's going to happen yet.' Annette knew that she was being ridiculously optimistic. The signs were unmistakeable. Hitler was not going to back down.

At eleven-fifteen, the café proprietor called for a hush and turned the wireless up. Neville Chamberlain's solemn voice crackled through the café, telling all about the ultimatum given to Germany. Britain was officially at war.

When the broadcast ended, the clientele sat in stunned silence. Everyone had won the impending war a million times in discussions at the pubs and in the factories. Now it was real, their confidence was shaken a little. Nothing was as certain as it had been.

At eleven-twenty-eight on the third of September nineteen thirty-nine, the first air raid siren in London sounded.

★ ★ ★

Most of the family was sitting in the drawing-room of the Priory. Veronica had excused herself, saying she could not bear the tension. Charles, George and Rebecca sat on chairs, whilst Ricky and Bobby sprawled on the floor, their lanky legs stretched out. Esther and Charlotte sat either side of Rebecca, holding her hands, their faces pensive. She stroked their hair and kissed their heads.

'I hate to say it,' said Charles, when the broadcast had ended, 'but this war could save Harcourt's.' They had already received preliminary approaches from the War Office, regarding supplying extra bandages to the armed forces and hospitals.

'Perhaps now you understand what we had to deal with during the Great War,' said George, without malice. 'I seem to remember you were quite scathing about it.'

'I didn't realise then how much responsibility we had to the community, and to the family,' said Charles. He glanced at Rebecca quickly then looked away. He could not remember the last time he had looked her in the eye. It was easier that way.

'We'll go and sign up in the morning,' said Ricky, speaking for himself and Bobby. 'It's our duty.' His eyes shone with excitement. It was all a game to him. He had dreamed of the war, and his part in it. Bobby was a little more serious about it, but nonetheless he was sure he would be needed.

'You don't have to enlist,' said Charles. 'You're students.'

'We want to, dad,' said Ricky.

'They'll need good engineers,' Bobby said. 'We're going in the same regiment. Right?'

'Right oh,' said Ricky. 'The Royal Engineers, here we come.'

'Boys,' said Rebecca, 'don't you think you ought to finish university?'

'All our friends will be going, mum. We can't get left behind,' Ricky said.

Rebecca got up and left the room, closely followed by Esther and Charlotte. The boys chatted for a few minutes, making their own plans for the war, then left Charles and his father alone.

'You should go and comfort Rebecca,' George said to Charles.

'Why?'

'She's worried about the boys. Aren't you?'

'Yes, of course. But it's their duty, as it was mine.'

'What's happened, Charles?'

'Hmm?' Charles lit a cigarette and sat back in his chair.

'With you and Rebecca. You used to be so happy. Now you barely speak to each other.'

'Things change.'

'Has she . . . well, is there another man?'

'No, not that I know of.'

'And you?'

'No, I don't have another man, either.'

'Don't be facetious, Charles.' George picked up the cigarette box and took one out.

'I thought you'd been ordered by the doctor to give up.'

'Old Latimer is a hypocrite who drinks a bottle of whisky a night. I won't take orders from him until he learns to practise what he preaches. Go and talk to Rebecca.'

Rebecca was sitting in the front garden, her eyes damp with tears. She hastily wiped them away when she saw him.

'Where are the children?' he asked.

'The girls have gone to telephone all their friends to talk about the war. I don't know where the boys are. I imagine Bobby has already got a tank or something built in the garage.'

'I'm sure they'll be fine,' he said, sitting opposite her.

'It's not just the war,' said Rebecca. 'It's us.'

'What about us?'

'You barely look at me anymore. You haven't touched me for God knows how long. What is it, Charles? What did I do?'

'Oh, let's not go over this again. Nothing is

wrong. Everything is fine. You can't expect the first passion to last forever. People change.'

'Stop loving each other?'

'No, not that. Never that.' He wanted to tell her that he loved her so much it hurt. No matter what lies she had told him, or what she had failed to tell him, he could never hate her. In the early days, after Maggie Alsop first told him the truth, he had pretended to himself it did not matter. He had still made love to Rebecca, still taken interest in her and everything she did. But gradually, over the years, as the lie cut him deeper and deeper, he had withdrawn from her. It was easier that way.

'I wish I could believe that. Is it because of Esther? It seems that everything dates back to when I brought her to live with us. Do you still resent her?'

'She's been a good child, and she's growing into a nice young woman.'

'Is there someone else?'

'My father just asked me that. No, there isn't. Why, is there for you?'

'My feelings for you haven't changed, Charles. You're the one who's changed. I don't know if I can bear it anymore. I've lost you, somehow, without really knowing how, and now I'll be losing the boys too.' She wiped her eyes again, smudging her mascara. 'I think you should move back in with your parents for a while. Because I can't go on lying next to you every night, wondering why you don't want me anymore. As soon as the girls are old enough, I'll leave. I promise I'll only take whatever I arrived with.' Her voice cracked. She stood up and ran back to the flat.

Charles stared into the distance. He hated hurting her, and yet he had been doing that for a long time. He could hardly blame her for having had enough of it. If only he had the courage to get things out into the open. But he had his own secret. If Rebecca told the truth, then he would have to, and he had promised Patty never to say a word.

He could plainly see the irony of his situation. He was hurt and angry with Rebecca for keeping a secret from him, and yet he also kept a secret. Perhaps it was easier to forgive one's own transgressions.

★ ★ ★

Esther stood at the bottom of the stairs to the flat, watching Ricky and Bobby talking in the yard. They were making plans about going to sign up. Ricky had fair hair, like his father, whereas Bobby was dark, like his mother.

226

'Bobby,' she said, coming out from the shadows of the hallway. 'Are you really going away?'

'Yes.'

'I wish you wouldn't.'

Ricky laughed. 'Aw, your best friend will be gone, Esther.'

'Shut up,' said Bobby. 'I'm not her best friend.'

'Yes, you are,' said Esther. She said it only wishing it was true. His indifference to her had been an itch she could not scratch. Ricky had been the one who accepted her, whereas Bobby had always been coldly polite.

'Go and play with Charlie,' Bobby said. 'We've got things to talk about.'

'I'm not a little girl,' said Esther, pouting. 'I'm thirteen.'

'Yes, that's right, you're thirteen. And we're eighteen. Which means we don't want you hanging around us all the time. Go on, go and play with your dolls or something.'

Esther's eyes filled with tears. 'I hope you get killed in the war!' She ran back up the flat, and lay sobbing on her bed.

'Come on, Bob, that was a bit harsh,' said Ricky, when she had gone. 'She's got a huge crush on you.'

'Harsh? She's the one wishing me dead. Besides, it's sick. She's our sister.'

'Not really. She's not even adopted.'

'It doesn't matter. Anyway, I was being cruel to be kind. I know how she feels, but it's wrong.'

'Like I said, she's not really our sister.'

'But she is thirteen years old. I don't go for schoolgirls.'

'Glad to hear it, mate. Hey, I was wondering.' Ricky's face settled into a rare show of solemnity. 'About mum and dad. They're not right, you know.'

'I know. But it's between them.'

'I don't like to think of us going away and them being unhappy.'

'Rick, not everyone can be happy, no matter how hard you try to make it so.'

'That's not going to stop me trying. I just wondered whether to take them out for a meal or something. Here's mum now. Mum!'

Rebecca rounded the corner of the Priory, stopping only to wipe her eyes. 'Mum, me and Bob, we thought we'd take you and dad out somewhere. Before we go away.'

'That's a nice idea,' she said, without showing much enthusiasm. 'We'll sort something out.'

'Mum . . . ' Bobby walked towards her and put his arms around her. 'What's wrong with you and dad?'

'We're just having a few problems that's all.

All couples go through it, I suppose.'

'Anything we can do?'

'No, darling. You've got your own lives to lead. Don't worry about us.'

'That's easier said than done,' said Ricky. 'Tell you what, you and dad just go out. We'll pay. Our treat. You never go out on dates anymore. I've read somewhere it helps keep a relationship alive.'

Rebecca laughed through her tears. 'Ricky, darling, stop trying to fix things.'

'That's what Bob just said.'

'Bobby's right. Your father and I need to sort this out for ourselves.'

'Come on, Bob.' Ricky slapped his brother on the shoulder, his concerns about his parents forgotten. 'Let's go and sign up.'

'Does it have to be today?' asked Rebecca.

'The sooner the better, mum,' said Bobby. 'Or all the good places will be gone.'

★　★　★

It occurred to Rebecca that there were no good places when it came to canon fodder, but she bit her tongue and kissed them both goodbye. She wondered how something that made them so happy could make her so miserable. But mostly she wondered how Charles could be so matter-of-fact about it.

She had never known him to be gung-ho, and his own wartime experiences had hardly been wonderful.

She wondered if their sons going to war was a way of punishing her.

Life for the past few years had taken her right back to the early times of her marriage, when George and Veronica barely spoke to her, and then only with icy politeness. She had never thought Charles would become the same, yet every day she saw him turning more and more into his parents. Only the children had remained the same towards her. At least, she thought as she climbed the stairs to the flat, she would still have Esther and Charlotte.

She arrived in the hall to hear sobs coming from the girl's bedroom. When she went in, Esther lay on the bed, crying, whilst Charlotte stroked her hair. 'Please don't cry, Esther,' said Charlotte.

'What's wrong, girls?' Rebecca sat on the bed next to Charlotte, and reached over to put her hand on Esther's hip. It was the closest she could get to comforting her. 'Are you afraid of the war, Esther? I'm sure we'll all be fine, darling. They won't expect you and Charlie to fight.'

'I told Bobby I hoped he'd die, and now I wish I hadn't said it,' Esther gulped.

'Esther!' Rebecca was more disappointed than angry. 'Why would you say such a thing?'

'He doesn't love me.'

'Of course he loves you, dearest. We all do.'

'She means he doesn't *love* her,' said Charlotte. 'Like the people in the films. All that kissy kissy stuff.'

'Oh.' Rebecca was shocked. Rebecca still saw Esther very much as a child, yet she had to concede that she was starting to develop into a young woman. She was a pretty girl, with freckles and strawberry blonde hair. 'But he's your brother, darling.'

'He's not my real brother.'

'No, that's true, but you have been raised as brother and sister. I'm sure Bobby thinks it wouldn't be right to love you in that way. Besides, you're only thirteen. You'll fall in love lots of times before you meet the right one.'

'He doesn't even like me, Aunt Rebecca.'

'Now that's not true. Bobby's not as demonstrative as the rest of us. He never has been. I learned when he was a little boy that I had to wait for him to come to me for cuddles.'

'Shall I make a cup of tea?' asked Charlotte. 'That's what they always do in books when someone is heartbroken. A cup

231

of tea and some laudanum.'

'The tea would be lovely, Charlotte.' Rebecca kissed her daughter's head. 'But we'll leave the laudanum for another day, shall we?'

'I really don't know what all the fuss is about,' said Charlotte with a dramatic sigh, as she crossed the room. 'I'm madly in love with Mackenzie Henderson, and he doesn't even know I exist.'

'As he's twenty-seven and you're only twelve, I'm very glad to hear it,' said Rebecca, sternly. When Charlie had left them, she comforted Esther. 'Please don't fret, darling. You can tell Bobby you're sorry later, and I'm sure he'll be sorry too.'

'Aunt Rebecca?' Esther had stopped crying, but her voice was filled with despair.

'What is it?'

'I think I'd like to go home and live with my dad and brothers now.'

Rebecca was taken aback. That was the last thing she expected to hear. 'Darling, why? If it's because you feel embarrassed about Bobby, he'll have forgotten about it by the time he gets back from enlisting.'

'It's not that.' Esther sat up and put her hand in Rebecca's. 'I'm really grateful for all you've done for me. Please don't think I'm not.'

'I know that, dearest, and we're very happy to have you here. I don't want you to leave.'

'I don't belong here. I'm sorry. It's not that anyone has ever been unkind to me. But I don't fit in. I don't fit in at home . . . I mean with my dad and brothers either . . . so I've got to settle somewhere.'

'So why not settle here?' Rebecca's heart ached. What could she say to change Esther's mind?

'Have you ever felt like that? As if you've got a foot in each world, but you don't belong in either of them?'

'For a long time,' said Rebecca, sadly. 'Though it got easier for a while . . . '

'Because of you and Uncle Charles, you mean?'

'Mmm . . . '

'I wish you could be happy again.'

'Is that why you're going, darling? Because if it is, there's no need. Uncle Charles is going to go and live in the main house for a while and . . . '

'No, see. It's all my fault,' said Esther, starting to cry again. 'Uncle Charles and Bobby are the same. They've just tolerated me. So it's my fault you're not happy.'

'No, Esther, whatever's happened, it's not you, I promise. Uncle Charles loves you. He was only just saying to me how well you've grown. Look.' She took Esther's hand. 'I know money isn't everything, but if you stay with us, you can have a good life. If you go to your father, well, there's you and four brothers to care for. I know your elder brothers are working down the pit now, but it's still a big family to feed. You might not be able to continue at the grammar school. Though of course, we'll do everything we can to help you.'

'Dad wants me to go home,' said Esther. 'He said so last week. He says they're struggling. I've got to help.'

'You shouldn't have that on your shoulders. It isn't fair.'

'It'll be awful though. My brothers resent me, because I've had the life they haven't.'

'So now you're going to punish yourself, by giving that life up?'

'No, it's not like that. Oh, Aunt Rebecca, I'm so confused. I want to do the right things, but I don't know what that is. I know you've all been good to me, but you're not my real family. But because I've never lived with my dad and brothers, it doesn't feel like they're my family either.'

'That isn't true,' said Charlotte, coming into the bedroom with a tray of teacups. 'You've got us. Tell her mum. You can't go, Esther. I won't have a sister anymore if you do.' She put the tray onto the other bed, then burst into tears. Mackenzie Henderson not loving her was an idea that appealed to her sense of the dramatic. It was the idea of Esther going that really broke her little heart.

Rebecca held them both while they cried. With one thing and another, their settled life had been thrown into turmoil.

19

Jack Daventry was in bed with Rosa when the news of war came. The wireless in the background did nothing to stop Rosa's demands. The subsequent air raid sirens did not quell her desire either. Her increasingly possessive arms wrapped around him, whilst she urged him on.

'Oh, Jack, yes, please. There, faster, there. No, not yet, darling.'

Jack lay down next to her. 'Damn you,' she said.

He ran his fingers through his hair. 'I can't keep up with your demands all the time,' he said. 'Most women would be grateful for the one orgasm.'

'You barely give me time for that nowadays. What's happened to us, Jackie?'

'For God's sake, don't call me Jackie. My mother calls me that.' He looked at her with distaste. Rosa was the wife of one of his father's fellow MPs. It had seemed fun when he was sixteen and she had seduced him. Rosa certainly knew a lot. But as a result, she expected a lot. Often more than Jack was able to give. She was not only looking more like his mother, she was starting to display the same tedious histrionics.

Jack got out of bed and put his trousers on.

'There's no need to go yet, darling. Rupert won't be back till this evening. We could play a while more.'

'I'm tired of playing,' said Jack. He added viciously, 'I'm tired of you, Rosa.'

'No, don't say that, Jack.' Her voice became harsh. 'I won't let you go. What would your mother say if she knew about us?'

'What would your husband say?'

'He'd divorce me and then we could be together.'

'That's not going to happen, Rosa. Sorry, but this is it.'

'You don't mean that. You've said it before, but you always come back.'

That much was true, but only because he knew Rosa was a soft touch. 'I won't this time.' He turned back to her, and put on his smoothest voice. 'I'm grateful for the time we've had, but we both knew it could never last.'

'Who is she?'

'I don't know yet. But she'll be young and pretty, and she'll be soft and supple in my arms.'

Rosa threw her head back and laughed. 'And where are you going to find a girl like

237

that with your track record, lover boy? If mummy and daddy didn't keep bailing you out, you'd be in prison by now. You think your young, pretty, soft, supple girl is going to risk a life with you? Unless there are so few men left after this war, the girls left will be grateful for anything.'

Jack reminded himself of his rule never to hit women. 'I'm not going to war, so I'll have my pick of them whilst I stay here,' he said, grinning, as he did up the buttons on his shirt.

'You'll have to. You're the right age, and in the peak of health.'

'Yes, but mummy and daddy know people. The same people who kept me out of jail will keep me out of the army.'

'You coward!'

'Maybe so, but I'll be alive when it's all over. I'll be rich too.'

'You're already rich.'

'No, mummy and daddy are rich and they keep a tight hold on my allowance. But I've got friends who know how to make money in wartime. Black market goods.'

'You're going to be a spiv.'

'Yep.'

Rosa looked at him with something like contempt. 'Get out. Don't come crawling back either.'

He leaned over and kissed her hard on the mouth. 'You don't mean that.'

'Oh, Jack, I . . . '

He pulled back and laughed. 'No, you don't mean it. I'll keep you in mind for if I'm ever desperate. So long, Rosa.'

Jack almost skipped out of Rosa's flat. Now he was free to do what he wanted, and to see who he wanted. What he had told Rosa was true. He wanted a girl of his own age. Unfortunately, what Rosa had said was also true. His reputation preceded him so that no decent girl would have anything to do with him.

The Old Brompton Road was busy, with people coming back up from the tube stations after the siren.

Jack spoke to one of the wardens who stood at the head of South Kensington tube station, marshalling people back out onto the street. 'Did I miss an air raid?'

The warden was a man with a sense of purpose. He had been training for this for months, and his time had finally come. 'Nah, mate. False alarm. I think someone must have panicked and hit the button when the Prime Minister declared war.' He sounded like a man thwarted.

'Oh, so we're officially at war, are we?'

'Where have you been for the last hour?'

'Wouldn't you like to know,' said Jack. He smirked and started down the steps of the tube, against the tide of frightened Londoners emerging into the light. He had a choice; go home and face his mother's questions about where he had been all night, or find a pub for a lunchtime drink. He chose The Ship Tavern at Holborn.

'Hey, Jackie, my old china.' Brian Miller raised a hand in salute as soon as Jack walked through the door. Brian was a born Londoner, not much older than Jack, with blonde good looks. He wore a black woolly cap over his hair, giving him the persona of a Jolly Jack Tar. That he had never even been on a boat in the park was irrelevant. Brian was not the sort of person Jack's parents wanted him to associate with, which made him irresistible as far as Jack was concerned.

'Brian, how's it going?'

'Buy us a pint and I'll tell you.'

'You always cost me money.'

Jack ordered two drinks, and then went to sit with his friend in the corner. 'Got some stuff coming in,' said Brian. 'But I'm a bit short of cash. I thought that if you could . . . '

'No chance, matey. Mummy and daddy have cut my allowance, and now I can't even ask Rosa for any.'

'You still tupping that old bint?'

'No, that's the point. I ended it this morning.'

'Not surprised, Jack. Who wants an old one when there are so many young pretty ones to choose from?' To illustrate Brian's point, two young women entered the bar. 'Mind you, don't like the look of yours, mate.' One of the girls looked as pretty as a picture, dressed in a yellow floral flock. She reminded Jack of a daffodil in spring; fresh and sweet. The other girl wore horn-rimmed glasses, and had wiry black hair.

When they noticed Jack and Brian looking, they both giggled and went to the bar, but the pretty girl kept looking at Jack and smiling.

'I think you're stuck with the other one, matey,' he said to Brian. 'The daffodil seems to prefer me.' He raised his glass in a salute to her.

'Jack?' she said, wandering over to them. 'It is Jack Daventry, isn't it?'

'He didn't do it. He wasn't there,' quipped Brian.

'Oh yes he was,' said the girl, smiling. 'He pulled me out of the river and saved my life.'

'Jesus . . . ' Jack sat open-mouthed. 'Not Lizzie Alsop?'

'That's me.'

Jack stood up, and was about to kiss her. She was too fragrant and lovely for the likes of him. Instead he held out his hand. 'It's good to see you're still alive, Lizzie.'

She reached up and kissed him on the cheek. 'Thanks to you. Have you saved any more lives since then?'

'No, but I did help an old lady across the road a few days later.'

'I know, I was with you, remember?'

Yes, he did remember then. Lizzie had followed him around for days. Funny how he had forgotten that. All he remembered was that when he told his Uncle Charles of his good deed, he might just as well have said that he murdered the old woman. 'What are you doing in London?'

'I've just come down to train at the Royal Free Hospital. I'm going to be a doctor.'

'A doctor? Well, that's fantastic, Lizzie.'

'A woman doctor?' Brian scoffed. 'God help us.'

Jack scowled at him. 'Lizzie's a clever girl. She can do it. Sit down and we'll get you and . . . '

'Marie.'

'We'll get you and Marie a drink.'

Lizzie and Marie joined them at their table, each with a glass of port and lemon. Marie sat holding her handbag tightly on her knees, as if she thought they might snatch it. 'How are your parents, Lizzie?' Jack hardly recognized himself. He was not the small talk type, and he never bothered about a girl's family.

'They're okay, thanks. We haven't seen you for ages at Stony Newton. Did you fall out with us all?'

'I was never that popular up there.'

'You were with me,' said Lizzie, gently.

'Thanks. So, erm ... Marie, are you training to be a doctor too?'

'No, I just live in the same building as Lizzie. We hardly know each other at all. I don't even know why she's asked me out today.'

'She's probably planning to sell you to white slave traders,' said Brian. Lizzie and Jack laughed, but Marie just held her handbag closer.

'I don't have many friends in London,' Lizzie explained. 'Marie is going to show me around. Aren't you, Marie?'

'Yes, I suppose so, though I do have things to be doing.'

'What's that, Marie?' Brian leaned over. 'Got to darn your stockings? Squeeze your blackheads?'

'No. Well yes, I do have to darn my stockings. But I've got ironing to do. I work at a bank and it's a very respectable position.'

'At a bank, eh?' Brian's ears almost visibly

pricked up. 'That's very interesting, Marie. Tell me all about it?'

'The friendship with Marie is going well then,' Jack muttered to Lizzie, whilst Brian pumped Marie for information about where she worked.

'Spiffing,' she said, rolling her eyes. 'Though, you know, sometimes you wish you hadn't . . . '

'Oh yes. Often.' Jack could hardly take his eyes off her. How had that clumsy child grown into this beautiful, self-possessed young woman? 'It really is good to see you, Lizzie. You, er . . . are you seeing anyone?'

'Yes, I am, though it's complicated.'

'In what way?'

Lizzie lowered her voice. 'Promise you won't be shocked? I think Marie might be.'

'No, go on.'

'He's married.'

Jack nodded. 'Just got out of a similar relationship myself. Can I give you a word of advice?'

'If it's to get out now, I probably won't take it.'

'You're in love with him?'

'Yes. No. I don't know, but I'm committed to the relationship, even if he isn't.'

'You can do better than him.'

'Can I, Jack?'

'You can do better than me too.'

'Don't put yourself down.'

'Why not? It saves everyone else the trouble.'

To his surprise Lizzie laughed. 'Oh, you poor hard-done-to thing. There you are, startlingly handsome and from a rich family, probably can have any girl you want, and you're upset because not everyone loves you.'

Jack gave a short bitter laugh. 'I don't even love myself.'

'Well, perhaps if you got off this path of self-destruction and started to like yourself, others would see your worth.'

'Well, thank you, Professor Freud.' He looked at her for a long time. 'How do you know I'm on a path of self-destruction?'

'We hear things, even in Stony Newton. After all, you may have been born in London and lived down here all your life, but you're one of the Harcourts.'

'I'm a Daventry.'

'On your mother's side, I mean. That makes you eminently fascinating to those of us from the lower orders. Of course, you're held up to us all as an example of how not to behave, but that doesn't mean we don't all love hearing about your latest escapades with the magistrates' court. It makes us feel superior.'

'Poor but honest, eh?'

'Exactly. Whereas you're rich and debauched. You're everything we want our wealthy citizens to be.'

'Can I see you, whilst you're in London, Lizzie? I don't have anyone in my life who really tells it to me like it is. Everyone takes me far too seriously. I suppose that's my fault. I'm always angry. Except with you.'

'Aren't you joining up, Jack?'

'No, mummy knows someone at the War Office.' He was not prepared for her look of disappointment.

'Well,' she said, quietly. 'You must do what you think best.'

'You think I should go.'

'I think you should do whatever makes you happy, Jack.' She picked up her glass and downed the rest of her drink, before standing up. 'Marie and I had better be getting on. Perhaps I'll see you around from time to time. Marie?'

Marie was deep in conversation with Brian. Her handbag had slipped to the floor, and she sat with her elbows on the table, hanging on his every word. 'I'll call on you, Marie,' Brian said.

'Lizzie.' Jack stood up. 'Lizzie, I hope I see you.'

'I'm sure you shall, Jack.'

'I'm sorry.'

'For what?'

'For not living up to your expectations of me.'

'Like I told you, Jack. You only have yourself to please. What I think, or what anyone else thinks, doesn't matter.'

'Like you're pleasing yourself with your married lover, I suppose.' The words were out before he could stop them, and it was too late to take them back. He wanted her admiration. Instead she despised him. No, not even that. She was disappointed in him, and that somehow made it worse. It reminded him of his Uncle Charles' disappointment when he found out that Jack had smashed up the twins' train set.

'Except that we're not letting our country down.' With her cheeks flaming crimson, Lizzie turned on her heel and stormed out of the pub.

'Well, what do you think of that, mate?' said Brian when the girls had left. 'Stuck-up little cow, isn't she?'

Jack caught Brian by the lapels and shoved him back into the corner seat. 'You don't talk about her like that, right?'

'Alright, alright.' Brian held up his hands in supplication. 'Christ, Jack, how was I to know you'd take on so? I mean, she's just a girl like any other girl, isn't she?'

'No, she isn't like any other girl. She's a nice girl.' Jack stepped back and wiped his brow on his sleeve.

'Okay, we've established that. Now, sit down and let's talk business. This stuff I've got coming in . . . '

★ ★ ★

Jack unlocked the door of the flat, and gingerly looked into the hall. A bedroom door opened and the human equivalent of a small pony came bounding out.

A gangly girl with braces came running along the corridor. 'Jackie! Where have you been? Mummy is furious and daddy just sat there at lunch all quiet, like he does.' Veronica threw herself into her brother's arms. She was one of the few people in Jack's life that he genuinely loved. Unfortunately that did not mean he treated her any better.

'Shh, Ronnie. Don't give the game away. Where are they?'

'Mummy is in bed with one of her headaches and daddy had to go out for war stuff. He's really happy because the Prime Minister needs his help. You've to go and see mummy as soon as you get back.'

'No, I'm not doing that. Hey, Ronnie, have

you still got that money grandmother and grandfather gave you for all those birthdays?'

'Ye-es. Why?'

'I need to borrow it. I'll pay you back. In fact, I'll double it.'

'Mummy said I'm not to give you money. You know I would if I could, because you're my favourite brother in the whole world, but I can't. Really, she'd be so cross, and mummy is horrid when she's cross.'

'Jack ... ' His mother stood at her bedroom door with her arms folded. 'Ronnie is not to give you any money. What do you want it for? It's not for another one of those deals is it?'

Jack looked at his mother's cocaine-ravaged face and raised an eyebrow.

'Ronnie, go to your bedroom,' Patty snapped.

'Aw, but mummy.'

'Now, go on.'

'Go on, pet,' said Jack. He gave his sister a kiss. 'I'll bring you back something nice. Mother?' He folded his arms and leaned against the wall. He tried to remember the last time he had been as far as the drawing-room. It was like living in a hotel, with his mother as the fierce concierge, blocking his way to either freedom or sleep.

Ronnie walked with exaggerated slowness

to her bedroom. 'Shut the door right up, Ronnie,' said Patricia. When Ronnie had done that, Patricia held out her hands in supplication to her son. 'Jack, darling, what happened to you? You used to be such a sweet little boy.'

Jack threw back his head and laughed. 'Oh, that's precious, mother. I was far from it. You made sure of that, teaching me the power of smashing crockery from an early age. It's a wonder Ronnie's not the same. She's determined to be decent despite your best efforts.'

'You have to stop this life you're leading, Jack. Think of your father . . . '

'My father barely notices I'm alive. All he cares about is his seat in parliament.'

'Why were you asking Ronnie for money?'

'I need it.'

'I won't have you dealing drugs, Jack.'

Jack laughed again. 'You're hardly in a position to speak, mother. Look at you. It's three o'clock on a Sunday afternoon and you're completely wasted. Who takes care of Ronnie when you're like this?'

'She's twelve. She can take care of herself now. And I've only got a headache.'

'Don't kid a kidder. I need a thousand pounds, mother.'

'Well, I'm not going to give it to you.'

'I saw Lizzie Alsop today,' said Jack, appearing to change the subject. 'You remember the little girl I saved from drowning, don't you? She was at The Ship Tavern. She's training to be a doctor.'

'Is she? That's very nice for her.'

'I didn't notice it when I was with her, but when I saw Ronnie . . . They're amazingly alike, aren't they? I've never told dad about everything that happened on the day the miners rioted at the Priory and what made me join in with them.'

'Jack.' Patricia's voice held a warning note. 'That has nothing to do with any of this.'

'Doesn't it? I think it has a lot to do with it.'

'You'd really cause Ronnie all that pain?'

'It wouldn't be my doing, mother. You're the one who had sex with another man and passed off his baby as dad's. It makes me wonder where I came from.'

Patricia looked panic-stricken. Jack would have liked to ask her more, because there was obviously a story there, but he did not want to change the subject. 'How much do you need?' she asked.

'A thousand.'

'That's a lot of money to lay one's hands on quickly. It will take me a couple of days.'

'I can wait. I need it by Wednesday night.'

'This is the only time, Jack.' Patricia's voice quivered. 'Do your deal, and then get out. I don't want you living here anymore.'

'That suits me. When this deal is done, I'll be able to buy a place of my own.' Jack opened the front door, and then paused. 'Do you want me to save you some of the stock, mother?'

'Get out!'

20

When Ricky and Bobby returned from enlisting the next morning, Bobby's mouth was set in a grim line. They joined their mother in the sitting-room of the flat, Charles having followed them across from the main house.

'What's wrong?' asked Rebecca. 'Did you fail to pass the medical?' She experienced a brief glimmer of hope, having prayed all night for such an outcome.

'No,' said Bobby. 'But we didn't get into the same regiment. I got into the engineers, but Ricky . . . '

'I got into the medical corps. They . . . er . . . they said they had enough engineers.'

'That's rubbish,' said Bobby. 'Jamie Linney got in after you went through.'

'Well, I don't know why it is. Maybe my arithmetic let me down,' said Ricky. 'I've never been as good at it as you.'

'We were supposed to go together,' said Bobby. 'Brothers, sticking it out.'

'Never mind, son,' said Charles. 'At a time like this, sacrifices have to be made. I'm proud of both of you.' He looked at Rebecca with a challenge in his eyes, as if he thought she might disagree.

'So am I,' she said, firmly. 'As your father says, sacrifices have to be made.'

'It stinks,' said Bobby, storming out of the room.

Ricky looked at the ground. Rebecca noticed that the tops of his ears were pink.

'Is there anything you want to tell us, darling?' she asked gently.

Ricky spoke in low tones, watching for the door. 'I know Bobby wanted us to go together, but . . . well, engineering has always been his dream, not mine. I want to be a doctor. Eventually, I mean. I can only go in as a combat medic for now. But I couldn't tell him that, could I? He'd think I betrayed him. So I got the sergeant to lie for me. How was I to know they'd take Jamie Linney in the engineers straight after?' Ricky took a deep breath. 'Besides, I'm sick of doing the twins thing. It's not that I don't love Bobby, I do. But I need room to breathe and I can't get that when I'm with him.' The words rushed from him, as if he had been holding them back for years. 'Tell me I did the right thing.'

'Of course you did,' said Rebecca. 'I just wish you'd have trusted Bobby with the truth. If he ever finds out . . . '

'Mum, you mustn't tell him. Dad, you mustn't either.'

'We won't,' said Charles. 'No one else need ever know.'

'I'd better go and see if he's okay,' said Ricky.

'I didn't know Ricky felt like that,' said Rebecca, to fill the awkward silence that followed his departure. 'Did you?'

'No, I always thought they did everything as a team.'

'Perhaps we've made a mistake in thinking that.' Rebecca turned her head to look out of the window. Anything so that she did not have to look at Charles' face. Another moment and she might beg him to stay. The night before, in bed alone, the enormity of her decision had hit her.

'We've done nothing wrong, Rebecca.' Charles started to light a cigarette but changed his mind. 'I'd better get back. Lunch will be ready soon. Are you and the children coming over?'

Rebecca shook her head. 'I've got a casserole in the oven. Why don't you invite the children?'

'I don't want you to be left alone.'

'You could stay with us. It's a momentous day, our boys joining the army.' A tear rolled down her cheek.

'Good idea. Make an event of it. Who knows when we'll all be together again?'

'And Esther is going back to her father.'

'Is she? When did this happen?'

'Yesterday. She's in love with Bobby. Or she thinks she is. So she's running away.' It amazed Rebecca how they could talk so normally about the children, when their marriage was falling apart. Inside she was screaming.

'Oh dear.' Charles laughed softly. 'Poor kid.'

'Don't say that to her. Oh, and Charlie is madly in love with Mack Henderson.' She smiled. 'But is being quite stoical about it.'

'I'm glad one of our children can take things lightly.'

'I'll miss them so much.'

'Rebecca . . . ' Charles went to reach out for her. 'I missed you last night.'

'No, don't, or I'll start sobbing and I don't want them to see me like that.'

'Do you still want me to go back to my parents' afterwards?'

'Yes, I think that's for the best. Nothing has changed, has it? You're still angry with me about something. I can see it in your eyes, even when you're trying to be nice to me.' She sighed. 'Charlie is going to be lonely when Esther has gone.'

'Not necessarily. Patty telephoned this morning to see if Ronnie could come up and stay while the war is on. John has to stay in London and Patty says she should be with him.'

Rebecca nodded. 'Ronnie's a nice girl. She could sleep here. It might be nicer for her than being in the big house with all the oldies.'

'Hey, I'm not that old.'

Rebecca smiled. 'I meant your parents.' As she spoke, the sitting-room door flew open and the twins burst in.

'Dad,' said Ricky. 'It's grandfather. He's collapsed.'

★ ★ ★

The wait was interminable. Charles paced the hospital corridor, whilst Rebecca sat with Veronica. The doctor had seen them once, and explained that George had suffered a heart attack. He was alive, but in a serious condition. 'We're doing all we can,' said the doctor.

Rebecca found it hard to talk to her mother-in-law. Even after nineteen years of living in close proximity she still knew less about Veronica than she did about the people who lived on the Stony Newton streets in

257

which she grew up. Even Veronica's relationship with George appeared cold and lifeless. She was like a ghost who haunted the Priory, leaving a tense atmosphere behind her.

George, on the other hand, was Rebecca's friend. The day of the riot had broken some considerable ice for them, and whilst — like Bobby — he was not very demonstrative, he did at least treat Rebecca kindly, taking an interest in the welfare of her and the children.

'I'm sure he'll be okay,' said Rebecca, just because she felt she ought to say something. 'Won't he, Charles?'

'What? Oh yes, of course, mother. Try not to worry.'

'I'm not worried,' said Veronica. 'The doctors will do all they can, and if they can't, it's in God's hands.'

'You, erm . . . you never told me how you and George met,' said Rebecca.

'Why would I?'

'Oh, no reason. Only . . . ' Rebecca looked at Charles as an appeal for help. He shrugged almost imperceptibly and continued pacing. 'I was just interested, that's all.' Her voice faded to a whisper.

They sat in uncomfortable silence for a few minutes longer, until Charles wandered off down the corridor mumbling about finding a doctor.

'George was one of twins, you know.' Veronica spoke so suddenly, it made Rebecca jump.

'Oh yes, I think Charles did mention that. His twin died, didn't he?'

'Yes. His name was Charles.'

'I didn't know that.'

'I was engaged to him.'

'Oh.'

'He died in a fire at the factory. We had to go and identify his body ... ' Veronica stopped, and swallowed hard. 'Well, there wasn't much left to identify. That's why when Charles ... our son, Charles, I mean. When he got burned ... it was so difficult.'

Suddenly it all made sense. 'Yes, it must have been. Does Charles know this?'

'No, why should he?' There was the Veronica that Rebecca knew and feared. Ice cold.

'I just thought it might help him to understand why you didn't go. It hurt him a lot.'

'Did it?'

'Yes, but that doesn't matter now. I'm sorry, you were telling me, you were engaged to George's brother, Charles. Then when he died, you fell in love with George?'

'Oh no. But George said he would take care of me and he has. He's been a good husband to me. I've never told him that. I've never told him a lot of things.'

Rebecca wondered just how much Veronica had locked up inside her and whether it might erupt in a torrent of emotion if George died. She sensed there was something that Veronica was not telling her. 'Do you love him?'

'Yes, I suppose I do. He's been very patient with me under the circumstances.' Veronica stopped. 'Well, I don't suppose I have to tell you everything.'

'No, of course not.' Poor George, thought Rebecca. No wonder he seemed so uptight all the time. She felt tears prick her eyes. He had given up a lot to make sure his brother's fiancée was cared for and had received very little affection in return. 'You should tell him that you love him.'

'I'm afraid it's too late.' For the first time, Rebecca heard real emotion in Veronica's voice. The old woman sighed. 'I suppose I always thought there would be time.' Rebecca reached out and took her hand. At first Veronica's hand felt icy and stiff, but gradually she relaxed and squeezed Rebecca's hand in return.

Charles came back along the corridor with a doctor. Rebecca looked up at him expectantly, but he shook his head, his face grim with the pain of loss. It really was too late.

21

Sam turned over in bed, and smiled. Marian lay next to him. Even with her mouth open a little, and the gentle snore emanating from her nostrils, she was a welcome sight. He brushed away a tendril of dark hair that covered her eyes.

'Hmm,' she said. 'Morning, love.'

'Morning, my darling. I was just thinking that you're a real picture.'

'Oh yes, with my hair a mess and my mascara all smudged. I bet I look like Merle Oberon.'

'She couldn't hold a candle to you.'

Marian snuggled up next to him. He revelled in her warmth and the happiness she brought with her. 'I'm going to look at divorcing Clara,' he said. 'So we can get married.'

She pulled her head back a little to look at him. 'Are you sure, love? Because I understand if you don't want to. We don't have to rush into anything.'

'Rush? We've been together for a year. Besides, Clara doesn't want us to go anymore. I didn't want to admit it to Annette, but it was a relief really. I've tried with Clara. But I've failed, and I've no more love left to give her. Is that rotten of me?'

'No, just human. It's like with my Reg. I poured so much love into him, helping him through his drink problems, that by the time he died, the pot was drained.'

'We're going to be happy, me and you, Marian. I was thinking, with the war on, we could move to the country. Surrey is nice. Or we could go back up north to Stony Newton. It's nice around there. Not in Stony Newton. Not with the pits and the factories. But in the Peak District. It's beautiful. Have you ever been there?'

'No.'

'Tell you what. We'll go this weekend. My sister, Hilda, will put us up. I can show you around. I'll take you to Chatsworth. And Hardwick Hall. Bess of Hardwick helped build them both. She was married four times. There's lots of history in the Peak District. I'll show you it all. It might be the last chance we get, with this war starting. It'll be all hands on deck in a bit. But there's time for a breather before it all starts, I reckon.'

'You're on,' said Marian. She kissed his nose. 'Now come here and say good morning to me properly.'

Sam had never expected to be happy. Most

of his life had been miserable, and the relationship with Clara had not helped. Marian had known sadness, but it had only made her stronger. The love she gave him was free and without condition.

★ ★ ★

On the Wednesday evening, Jack and Brian met the seller, Steve, in a disused warehouse in the docklands area of London. 'It's good stuff,' said Brian Miller. 'Do you want to try some, Jack?' He held up the tiny spoonful of white powder. A clear plastic bag filled with cocaine sat on the table between them. Steve stood at the end, counting his money.

'I never touch the stuff,' said Jack. 'I've seen what it's done to my mother.'

Miller sniffed up the small mountain of cocaine himself, despite having just tried some. He shuddered theatrically.

'Try not to use all our stocks,' said Jack.

'Don't worry, mate. If we mix it with some cornflour, we'll make a fortune out of this. We'll take it back to my place and split it into smaller bags. Thanks Steve.'

Steve nodded and pocketed the money. 'Supplies might be harder to get with the war on. They'll be monitoring shipping for a while to come. But I've got a mate in the Royal

Army Med Corps. He might be able to get some amphetamines. Uppers, downers, that sort of thing. Or some black market stuff, like bandages and other medical supplies.'

Jack burst out laughing. 'Bandages? My grandparents own Harcourt's. I can get those by the truckload and cut out the middle-man. You just keep supplying us with the dope. Leave the medical supplies to me.'

Jack and Brian headed back towards the city, keeping on foot and in the back lanes. After five minutes they became aware of being followed. 'I bet they're Steve's goons,' said Brian. 'He's not above pocketing the money then stealing the stuff back.'

'Come on,' said Jack. 'We'll get to the main road and hop in a taxi. It's no good going to your place. They know where you live.'

'Where will we take it?'

'Rosa's. Might as well use her for something. I'll keep her occupied while you hide the stuff in her flat. We'll come back for it another day.'

'How do I know you won't get it before me?'

'Because I won't know where you've hidden it, idiot.'

'How do you know I won't go back and get it?'

'Because Rosa won't let you in. Leave the

thinking to me, Brian. You're not very good at it.' They started walking faster, making their way towards the main road, where it was busier. The men behind them dropped all pretence and speeded up.

'I'll kill Steve when I see him,' said Brian, struggling to keep up with Jack's longer stride.

'No you won't. You'll just do business again like this never happened. In the meantime we work out a way to get back at him, right?'

'Yeah, good idea. I say we stick him.'

Jack stopped and took Brian by the lapels. 'We're not sticking anyone. I've told you before; I'm not getting into killing.'

'You're a pussy, Jack.' Brian looked behind him. 'And you'll be a dead pussy if we don't get going. They're getting closer.'

They picked up speed reaching the main road just as it began to get dark. Jack hailed a taxi. Several drivers, seeing that they were running from something, drove straight past. Steve's goons had almost reached them when a taxi pulled up to the kerb.

'Thanks,' said Jack, falling into the back of the cab, with Brian closely behind him.

'Where to, mate?' said the cabby.

'Get going first, and then I'll tell you,' said Jack. He noticed that Brian had not yet closed the door. 'Shut that, you idiot!'

Brian slammed the door and the cabby pulled away from the kerb. 'The Old Brompton Road,' said Jack. 'Near to the tube will do.'

'Right ho.'

Jack looked at Brian thoughtfully, wondering why he had left the cab door open, knowing that the men were after them. What if it was not just Steve trying to double-cross them? What if Brian had set it up, so that he got the dope, whilst Jack was out of pocket?

'So,' said Brian as they travelled. 'Your family own Harcourt's, hey?'

'Yes.'

'I never knew that. It's handy though. Very handy. Like you said, you'd be able to cut out the middle-man.'

'Shh,' said Jack, pointing to the cabby.

'Did I hear you mention Harcourt's, mate?' said the cabby.

'Yes, that's right,' said Jack.

'They're up in Stony Newton. I'm from there.'

'Yeah?'

'Yeah. The name's Sam Jenkins. I don't suppose you know my sister, Hilda. She lives on South Street.'

'No, I can't say I do.'

'Do you get up there much?'

'I did when I was a child, but not so often nowadays.'

'I used to work at the factory, before the war. I got called up in the last year. Then I moved to London and became a cabby.'

'Fascinating,' said Brian, wryly.

'I remember your family's house. The Priory, isn't it?' said Sam Jenkins.

'Yes, that's right.'

'Lovely place. I used to knock around with some kids in the area. Probably before your time though. Don't suppose you knew Clara Peters? Jed Alsop? Maggie Fletcher?'

'Yes, I've heard their names, I think,' said Jack, his lips tightening. Yes, he had definitely heard Jed Alsop's name. He had also seen him naked. A fact he did not share with Sam Jenkins.

'And who else was there? Oh yes, Becky Wilson.'

'Rebecca Wilson? She's married to my uncle Charles.'

'Yeah? Nice girl, Becky. I always thought she'd do well. Small world, eh?'

'Yes, it is.'

Just as they reached Tower Bridge, Brian took the package out of his pocket and started fingering it. Jack saw Jenkins' reflection in the rear view mirror. 'Hey mate,' said Sam. 'I don't want none of that in my cab.' He pulled up the pavement. 'Come on, get out.' There were few pedestrians on the bridge, but some cars passed them.

With his free hand, Brian pulled a knife from his pocket and dived at the front of the cab, catching Sam around the throat. 'You'll take us where we want to go.'

'For Christ's sake, Brian,' cried Jack. 'Put that away.'

'No, I'm sick of playing it your way, Gentleman Jack. Think you're better than I am, do you? Well you're not. Now . . . ' Brian yanked Sam's throat back. 'Take us to where we want to go and I might let you live to go home.'

Brian sat back, whilst Sam took some deep breaths. 'He won't hurt you, mate,' said Jack. 'I won't let him. Just take us to Old Brompton Road. Doesn't matter which end.' Sam started the car again, and they drove in tense silence until Knightsbridge.

The streets were lined with sandbags, as others prepared for war, whilst in the taxi a difficult peace ensued. 'I don't think your grandfather would be very proud of you,' Sam said to Jack, his voice quivering slightly.

'He's dead,' said Jack. 'He died on Monday.'

'I'm sorry to hear that. He was a grand old bloke, Mr. Harcourt. Your mother married a

Daventry, didn't she?'

'What's he up to?' said Brian. 'Trying to get information about you.'

'He got all that when we first got in the cab, thanks to you mentioning Harcourt's,' said Jack, grimly.

'So we should kill him,' Brian muttered.

'We're not killing anyone.' He leaned in to Brian. 'Have you seen it out there? There are air raid wardens, Home Guard, and people. They're everywhere and the Old Brompton Road is going to be even busier. Let's just let the man go on his way.'

'Pull up here,' said Brian. They had reached a quiet street near Knightsbridge. 'We'll walk the rest of the way.'

Jack took some money out of his pocket and handed it to Sam. Sam hesitated before taking it with trembling hands. 'Thanks. And don't worry, I won't say anything.'

'Thanks mate.'

'Sorry about your grandfather. He was a good man.'

Never before had he felt so ashamed of himself. 'Yeah, he was a good man.'

'Come on, Jack,' said Brian. He was already standing on the pavement, near to the front passenger door. 'Get out of the bloody cab. You can catch up on family stuff another time.'

Jack got out. 'This way,' he said, turning away from Brian. He began walking, but then realised Brian had not followed him. He turned back several yards from the taxi to see Brian leaning in through the front passenger door. Jack did not know if he imagined Brian's lunge forward, or just guessed what he had done, but he knew it was bad. He ran back, but by the time he had, Brian was out and running in the other direction.

Sam Jenkins lay slumped over the steering wheel, leaving Jack with a dilemma. Did he follow Brian, who had the dope bought with his thousand pounds, or did he help the taxi driver? And if he helped Sam Jenkins, would Jenkins then rat on him to the police?

Thinking he was probably dead anyway, Jack started to walk away, but then he heard Sam groan. He was still alive. Jack went around the end of the taxi to the driver's door. 'It's alright, mate,' he said, on opening the door. 'I'll get you some help.'

With some difficulty, Jack moved Sam onto the passenger seat, realising he was probably doing more damage. He could see the hilt of Brian's knife poking out from Sam's shirt. 'Whatever you do, don't pull that out. I know someone who can help us,' Jack said, before starting up the taxi. He switched off the 'for hire' sign, and drove off into the night.

Sam replied with a groan. His face was ashen, as blood drained from him.

'I'm sorry, mate,' said Jack as he drove towards Hampstead. 'I didn't mean for anything like that to happen. Hey? Hey, wake up and talk to me.' He reached over with one hand and gave Sam's cheek a shove. 'Wake up and talk.'

'Wha . . . ?'

'Don't you dare go to sleep. I'm going to take you to a friend of mine. Lizzie. She's Jed Alsop's daughter. You remember Jed Alsop, don't you?'

'Used to play with him when we were kids.'

'That's right. And my Aunt Rebecca . . . Becky. And . . . who else was it? Who was it, Sam?'

'Maggie Fletcher.'

'That's right. I think she's Lizzie's mother. Yeah, I remember now. She married Jed. What was the other one? The other girl you mentioned?'

'Clara . . . Oh God, Clara. Annette!'

'Annette? No, you didn't mention an Annette. Was she another playmate from Stony Newton?'

'My daughter. Annette. She's my daughter. Mine and Clara's.'

'So Clara is your wife. Okay, I get it. Well don't worry, we'll get Lizzie to sort you out and then you can go home to Clara and Annette. Think about that, Sam.'

'Marian.'

'Who the bloody hell is Marian?'

'Ladyfriend.'

'Oh right. So Clara doesn't know about her. Okay, I can keep that secret if you can keep mine.'

Sam shook his head. 'Clara is in a hospital for the insane. She killed a man.'

'We've barely scratched the surface of your story, Sam.' Jack reached over and shook Sam's shoulder. 'Stay awake, mate, and you can tell me all about it. Sounds like you've lived a full life there, with all those pretty girls from Stony Newton. And who else? Yes. Annette. Tell me about Annette, Sam. Tell me about your daughter. Sam!' Tears stung Jack's eyes. How had he come to this? He was clever. He could do anything. Yet here he was, a drug dealer indirectly responsible for a man's stabbing. No, not indirectly. If he had not got into Sam's cab with Brian, this would not have happened.

'Annette's a policewoman.'

'She would be, wouldn't she?' Jack's blood ran cold.

'Good girl. My Annette. He was going to hurt her, you see. Annette. And she was only a little girl. Clara wouldn't let him.'

'Annette? Some chap was going to hurt Annette and Clara stopped him? Is that it? Well good for her, Sam. Good for her. And they locked her up.'

'She couldn't stop. Once she started stabbing him. She couldn't stop.'

'You'll be back with them all soon, mate. I promise. Just as soon as we get to Lizzie.'

'Lizzie Alsop. Jed Alsop's girl.'

'That's right, Sam. Lizzie Alsop. She's lovely. Like a picture. Her smile alone will make you better. I promise.' Jack felt tears roll down his cheeks, and stifled a sob. He knew involving Lizzie was wrong, but he had no one else he could turn to. He did not want to dump Sam on the steps of a hospital in case no one found him.

He thought back to several days before when he had wished for a sweet, innocent girl, but known he would corrupt her. It was already happening. Lizzie had walked back into his life as pretty as a daffodil, and he already planned to put her in an impossible situation.

'I won't tell,' said Sam. 'I won't ever tell. Just let me out.' He fumbled for the door handle. Jack just stopped him from opening it and falling out of the cab.

'No, look Sam, I'm not taking you anywhere to hurt you or dump you. I'm taking you to Lizzie. I promise. I don't want you to die. I'm not like Brian Miller. I know I've done some bad things but I don't want to be responsible for killing anyone.'

'You don't think those drugs you peddle kill people?'

'It's their choice to take them.'

'Is that what you tell yourself, Jack? Is that how you sleep at night?' Sam clutched his chest where the knife still protruded. His face was deathly pale.

'Don't pull that out, Sam. You'll bleed to death.'

When they arrived at Lizzie's block of flats, Jack jumped out of the car and told Sam to wait where he was. Not that Sam was in any condition to run. His speech had become more and more slurred as the journey progressed.

Jack ran up to the front door and looked for the list of tenants. Lizzie was on the top, three floors up. That was all he needed. He took the stairs two at a time, gasping for breath by the time he reached the top landing. He hammered on her door.

'Jack! What brings you here?' Lizzie opened the door slightly.

'I need your help, Lizzie. There's a man. A taxi driver. My friend stabbed him.'

Another door opened down the hall, and

Jack saw Lizzie's friend, Marie, stick her head out.

'What?'

Jack dropped his voice to a whisper. 'He's in a taxi downstairs. I didn't know what to do, Lizzie. I thought you could help.'

Lizzie was already halfway down the stairs, heading for Sam Jenkins' taxi. When she reached the street, she yanked open the passenger door and knelt down. Sam's limp arm fell out. When Jack arrived at the car, Lizzie's face was grave. 'He's already dead, Jack.'

'No. He can't be. I've been trying to help him, Lizzie. I kept him talking. He can't be dead.'

'You should have taken him straight to the hospital. We have to get the police.'

'Lizzie, I can't. I'm on a last warning. If this comes out I'm finished.'

'Jack, you helped him. You did a good thing.'

Jack shook his head. 'No, they'll want names, and if I do that, I'm dead. Brian Miller . . . this friend . . . I think he's already tried to double-cross me once tonight. You've seen what he did to the taxi driver. He'll have me killed.'

'Are you sure it was your friend who did this?' Lizzie stood up and looked Jack square in the eyes.

'I swear it, Lizzie. I didn't want the poor bloke to die. I've got to get away. Please, can you just say he was dumped here?'

'People might have seen you, Jack. Marie certainly did. She'll remember you were here.'

'You can say you didn't know who I was.'

'She met you today! You've put me in a difficult situation, Jack.'

'Please, Lizzie. Help me.'

She pressed her lips together. 'I resent you involving me in this.'

'Yes, I understand that. But I had nowhere else to turn.'

'You've made me an accessory.'

'I know. I didn't want to. If there was any other way . . . '

'Go on, Jack. Get out of here before anyone sees you for long enough to remember you.'

'Thanks Lizzie. Look, his name is Sam Jenkins. He's from your neck of the woods originally. Stony Newton. He's got a daughter, Annette, and a girlfriend, Marian. They'll need to know.'

'You found all that out?'

'I had to keep him talking.'

Lizzie looked at him for a long moment. 'I can't work you out, Jack Daventry. Go on, get out of here. But, Jack . . . '

'What?'

'I never want to see you again.'

He nodded, as his one chance of happiness slipped away from him. He had known he would end up corrupting Lizzie. He had just not realised how soon it would happen. 'I'm sorry I'm not the person you'd like me to be, Lizzie. The boy who saved you from the river and helped an old lady across the road doesn't exist. He's never existed. I only did those things because I thought it would reflect well on me and make my family like me more. I'm a waste of space. Always have been.'

He turned and high-tailed it away from the block of flats, running through the streets of London without really knowing where he was going. He thought of going to Rosa's, but she would expect too much of him. More than he was willing to give her any more. If he went home his mother would want to know what happened to her money. Brian Miller's place was definitely out. The truth was he had no one.

After several hours of walking he found himself near St Pancras station. He could go to Stony Newton. Nothing would be more natural than him arriving for his grandfather's funeral. Something stopped him. Some glimmer of common decency he did not realise he possessed. He had already used

Lizzie, and he hated the bitter taste it left in his mouth. He could not use his grandfather's death in the same way.

He glanced up at the station, and saw an air force recruitment poster. He thought about his uncle Charles and the quiet courage he had always shown. Jack did not deceive himself that he would join the air force for the same noble reasons. Joining up was simply the best way to run away. With any luck he would get killed in action. Only then could he forget the look of disappointment on Lizzie's face when she realised just how toxic he was.

★　★　★

The streets of Stony Newton were lined with people as George Harcourt's funeral procession made its way to the churchyard. The men took off their caps, and the women bowed their heads. When the hearse reached the gates of the church, the pallbearers took over. Ricky and Bobby Harcourt; their father, Charles; Jed Alsop, Len Peters and Arthur Taylor. The latter two had requested the role as a way of making amends for the riot in nineteen twenty-six. Though both old men, they stood ramrod-straight, pushing away the aches and pains of their age in order to give George Harcourt a good send-off.

After the service, the family and close friends stood around the grave, as the reverend said the final prayers. Esther and Charlotte were either side of Rebecca, crying into her shoulder, whilst Charles stood next to his mother.

On the way home in the car, Charlotte and Esther still cried, whilst Rebecca shushed them gently. Veronica turned to them and said, 'It's all over now. You can stop crying.' It was a testament to her formidable personality that they both did. Immediately.

★ ★ ★

In London a flank of black cabs, decorated with black ribbons, followed Sam Jenkins' hearse to Highgate cemetery. Despite the high turnout, there were only two people in the lead car: Annette and Marian. Annette had contacted Sam's sister, Hilda, who had declined to attend. Sam's uncle had died some years earlier.

'It's good of them all to come,' said Marian, gesturing to the convoy following them. Her face was grey with grief. 'He deserves a good send-off.'

'Yes, he does.'

'Did you manage to see your mother yesterday?'

'No. I was going to go but I telephoned instead, and asked them to tell her.'

'Oh, Annette . . . '

'I know I should have. But I was afraid of how she would react. They can deal with her if she gets out of control.'

'What have the police said?'

'Not much. Only that he was dumped at that block of flats and that young woman, Elizabeth Alsop, found him.'

'It makes me shudder to think of the evil that's out there, Annette. Hitler is bad enough, but to think this is happening in our own country and to a hardworking, honest man. Poor Sam. He must have felt so alone.'

Annette took her hand. 'We'll stick together, won't we, Marian? I mean, I know you'll want to move on one day, perhaps even meet someone else, but . . . '

'Oh, love, of course we will. We're family, aren't we?'

'I hope so. I don't have anyone else.' The last words got caught in Annette's throat.

'We'll get through this, pet, don't you worry.'

'I'm going to find him, Marian. One day, I'm going to find the man who killed my father.'

22

Within days of Chamberlain declaring war, men between the ages of eighteen and forty-one began to move from their hometowns and off to army camps, airfields and ports. Young women between the ages of twenty and thirty were also called up. Others joined the Land Army. Families wept as they said goodbye to loved ones who were entering the war, and others in the cities wept as their children were taken off to strange towns and villages as evacuees.

Rebecca, Charles and Charlotte waited with Ricky and Bobby at Stony Newton station. Esther had been invited, but declined. She was too embarrassed to face Bobby after her outburst.

'We're not even being sent overseas,' said Ricky, his voice full of disappointment. 'Not until we're twenty.'

'I can't say I'm sorry about that,' said Rebecca, straightening his collar. 'The war will be over by then.' His uniform made him look like a child playing at being a soldier. He was so ridiculously young. Tiny pieces of blood-soaked tissue stuck to his chin. He had started shaving a few days earlier, not because he needed to, but because he did not want his fellow soldiers to know that he had no whiskers.

'Mum, what's the point of us joining up if we can't help in the fighting?'

'If Hitler invades Britain, you might get a chance soon enough,' said Charles.

A cloud seemed to pass over the sun. 'He won't though, will he?' said Charlotte.

'No one has ever been able to invade Britain before,' said Charles soothingly.

'Apart from the Romans,' said Ricky.

'And the Vikings,' said Bobby.

'Not to mention William the Conqueror,' Ricky added for good measure.

'Yes, alright you two,' said Rebecca. 'This was not the time to show off your grasp of history.'

'No,' said Charles. 'Though it would have been nice if you'd bothered at school.'

'Look, there's Mr. Alsop,' said Charlie.

Jed stood at the end of the platform with some of the older conscripts. Rebecca waved him over. 'I didn't realise you were going, Jed. Is Maggie with you?'

Jed shook his head. 'No, she disagrees with me joining up. But a man's got to do his duty, hasn't he? Even if he is getting on a bit.'

'We could use you at the factory, Jed,' said Charles. 'Especially now. I wish you'd said something earlier.'

'Sorry, Mr. Harcourt, but I didn't decide till last night.'

'Don't worry about it. There'll be a job waiting at Harcourt's when you get back.' The two men shook hands.

The train pulled into the station, and the next few minutes were lost in a sea of kisses and tears, as everyone held on to their loved one for as long as possible before letting them go. There was no one to kiss Jed, so Rebecca reached up and gave him a peck on the cheek. 'Take care, Jed. Come back to us.'

'I'll do my best, Becky.'

She felt a pang at hearing him call her by her old familiar name. It was a long time since she had been Becky Wilson.

She watched until the train was completely out of sight, as did everyone else. Her instinct was to put her head on Charles' shoulder, but the rules between them had changed. She could no longer do that. Instead she took her daughter's hand and they walked home together, whilst Charles muttered something about doing some paperwork at the factory.

* * *

Maggie Alsop was just finishing up for the day. She put the files away with a smile of satisfaction. She was easily as good at keeping the accounts as Rebecca Harcourt. She was also good at siphoning a few pounds off here and there. If Charles Harcourt knew, he kept it very much to himself.

She heard the office door open, and turned around to find Charles. 'I thought you'd be at home with the family.'

'No, my presence is not required. I thought I'd come in and do some work. I didn't expect to find you here, Maggie.'

'Didn't you?' She moved towards him, and put her arms around his neck. 'Didn't you really, Charles?'

He kicked the office door shut with his foot, and backed Maggie up to the desk, pressing his hips against hers. 'I see you didn't pretend to play the dutiful wife,' he murmured against her neck.

'I'm not as good at that as Becky.' She wrapped her legs around his waist, and bit his lower lip. 'I knew you'd come here though. You can't resist it, can you?'

He pushed her back roughly, and yanked her skirt up. 'I might as well get something for all the money you steal from us.'

'You are getting something. You're getting my silence.'

23

1944

Rebecca raked over the soil, ready to put in the new seedlings. Charlie and Ronnie worked a plot each, whilst Veronica, despite her age and Rebecca's protestations, knelt down picking out the weeds. The vegetable patch was at the front of the Priory, in a small part of the field where eighteen years before a fairground had stood for the twins' birthday. Had she the time she might have reflected on how much had happened since that day. She might concede that the war had made many other problems fade away.

Veronica's presence in the vegetable garden had been something of a surprise. Not that Rebecca had refused, a couple of years previously, when Veronica asked if she could be of any help. But it was indicative of how much this war, even more than the war they had previously survived, had changed so much. Whilst the Great War had not broken down all class barriers, the current war had struck a sword right thought them. Rebecca and her mother-in-law had found common

285

ground in adversity, and they shared that with every other woman left in Stony Newton.

The rest of the Priory fields had been given over to the war effort, and were being worked by Land Army girls. The wrought-iron gates that used to keep out the world had also gone, along with much of the fencing. The house itself had, for a short time, become a home for evacuees, before most of them returned to their families in London. Now they gave rooms to soldiers recovering from the war, and the nurses who cared for them. Charles and his mother had moved into the flat with Rebecca, Charlie and Ronnie, but it had done nothing to help their marriage. He slept in the twins' old room, whilst Veronica shared with the girls. It was an uncomfortable arrangement for all, but they had very little choice other than to do their bit for the war effort. Harcourt's Surgical Supplies as a business was booming, and they all tried not to think too hard about why that was. Besides, it did not ensure them any privileges. They had the same ration allowance as everyone else, even if they might have had more money to spend on little luxuries.

'I think we'll have a nice crop this year,' said Rebecca, wiping sweat from her brow. 'And with any luck the war will be over and the boys will be able to share it all with us.'

'You said that last year, mum,' said Charlotte. 'And the year before that.' At seventeen she was already beginning to show signs of becoming a stunning woman. She had inherited her father's fair hair and finely-carved features, given her a slightly androgynous look, which was accentuated by the fact she kept her hair very short. The boyishness was softened slightly by the fact her hair curled around her brow.

'I can dream, can't I?'

'Yes,' said Veronica, pulling herself up off the ground with great difficulty. 'We should remain optimistic.'

'That's not like you, grandmother.'

'Now, don't be cheeky. I never realised how much fun keeping a vegetable garden would be. I should have tried it years ago. There's pleasure in hard work.'

Rebecca smiled. 'I got a letter from Clementine the other day. She said they're playing tennis at Vittel to keep their spirits up. It sounds like she's having a better time of it then we are.'

'Only Aunty Clementine could get caught in the middle of a war and end up interred in a luxury hotel,' said Charlie. 'I wonder where Mack is.'

'You're not still mooning over him, are you, sweetheart?'

'Well, I'm not about to die of despair. I'm not Esther.'

'That's very cruel.'

'I know. But the way she was over Bobby. It's all a bit silly, really.'

'It wasn't silly to her.' Rebecca looked up for a second. 'Talk of the devil . . . '

Esther was walking along Factory Lane towards the Priory. She waved to Rebecca, who waved back. Esther was dressed in the uniform of the Royal Army Medical Corps.

'Hello, dear,' said Rebecca when Esther had reached the vegetable patch. 'What brings you here? Not that you're not welcome.'

'I've come to say goodbye, Aunt Rebecca.'

'Goodbye?'

'I've finished my training. I'm being sent overseas.'

'Oh, my darling girl.' Rebecca pulled Esther into her arms, hardly wanting to let her go. 'Please keep safe.'

'I will.'

Charlotte, despite her previous bitchy comments about Esther, started to cry, and ran to embrace her foster sister. 'It isn't right that all the people we love have to go away,' she said.

'Come back to us soon, Esther,' said Veronica, with her usual reserve. But it was meant kindly, and Esther smiled her appreciation.

'We heard about Artie,' said Rebecca. 'I'm so sorry.'

Esther nodded, sadly. 'Yes, dad is beside himself. And with the other three boys out there . . . '

'Yes, it's a huge worry. For all of us,' said Rebecca, thinking of her own sons.

'They do say that if you lose all but one of your children, they send the last one home,' said Charlotte.

'That's not very helpful, Charlotte,' said Veronica. Thankfully, Esther smiled. She was well used to Charlie's way of saying whatever happened to be in her head.

'Oh,' said Esther. 'Sorry, Aunty Rebecca. I forgot. Mrs. Price at the Post Office asked me to bring you this.' She took a letter out of her pocket, which had the Royal Engineers insignia on it. Rebecca's blood ran cold. 'It's not a telegram,' said Esther.

'No, no, that's something, I suppose,' said Rebecca. Despite the fact it was addressed to Charles, as the head of the house, she opened the letter, and then put her hand to her mouth to quell a cry of pain. 'Bobby has been captured. They're holding him in a transit camp in Poland.'

'No!' The other three women spoke together.

'But he's alive, Rebecca,' said Veronica, putting her hand on her daughter-in-law's shoulder. 'He's alive, dear.'

Rebecca nodded. 'Yes, he's alive. That's something, isn't it? I'd better go down to the factory and let Charles know.' She threw off the overall she had been wearing over her shirt and slacks. 'Oh, Veronica, can you find out about sending a Red Cross parcel. He'll need something nice to eat. And we'll write to Ricky and let him know. Oh . . . ' She hugged Esther again. 'I'm sorry. I'm forgetting all about you leaving.'

'It doesn't matter, Aunt Rebecca. If . . . if you write to Bobby, will you tell him I'm sorry for what I said.'

'He'll know that, my darling.'

'But I'd like him to know anyway. I'd write to him myself, but I made such a fool of myself over him.'

'Yes, you did rather,' said Charlotte. She added dramatically, 'Oh Esther, will we ever see you again?'

'We're not in a film, Charlie,' said Esther, with pretty dimples appearing in her cheeks. 'I'm sure that being in an army hospital, I'll be safer than most people. I'd better go. I've got a train to catch.'

'I'll walk so far with you,' said Rebecca, linking her arm in Esther's.

The factory was busier than ever. Crates of medical supplies were being loaded onto army trucks ready to be taken off to army hospitals all over the world. Somewhere out there one of Rebecca's sons was helping to heal those wounds. Elsewhere her other son was, for the moment, safe from the fighting, though rumour had it that those in the prisoner of war camps suffered great hardships. And now, Esther was going to join them, having already lost one of her natural brothers. If the war continued, it would be Charlotte's turn to officially join in the effort.

It was with all this in mind that she opened the door to the office and found Charles in Maggie Alsop's arms.

He pulled back quickly. 'Rebecca. It's not what you think.'

Ignoring the dagger piercing her heart, Rebecca spoke calmly. 'I thought you should know that whilst you're here — fiddling — Bobby is in a prisoner of war camp.'

'Dear God. Is he alright?'

'He is at the moment.'

'I'll come home.'

'That's the very last thing I want you to do.'

Rebecca left the office, slamming the door behind her.

24

As far as Bobby Harcourt could make out, the transit camp was somewhere near the German-Swiss border. Their captors had done much to hide their destination from them, including keeping them in closed carriages, but he recognised the landscape from a road trip he had taken with his brother Ricky and Mack Henderson, not long before the war started. The current trip had been a difficult one, packed into freight trains like cattle with a bucket for a toilet. It left the carriage smelling of fear, urine and excrement.

The Allied prisoners complained amongst themselves until they reached one station to take on water. They saw Jewish prisoners being loaded onto a cattle truck, misery and despair lining their faces. Nazi guards jostled them. One brute of a soldier clubbed an elderly rabbi around the head, after the old man had stopped to help up a falling child.

'Is it true? What's happening to them, sir?' Brian Miller asked. 'I've heard Hitler's killed millions of them.'

'I think the evidence speaks for itself,' said Bobby. 'Poor buggers.' He stood as close to the edge of the carriage as possible, desperate for a bit of space he could call his own.

'Yeah, not lucky, like us?' said Miller, spitting on the ground. As if there wasn't enough mess down there, thought Bobby.

'We are compared to them,' Bobby said brusquely. 'The Germans have to look after us, even if they do it badly. The Jews aren't protected by the Geneva Convention.' As he looked out of the tiny gap in the freight train door, a woman broke free from the group of detainees and tried to run across the tracks. The Germans shot her, and then turned back to what they were doing as if nothing had happened. Bobby closed his eyes and said a silent prayer for the woman. She must have known escaping was futile. He wondered if she had deliberately chosen death instead of what might await her in the concentration camps.

'If the rumours are true, the Geneva Convention didn't protect those from Stalag Luft III,' said Miller. Bobby almost envied Miller's ability to be completely unmoved by the woman's death. But only almost. The man's coldness disturbed him. If it had only been towards those Miller saw as the enemy he might have understood it, but during the

293

shooting before they were captured, Bobby had seen the man next to Miller fall down dead. Miller barely batted an eyelid.

'No,' said Bobby, his lips set in a grim line. He looked around the carriage, where men slept standing up, leaning against the walls. 'But let's not talk about that amongst the men whilst we're on the train, okay?'

They travelled for a few more hours, before being unloaded from the freight train, and then marched along bomb-cracked roadways to the camp.

They were assembled in a large yard. Bobby did a quick reconnaissance of the area and saw that there were about fifty huts, surrounding an old château. And it was all surrounded by a barbed-wire fence, with a sentry post every hundred yards. The forest had been cut back to around two hundred yards from the fence. All open land, with nowhere to hide. Bobby knew it was what went on underground that mattered, and what he hoped was that tunnels had already been started on.

'You will stay here for a short time, before being split up and taken to different camps according to your service,' the German officer in command of the camp told them. 'There will be no escape attempts.'

'Is it true what happened to the fifty men

who escaped from Stalag Luft III?' asked Bobby.

'I do not have that information, Captain Harcourt. You will do better not to ask questions.'

The officer ran through a few more rules and regulations, before dismissing them.

'Captain Harcourt, sir?' A young airman walked up to Bobby and saluted. 'Flying Officer Greaves, sir. I've been asked to accompany you to see the British CO.'

'Thank you.' Bobby breathed a sigh of relief. He had been the highest-ranking officer thus far. It would be good to hand the reins and responsibility to someone else. 'Sergeant Miller, find us somewhere to sleep, and get the other men settled in.'

'Yes, sir.'

'I believe you already know the Group Captain, sir?' said Greaves as he led Bobby to the château. 'Group Captain Daventry?'

'Jack Daventry?'

When Greaves nodded, Bobby's relief turned to a sinking feeling. Playing second fiddle to Jack was not his idea of sitting out the war. He braced himself for the meeting, and made a silent vow to have as little to do with his cousin as possible.

Any thoughts Bobby might have had about the château lending them some luxury was very quickly eradicated. Anything of value had been stripped, leaving only bare walls. Bobby imagined that some general in Berlin, or even Hitler himself, was enjoying the additions to their own homes. Or maybe, given the Nazi propensity to destroy everything they touched, it had all been smashed up and used for firewood.

Greaves led him to a small room at the top of the stairs, and he found himself face to face with the cousin he hated.

'At ease, Bobby,' said Jack. He sat behind a large table, on which stood a pile of folders. He looked tired and harassed. 'It's good to see you again. Please, sit down. I'll see if I can get the men to rustle you and the other men up some decent food. We've just had a delivery of Red Cross parcels. First for months. Mother sent some Turkish Delight. She's nothing if not practical.'

Bobby sat down, slightly confused and wary about Jack's apparent friendliness. He doubted it could last, but he was too tired to even think of getting into all the stuff from their childhood. 'I've just asked the German CO about Stalag Luft III. Do you know if it's true, Jack? Sorry, I mean, sir.'

'Jack will do in private. We are family after all. That's important now, don't you think, Bobby?'

Bobby nodded, still wondering if this was all an act for Greaves who stood at the side, awaiting orders.

'Yes, it's true,' Jack continued. 'Fifty of them. We're trying to play it down amongst the men. It's not good for morale. We have to keep believing we can beat them.'

'I agree. But what does that mean for those of us still locked up?'

'So you're already thinking of escaping?'

'Aren't you?'

'There are attempts taking place.' It seemed to Bobby that Jack was dodging the question, even though his answer seemed straightforward enough. 'That's why I wanted to see you, Bobby. Not just to say hello, but because we could use an engineer. I'm not sure the Germans always think carefully about what they've done, putting so many different services together in this transit camp. But for us it means we've got lots of different areas of expertise. Only we were lacking a good engineer till you arrived.'

'What's the plan? A tunnel.'

'Yes. We've got one already started, but we can't get air into it. Can you help us?'

'Yes, give me the tools and I can fit up some air ducts. Maybe even help out on other things. But I want a place in it when we break.'

'Of course.'

'How are you for scroungers?'

'Why?'

'My sergeant, Brian Miller, he's good at getting what's needed.'

'Brian Miller?' Jack took a handkerchief out of his pocket and wiped his head. 'I used to know a Brian Miller, back in London in peacetime.'

'Tall, fair-haired. Got a chip in his front tooth.'

'That's him.' Jack sat back and sighed, flicking through the files in front of him. He clearly had not had time to read them all. 'Look, Bobby, I don't want to interfere with your plans, but he's a spiv. A crook.'

'That might have been a problem in peacetime, Jack, but it's bloody useful in this place.'

Jack nodded. 'Yes, all the old rules have gone, haven't they? Okay, I'll trust your judgement. Just . . . just keep him away from me, Bob. We don't get on.'

'Fair enough, but as you're the highest-ranking officer here, he should behave himself.'

'I doubt that, if I know Miller as well as I think I do.'

'I'll get some rest, then you, or your man here,' Bobby gestured towards Greaves, 'can

298

fill me in on where we are so far.'

'Great. It'll be good to work with you, Bob.'

'You didn't answer my question. About whether you're going to be escaping.' Bobby had been watching Jack closely. He did not only sweat when Miller was mentioned. He seemed to have a faint sheen of perspiration on his face the whole time. And he was pale. Deathly pale.

'I'd only hold things up.'

'Why?'

Jack nodded to Greaves, who brought a pair of crutches that had been leaning against the wall. Jack hauled himself up onto them and pulled himself around the desk.

'Dear God,' said Bobby. 'Jack, I'm so sorry.'

Jack's left leg was missing below the knee.

★ ★ ★

Jack waited till Bobby had left the room before sitting down again. 'Greaves.'

'Yes, sir.'

'You give my cousin whatever he needs to escape, okay?'

'Yes, sir.'

'When we were kids, I smashed his train set up. I owe him big time.'

'Don't be so hard on yourself, sir. Kids do

stupid things sometimes.'

'No, I knew exactly what I was doing. Also, find out more about Miller. What he's been up to since he joined up. I want to keep an eye on him.'

'You think he could be trouble, sir?'

'Not for the escape, perhaps. But for me personally. It goes back to the stupid things we do when we're kids.' Jack had been sure he had dodged all the problems that Miller brought with him. Now they were stuck together in this camp.

'Do you want to talk about it, sir?'

'No, I'd much rather leave it in the past where it belongs. If he lets me. Go and tell the Commandant that I need to see the doctor, will you? The morphine he gives me barely hits the spot.'

'Sir, I wish you'd fight more for repatriation.'

'Maybe I will now my cousin is here and I know the lads will be in good hands. It'll be nice to hand over the reins.'

'Sir, if you like your cousin so much, why did you smash up his train set?'

'I don't know that I like Bobby, but he's a smart one. People don't realise it, because he's so quiet. He's honest too. We can trust him. Miller, on the other hand . . . '

Greaves left the room, and Jack reflected

on what a good lad he was. He had looked up to Jack from the very beginning. Jack wondered what the kid would think if he knew the truth. That the man he admired had been an accessory to a murder. The problem was whether Greaves, and everyone else in the camp, might find out soon.

Miller was not known for his discretion, even if it came to the murder of a taxi driver five years earlier. No, it was the sort of thing Miller liked to boast about, to give off the air of being like an American gangster.

25

Rebecca received the call after a sleepless night trying not to think about Charles and Maggie in each other's arms.

'We thought that as you were his only living relative, you should know,' the nurse at the other end of the phone said. 'Mr. Wilson has had a stroke.'

Rebecca tried to remember if Doris had died, but could not recall hearing the news. She had not spoken to her stepfather since the day of the riot, and had heard very little about him. She knew that he had run for the council as a Labour candidate, but had been heckled and booed so much during a speech in the town centre that he had withdrawn from the race. The people of Stony Newton had long memories, and none of them would forget how he betrayed his own.

As for Frank Wilson's private life, she had refused to take an interest, gradually limiting his access to Ricky and Bobby, so that over the past ten years, they had lost touch completely. That suited Rebecca, and if Ricky and Bobby had any problems with not seeing him, they kept it to themselves. On some level, Rebecca believed they absorbed some of what had happened on the day of the riot and the fact that the grandfather they loved had something to do with it.

'Hello, Mrs. Harcourt. It's nice to see you again. I wish it were under better circumstances.' Lizzie Alsop met Rebecca in the hospital reception area.

'Hello, Lizzie, it's good to see you too. Or should I say, Doctor Alsop?' Rebecca struggled to put aside her intense hatred for Maggie. She was genuinely fond of Lizzie, but found it hard to remember when her emotions regarding the Alsop family were so tied up in Maggie and Charles' betrayal.

'It's still Lizzie to you.'

'How is your father?'

'He's doing okay. His shoulder is a bit shot up, but they say he should be home from the army hospital soon. Mum will be pleased.'

Rebecca did not answer that. 'Where is Frank? My father.'

'I'll take you to him. Mister Latimer is with him now.'

'I thought he'd retired.'

'Sorry, not old Doctor Latimer. Young Mister Latimer. His son. He's in charge of the geriatric ward.' For some reason Lizzie blushed when she mentioned Mister Latimer's name. They walked to the ward together, whilst Lizzie explained Frank's illness. 'He's had a stroke, as you were told, and is in a coma. We're doing all we can. The next few hours are crucial. If he wakes up in that time, then the prognosis is good. If he doesn't then the chances are he could be like it for a long time. Or until he has another stroke. I'm sorry, Mrs. Harcourt, but things are not hopeful.'

'Don't be, Lizzie.'

'He's not very old. Only fifty-five. But from what his ex-wife tells us, he drank quite heavily, and had put on a lot of weight. We also think he had developed type two diabetes without realising it. What we were hoping is that you might be able to fill in some blanks about his health. He's seldom gone to see the doctor, apart from when he was injured in the Great War.'

'I'm sorry, Lizzie, I'm the wrong person to ask. I didn't even know that he and Doris were divorced.' Rebecca began to bristle. There was something annoying about the way she was expected to know all about Frank. She hated that Lizzie was troubling her with it, even though her more rational mind knew that it was not Lizzie's fault.

'Doris?'

'His wife. Or ex-wife, as you say.'

'That's not the lady with him now. Her name is Rita.'

'Rita?' Rebecca racked her brains to remember if she knew anyone of that name. 'I've no idea who she is. Frank . . . my father . . . and I haven't spoken for a long time.'

Rita turned out to be a rather haggard woman who could have been anywhere between thirty-five and fifty-five. It was hard to tell. She had shaved her eyebrows and redrawn them some three inches above the original line, giving herself a perpetually surprised look. Her make-up was thick and it looked as if she did not wash, but just put fresh foundation on over the existing cream. Her lipstick spread like a centipede's legs into the creases around her mouth.

They met in the corridor outside the ward, where Rita smoked a thinly-rolled cigarette, holding it much like a sailor. Mister Latimer, a startlingly handsome man in his early forties, was trying, and seemingly failing, to explain to Rita what Lizzie had just explained to Rebecca.

'Hello, Becky, love. I've wanted to meet you for a long time.' Rita held out a grubby hand, which Rebecca took reluctantly.

'Hello. It's Rita, isn't it?'

'That's right, love. Me and your dad have

been together since old Doris died.'

'I'm sorry. I had no idea about Doris.'

'Yes, three years ago now. She was a good 'un, was Doris. We were friends, you know, and she asked me to take care of him. He talks about you all the time. You're just as pretty as he said you were. He loved you a lot, you know.'

Rebecca felt unwelcome tears prick her eyes. 'How long have you been married?'

Rita looked at Lizzie and Mister Latimer, and then whispered, 'Well, we're not really married yet. We were going to be, which is why I said I was his wife. By the way, he said I could have his stove. If he died. He said I could have it.'

Rebecca fought a strange compulsion to laugh. She was afraid that if she started it would end in bitter tears. 'I'll just go in and see him.'

She was glad that they let her go in alone. She was unprepared for the wave of pity that crashed over her on seeing Frank lying on his side, almost as if he were asleep. She wondered what he was dreaming about, if he was dreaming at all. Had all his sins come to haunt him? Or did his indifference to the suffering he had caused carry over into whichever world he inhabited?

Leaning over him Rebecca whispered,

'Dad. It's me, Becky.' A hot tear fell from her eye, and she brushed it away impatiently, along with a memory of him hoisting her up on his shoulders when she was about five years old, and carrying her through Stony Newton to the fair. She sat down on a chair next to the bed and watched him for several minutes, fighting her emotions. Not just about Frank letting her down, but about Charles betraying her with Maggie. She had trusted him never to be like her stepfather.

After a while, she leaned forward and whispered, 'I hate you.' She checked to make sure no one else could hear her. 'I hate that I have to feel sorry for you, and that I have to be kind to you when you've no ounce of pity or kindness in you. You've only managed to destroy anyone who ever loved and respected you, whilst you kept on surviving. You never even asked about him, did you? Not once did you ever stop to wonder if he was alright. She did. She asked every single day. That's why I know she's in heaven and you're going straight to hell.'

Unable to bear the pain anymore, she ran from the ward, sobbing.

'Aw,' said Rita, lighting up another cigarette. 'She's heartbroken about her old dad.'

★ ★ ★

Simon Latimer called Lizzie into his office at around ten o'clock that night. 'Lizzie . . . ' He held a glass of whisky in his hand, but seemed undecided whether to drink it or not. His hands shook as he tried to raise the glass to his lips, which were set in a thin, pale line.

'What is it, Simon? What's wrong?' She shut the door behind her, and went to his outstretched arms, placing herself on his knee. 'Darling, tell me? Is it Thelma? Has she found out about us?'

'No, not that. I've made a dreadful mistake. I was giving Frank Wilson some morphine . . . I'm so tired, Lizzie.'

'What?'

'I gave him the wrong dose. He's dead, Lizzie.'

'What? How?' Her first instinct was to jump up, but she remained on his knee, waiting for him to tell her he was joking, or that he only thought he had killed Frank Wilson.

'I've told you, I gave him the wrong dose. I got the arithmetic wrong. You know it's not my strong point. I need you to cover for me, Lizzie. Write his death certificate. Say it was another stroke.'

'Simon, are you mad? Look, just come

308

clean. I'm sure they'll understand. We're understaffed because of the war.'

'For God's sake, Lizzie, I killed a man! They're not going to understand that. Darling, if you love me. If you care about me. I can't let this get out. It'll be like Brighton all over again.'

'Everyone understood that was a mistake, Simon. You weren't to blame. It was the daughter who gave her mother the wrong dose. Wasn't it?'

'What the hell are you suggesting? You think I make a habit of killing old people?'

'Of course not! But think about what you're asking me to do. It's hard enough being a woman in the medical profession. If I get found out . . .'

'You won't be, Lizzie. The only people who will know will be us. Please, darling. I can't risk being struck off. Think about it. The man was going to die anyway. Given the state of his arteries, he was an accident waiting to happen. It's a wonder he's lived this long.'

'And that makes it alright, does it?' Lizzie's stomach curled into an uneasy knot. She sighed. 'What do you want me to do?'

'Sign his death certificate. Say he died as a direct result of the stroke. No one is going to question it, not with a war going on.'

'He wasn't a very old man, Simon. There

could be an inquest.'

'But he was unfit. A heavy drinker and smoker who lived on meat pies and chips. Please, darling. If you have any feelings for me, then do this.'

Lizzie nodded miserably. She understood how tired Simon was. They all were, with so few staff to run the hospital. She pushed aside the doubts about how two of his patients could have died of a morphine overdose. The girl in Brighton had admitted giving her mother the wrong dose. As she was young and had so much on her plate, with four younger siblings to care for, it was recognised as a tragic accident brought on by exhaustion.

Only later, when she was alone, did she begin to think Simon's argument was too practised. She could almost imagine him saying the same to the other girl. Had she been naïve and impressed by a mature handsome man? Just as Lizzie had been when she had given her virginity to him, despite knowing he had a wife and two children at home. There were no innocents as far as Lizzie could tell. Not even her. She remembered Jack Daventry and how she had covered for him when the taxi driver died. What made it worse was that, having seen so many patients over the years, she could not even remember what the taxi driver looked like, and she had to think for a while before recalling his name.

The days passed, and as Simon had suspected, no questions were asked about Frank Wilson's death. There were too many other things going on in Britain.

Eaten up with guilt, Lizzie eventually went to see Rebecca Harcourt. She found her digging in the garden, punishing the soil with a spade. Mrs. Harcourt wore drill trousers, a plain sweater and a wide-brimmed hat which looked incongruous and as though it belonged at a Buckingham Palace Garden party rather than in a muddy vegetable patch. She looked up and shielded her eyes from the morning sunshine.

'Lizzie, how nice to see you.'

'Mrs. Harcourt, I wanted to come and offer my condolences on your father's death.'

'That's very kind of you, dear. Why don't you come into the house? I'm sure we could rustle up a cup of tea, and Charlotte has learned how to make a fruit cake with barely any fruit — and not much in the way of cake for that matter. It has to be eaten to be believed.'

'Thanks, but my shift starts soon. I just wanted to say . . . It's your father's funeral tomorrow, isn't it?'

'Yes. Did you want to come? I didn't realise you knew him that well. Not that you wouldn't be very welcome. Otherwise it will just be me and his girlfriend making sure she goes home with his stove. I'm debating whether we could do with it ourselves, given that the one in the Priory kitchen is almost falling to pieces.'

Lizzie was not sure whether the comment required her laughter or not. Mrs. Harcourt's manner mystified her. She did not seem like a woman grieving for a lost father. 'What I wanted to say, Mrs. Harcourt, was that if you had any questions about your father's death, any doubts about why he died at a relatively young age, then you do have the option of insisting on a post-mortem.'

'Is he the first patient you've lost? Is that it? You poor, dear girl. There's no need for you to feel guilty. I'm sure there's no need for a post-mortem, Lizzie. I know you and Mr. Latimer did all you could for him. It was his time. You mustn't tie yourself up in knots about it.'

'No. That isn't it. He wasn't the first patient I've lost . . . not that I lose hundreds.' Lizzie's voice died away. She thought of just coming out with it and telling Mrs. Harcourt the truth. But some spark of self-preservation stopped her. Had Mrs. Harcourt called for a post-mortem and the truth been found, Lizzie would have faced the consequences. But there is a difference between being pushed and jumping. Lizzie was willing to be pushed, but had not quite reached the stage of wanting to jump. 'I just thought I'd point out your options to you.'

'That's very kind but, as I said, there's no need to worry about it. Now please do come in for a cup of tea and some of Charlie's cake.'

Lizzie shook her head. 'Thank you, no. I'd better go or I'll be late.' It was a lie. Her shift did not start for another two hours, but having come all the way to the Priory, she now felt she wanted to be as far away from it as possible. How could she possibly take tea and cake with Mrs. Harcourt knowing what she knew about Frank Wilson's death?

'Well, do come and see us again,' said Rebecca. 'You're always welcome here. Perhaps you could come to dinner one night. We see so few people nowadays.'

There was something brittle about her manner that surprised Lizzie. Rebecca Harcourt had always seemed such a kind, albeit quiet and shy, woman. But at that moment she was doing the best impression of a manor-born country squire's wife that Lizzie had ever seen. Behind the brittleness and lodged deep in her eyes was some other emotion. But it was not grief, Lizzie felt sure of that. She had the strange feeling that it was something to do with her. Perhaps Mrs. Harcourt did have suspicions about her father's death. But that did not seem to be it. Whatever sin Lizzie had committed in Mrs. Harcourt's eyes had nothing to do with Frank Wilson. She was not even sure it was about anything she herself had done. Only that Rebecca Harcourt's manner seemed artificial, as though she was forcing herself to be nice to Lizzie, despite . . . despite what?

Lizzie thanked her and started to walk away, feeling at that moment that she never wanted to set foot in the Priory grounds again.

'Lizzie . . . ' Mrs. Harcourt called her back briefly.

'Yes.'

'Give your father my best regards, won't you? I often think of him and wonder how he's getting on. We grew up together you know.'

Lizzie frowned, and hid it quickly with a smile. Mrs. Harcourt's sudden misty-eyed nostalgia regarding her father confused her. She had often heard her mother and father mention Rebecca Harcourt, and had sensed the mention of her name caused some tension between them. She wondered if there

314

were things she did not know; and decided, given her own current state of mind, she did not want to know. 'I'll be sure to mention you to him,' she said, before waving and saying goodbye.

* * *

The funeral was every bit as soulless as Rebecca expected it to be. Frank had few friends, having sold them all out during the strike. The pit owner, Blake, attended. Rita also attended, with a friend at her side. Both took what appeared to be a ghoulish enjoyment in the proceedings. Rita certainly seemed to relish playing the grieving widow, looking up at the vicar with a comically tragic gleam in her eyes.

Afterwards, she moaned against her friend's shoulder, 'I want to be alone,' reminding Rebecca of a poor man's Greta Garbo. Despite her statement, Rita made no attempt to leave the spotlight, but instead appeared to be waiting for someone to challenge her.

Charles insisted on accompanying Rebecca, she suspected more for society's sake than from any real feeling for her or Frank. They had not spoken about her catching him with Maggie, and she had no intentions of broaching the subject. They stood side by

315

side, both lost in their own thoughts. After the final words had been spoken and the coffin had been lowered into the ground, Rebecca walked away, without inviting Charles to go with her.

She made her way up to the castle, as she had after her mother's funeral, and fought back the tears that threatened to engulf her. She found herself grieving for Frank more than she would ever admit. Perhaps not for the man he had become, but for the eager boy who had come into their lives and promised to be a good father to her. And he had kept that promise for a short time, before his true nature, or perhaps just his immaturity, came through and he began to assert his authority with Myra. Rebecca had trusted him and he had betrayed her. Just as she had trusted Charles.

'I remember coming here on the day of your mother's funeral.' Charles' voice startled her. 'Are you alright, Rebecca?'

'What do you think?'

'I'm sorry. I didn't think Frank's death would bother you that much. You've always seemed to hate him.'

'I did. I do. But that's hardly my most pressing concern at the moment, is it?'

'Rebecca, about Maggie. It's nothing. It's over.'

She spun around, with tears splashing onto her cheeks. 'And that makes it alright, does it? That it's over? What did I do, Charles? Tell me. What did I do that sent you into the arms of not just any woman, but that, that thieving, conniving bitch?'

'You lied to me.'

'Lied? About what?'

He looked at her for a long time, and then laughed bitterly. 'You don't even remember, do you? You've just put it right out of your mind. That's one thing I've noticed about you, Rebecca. How good you are at shutting out the bad things. The things that don't fit with your image of yourself as lady of the manor.'

'What?'

'I can't say I blame you. It's not easy to break away from bad beginnings, but you've managed it. You should be happy. Everyone knows the Priory is yours now. Even my mother concedes it. Congratulations. You got what you wanted. And all you had to do was hide your nausea whilst a disfigured man made love to you.'

His words struck her like the swords of a bad knife thrower, chipping away at her and leaving deep, dark cuts. And yet she could see some truth in what he had said. She had spent most of her teenage years dreaming of

317

being mistress of the Priory. She had also done much to put herself in his way in the hopes he would notice her. Had she wanted the Priory so much that she only thought she loved Charles? No, that part was not true. She still loved him, which made his words all the more hurtful.

'It's true I used to dream of living in the Priory,' she said, struggling to keep her voice on an even keel. 'But I never had to pretend to love you, Charles, and I'm sorry for whatever self-hatred you feel that makes you believe that. But the Priory isn't mine. It's yours. I'll pack my things and leave today.'

'There's no need for that. I'm sure we can come to some amicable arrangement. Think of the children. Think of what people will say.'

'Did you worry about the children and other people whilst you were screwing Maggie Fletcher? Because whatever you believe I've done to betray you, Charles, it was nothing compared to your betrayal.' Her voice broke, and she rushed past him, out of the castle and down the hill.

26

The days in the transit camp spread into weeks and then into months, whilst the men played cricket (in good weather) and cards (in bad weather). They performed shows for each other in the château's ballroom, which had become the theatre. They started choirs. They painted, albeit only still life, as the guards would not permit them to draw the camp. If the guards guessed that the drawing classes were a good front for forgery, they kept it to themselves. And the captured men wrote letters home to their loved ones, eagerly awaiting the replies that would be full of all the normal everyday things they were denied, such as going to the pub, or a film at the picture house, or a trip to the seaside for fish and chips.

Meanwhile beneath the camp, they took it in turns to dig, on the basis that it would not do for the same men to be absent from the other activities too much. Only Bobby Harcourt, who had little interest in all the other activities — apart from writing home to his mother — stayed on task all the time, and even then, Jack would often have to order him to stand down in case the guards began to get suspicious. Often he would disappear into one of the huts, messing around with some project that he refused to share with the others.

'I need to get out of here, Jack,' he would protest. 'The war will be over soon and I want to be a part of the push into Berlin. They'll need good engineers like me. Don't you want to get out?'

Jack pointed to his amputated leg in response. They were sitting in Jack's room, drinking watery coffee, and discussing the final plans for the escape, whilst outside one of the other internees kept watch for the guards.

'They say Bader still flies,' said Bobby. 'He's lost both his legs.'

'Bader is an egomaniac,' said Jack. It was not a popular view of the war hero, thought Bobby, but Jack never did care about being popular. 'We've had this conversation before, Bobby. I'm not going with you. I'd slow you down.'

'Jack, no one knows what's going to happen in the final push by the Allies. The Nazis might decide to kill everyone in a camp. You need to get out now. I'll take care of you.'

'Why?' Jack frowned. 'You hated me when

we were kids. I gave you good reason to. Why should you care now if I live or die?'

'You're family. We should stick together.'

'Excuse me whilst I find my violin.'

'Take the piss if you want.' Bobby stood up and got ready to leave. He could not explain it to Jack in the way he wanted to. If he had said, 'we belong to each other', Jack would probably have thought he was making a pass at him. Only Bobby's mother, Rebecca, ever really understood what he meant. It was about having the same blood. Being a part of one another in a way no one else ever could be. Jack and he might not be the best of friends, but in a place where there was no one else that Bobby could call his own, Jack mattered. He was a link to home and normality. Instead he settled on, 'I'm responsible for you. We're responsible for each other, because we're blood.'

'Bob.' Jack called him back just as he was about to leave the room. 'I appreciate it, I really do. But the fact is, I can't just be responsible for you, even if we are family. At the moment, I'm the allied CO. If I leave, along with all the other officers on the escape list, there'll only be non-coms left.'

'Some of the sergeants are just as capable of commanding the men, Jack. You know as well as I do that it's our duty to try and escape. Miller said you were afraid to go back.'

Jack's head snapped up and he looked at Bobby sharply. 'Why?'

'I don't know. He says you've got wire-happy, and you feared going back to the real world. Something about you didn't know what awaited you there.'

'Look, Bob, you know Miller is a shark, don't you?'

'He's a bit shady, yes, but that works against the guards.'

'It's a funny thing, how a man of his talents can come into his own during wartime. At home he'd be locked up for stealing.'

'He is locked up.'

'Touché. But you know what I mean.' Jack began to massage the stump of his leg. He had that haunted look again, and Bobby was not sure if it was the pain or something else causing it.

'Yes, okay, he's perhaps not the sort of person I'd have as a friend at home. Then again, he tells me you and he were really thick at one time. You seem to hate him now. What happened?'

'Nothing. Forget it.'

Bobby left Jack massaging the stump. One of the German guards stood at the end of the corridor. 'My cousin . . . the Allied CO . . .

322

needs some medicine.'

'The doctor has given him a dose today already.'

'He needs more. You should repatriate him, you know. Extenuating circumstances.'

'No repatriation. Soon the war will be over, and you will be servants of the Reich.'

'Yeah, keep dreaming son. Get medicine for my cousin or I invoke the Geneva Convention.'

Miller stood in the grounds with some other men, smoking a cigarette that was thinner than the matchstick with which he had lit it.

'I don't know why you bother, sir,' said Miller, when he saw Bobby's defeated expression. 'I told you, the Group Captain is wire-happy.'

'I didn't ask your opinion,' Bobby snapped. He sighed. 'Sorry, Miller, but it's a sore subject. I'm beginning to think you're right. He doesn't want to go home. I get the feeling you know why, too?'

Miller looked around at the other men and shrugged. 'Nothing I can talk about here. But let's just say that your cousin might not be as worth saving as you think.'

Bobby dropped his voice. 'You're on tunnel duty with me later. You can tell me then.' It was not a request.

They took over from the digging team at around five in the afternoon, hoping to get another hour of digging before the evening roll call. It was harder to dig safely in the evenings, because the camp quietened down. During the day, when men were hanging around in the yard, or going from hut to hut, the guards did not miss people. At night, when most of the prisoners should be in their own huts, with a guard checking each one, it was more difficult for the presence of one or two men to go unnoticed. Plus the quieter atmosphere might make it easier for underground vibrations to be detected. Generally those who worked in the tunnels at night were those who resided in that hut.

Bobby and Miller had been digging for half an hour, making painfully slow progress. 'So,' said Bobby. 'Tell me why my cousin doesn't want to go back. It's obvious you and he hate each other. Why?'

'Killed a bloke, didn't he?' said Miller.

'What?'

'Yeah, before the war. We were both into some stuff, and had done a deal. We had to get a taxi. Jack went mental. The drugs, I reckon. They say his mother is a junkie.'

Bobby said nothing, but silently conceded that point. His aunt Patricia was known for her predilection for the white stuff. She thought she hid it from the family, which made her addiction even more pathetic.

'He stabs this poor taxi driver, and then ran off, leaving me to carry the can. I did what I could for the bloke. Got a girlfriend who's a doctor to help him out. But it was too late. I thought I was going to be arrested, but the girlfriend put in a good word for me.'

Bobby stopped digging, and lay on his belly, contemplating Miller's words. 'So if he goes back, he'll be arrested?' said Bobby.

'Yep. Most likely. They'd hang him for it.'

Bobby started tunnelling again, but for the rest of the dig, he kept a close eye on where Miller was.

★ ★ ★

'Thank you for your help, Jed,' said Rebecca, pushing the sofa into place. He had just entered the small sitting-room with a box of books. 'You shouldn't be carrying with your bad shoulder. Especially up all those flights of stairs.' She had taken a flat in an old pit manager's house near to the castle.

'It's not so bad now. Besides, I can't leave a lady to struggle all on her own.'

'That's the problem with having sons away in the war. Charlotte and Ronnie are working on the land today.' Rebecca did not want to

325

tell him that she had deliberately waited until the girls were busy so as not to cause them too much distress by her leaving.

She went to the window and looked down over the changing landscape. Where there had once been fields in Stony Newton were council properties, built to house those bombed out by the war. Rebecca thought they were ugly, grey square buildings, but she did not doubt they were needed. Only the field directly in front of the castle had been left unchanged.

'Do you remember when we could run all the way along the edge of Stony Newton and never have to step on a pavement?' she asked.

Jed joined her at the window. 'Yeah, those were the days, weren't they? I hate to sound a snob, but this new bunch of kids they've brought in from the cities are a rum lot. I don't think their parents ever watch them.'

'We were a rum lot,' Rebecca said, laughing. 'We were damn near feral as children.'

'Ah, I reckon so. I'm probably just getting old.'

'Well you look good on it,' she said, turning to face him. He did look good too. Jed had grown into his looks, and was much more attractive as a middle-aged man than he had ever been as a teenager. Not that he had been bad-looking then. But the grey in his hair suited him, giving him a distinguished air.

'So do you, Becky.'

She stifled a pang. 'No one has called me Becky for a very long time. I'm not sure that girl even exists anymore.'

'She's in there somewhere, lass.'

She shook her head. 'No, I think she died on that night all those years ago.' One thing about being with Jed was that she did not have to pretend. He knew the story as well as she did. 'Do you ever think about it?'

Jed seemed a little uncomfortable. He turned away from the window. 'Ay, every now and then I do.'

'I've thought about it all the time recently. I had almost forgotten little Charlie. Well, not forgotten him, but buried him deep.' Rebecca shivered and wrapped her arms around her. 'I wonder what did happen to him.'

'What's the point of wondering after all this time? Let it go, Becky. You'll only make yourself unhappy thinking about it. And you deserve to be happy. More than anyone I know.'

'I was happy until . . . ' Rebecca paused. She had no idea if Jed knew about Maggie and Charles. She could tell him, and pay Maggie back. But even if the woman she still thought of as Fletcher the Filcher deserved everything she had coming to her, Jed did not. 'Tell you what,' she said instead. 'Why don't you stay and have dinner with me? Unless you have to get back to Maggie.'

'She's working late tonight,' he said. 'Charles keeps her very busy in the office.'

'Yes,' Rebecca said sharply, annoyed that the mood of a few moments ago had changed to one of darkness. 'He does that.'

Jed reached over and stroked her cheek. 'I'd love to have dinner with you.'

Rebecca realized she would have to put him straight. She had not meant to sound as if she was seducing him. Had she?

27

'I shouldn't have come.' Jack groaned loudly in the early morning light. They were in a French forest, with no real idea of how far from the camp they were. As soon as they reached the end of the tunnel, they kept going, facing the general direction of Switzerland. They could not run, because of Jack, but they had managed a fairly brisk pace. 'I'm holding you back, Bob.'

'Shh.' Bobby clamped his hand over his cousin's mouth. 'And I told you that I'm not going back home and explaining to Aunty Patty why I left you behind in a Nazi prisoner of war camp.'

They moved further into the woods, and found an old hunter's cabin. Bobby helped Jack inside, closely followed by Brian Miller. 'We should be able to talk in here. Rest a while, Jack. Then we'll move on. Miller, where are we?'

'Not as far as we'd be without him,' said Miller, churlishly.

'Don't start all that again. He's doing well, even with the false leg.'

'It bloody hurts,' said Jack, sitting on the

floor. He pulled the prosthetic off and rubbed at his stump.

'I did the best I could,' said Bobby. He had worked day and night to create a limb after the Germans had denied Jack one, determined that he would not leave the camp without him. Unfortunately, Jack had no time to get used to it, and Bobby had to create it without being able to do any fittings. He had guessed, almost perfectly as it turned out, Jack's measurements.

'I know you did. I'm not ungrateful. I'm only saying . . . I wish I'd had more time to get used to it, that's all.'

'I know, Jack. But it was tonight or never with them saying they'd be moving us out next week. Miller, I asked you two minutes ago where we were.' Despite Jack's superior rank there was no doubt about who was really in charge. Bobby had made all the plans, and Bobby had the last say in everything.

Miller looked at the map and compass. 'We're about three miles from the Swiss border. It's due east from here. I say we leave Jack to his own devices.'

'Miller, if you want to go on alone, you can suit yourself. It's probably better if we split up. But I'm not leaving my cousin. Is that clear?'

'He's a liability. Why would you want to

330

save him anyway, after what I've told you about him?'

'What have you told Bobby?' Jack's face became even paler.

'That you're a bloody killer. Stabbed a taxi driver and left him for dead. I was there with my girlfriend when you came asking your bit of fluff to help the bloke.'

'You're a bloody liar,' said Jack, struggling to get up off the ground. Miller piled on top of him in a furious assault. Bobby, weakened by months of bad food, struggled to contain him, but eventually managed to pull him off.

'I thought you said it was you who went to your girlfriend for help,' he said to Miller.

'What?'

Bobby slammed the little sergeant up against the wall. 'You heard me, Miller. Your story has got so many holes in it and it changes every time you tell me. Not to mention the fact that you knew stuff you couldn't have known unless you'd been there. I'm not nearly as stupid as you think I am.'

'Then why have you let me come with you?'

'I needed men to dig the tunnel. You're strong and healthy. But to be honest, I didn't really care what you and Jack did in your previous lives. Nothing that happened before the war matters anymore. We're here, in this situation now, escaping a common enemy. Anything else is not important.'

'I'm not getting captured again because of Long John Silver there,' said Miller. 'I should have killed him before we left the camp.'

Jack glowered back up at Miller.

'Okay, enough,' said Bobby. 'We're moving on. We need to get to the Swiss border and freedom.'

'You do what you want,' said Miller. 'I'm out of here.'

Miller matched the action to the words, dashing out of the hut. Bobby went to follow him, but changed his mind. There was no way he could leave Jack, not even for a moment.

'Go on, Bobby,' said Jack. 'Get out of here. I'll manage.'

'I'm not leaving you, Jack.'

'Why would you bother saving me?' said Jack. 'We hate each other.'

'I thought we'd gone past all that childhood stuff,' said Bobby. 'Look, I know you're not much of a one for family, but that's what we are, whether you like it or not. And family matters now, more than at any other time. It's not just because of Aunty Patty I'm saving you. It's not as if she ever really liked me either. It's because I couldn't live with myself if I left you behind.'

'I appreciate it. More than you know. But we're stuffed, Bobby. Miller has the map and compass.'

'Yeah, that is a problem, but he won't have gone far. I'll go after him and get them back. Wait here.' Bobby left him alone in the hut.

When Bobby first mentioned the prosthetic limb, Jack had scoffed at the idea. But his cousin had been adamant. 'It's just engineering, Jack, like anything else. It'll be heavy and cumbersome, and you won't win any marathons, but you will be able to walk on it. If Bader can escape with two false legs, you can manage it with one.'

Bobby had fashioned it out of wood from bunk bed legs, and old shoe leather, taken from fellow prisoners' boots. When the rumour started to spread that they were being moved out, Jack had just a few days to learn how to walk on it, and only then when there were no guards around.

Something about Bobby's certainty gave Jack hope. It was mad to even think of trying to escape in his condition, but it was still better than remaining in the POW camp. Even if Jack never reached home, he would at least have done his duty as a British officer. If he were truly honest, he wanted to be free. Free from the camp and free from his growing reliance on morphine. He began to suspect that the Germans only gave it to him to keep him docile.

He had gradually begun to wean himself off it, but sitting in the gamekeeper's hut, somewhere in France, his stump screaming with pain and with beads of sweat covering his brow, he craved it more than ever. He had to move. It was the only way to fight the pain.

Assuming his cousin had been persuaded by Miller to go on without him, Jack put the prosthetic leg back on and started an agonizing walk in the direction of the rising sun. He found Bobby and Miller, covered in blood and lying in a ditch, less than a mile from the gamekeeper's cabin. They had been shot, but judging by bruising on their faces, they had also been fighting each other just beforehand.

He slumped down onto the ground and sobbed for the cousin who had set him free. Eventually, realizing he was in a vulnerable position, he pulled the map and compass from inside Miller's coat, and took Bobby's identity discs, intending to show them to Charles and Rebecca as proof of their son's courage.

It humbled Jack, the way Bobby had insisted on saving him, despite the fact they were never the best of friends. He wished he had known his cousin better and for longer so he could at least put that right. He would shake his hand and then maybe they could start afresh. It was too late for that. Bobby was gone, sacrificing himself to save a man to whom he owed nothing.

'Thanks, Bobby,' Jack murmured, as he headed towards freedom and home.

28

1947

They told him that his name was Brian Miller and that he had lost his eye. They also assured him that his memory would return one day.

'You've been in a coma for a long time,' the consultant told him. 'So some memory loss is to be expected. We're grateful that there's no permanent brain damage. Now, would you like to see your wife?'

He nodded, whilst trying to conjure up an image of the sort of woman he would have married. He had to admit to himself that the mousy girl in horn-rimmed spectacles who walked hesitantly into the ward was not what he had imagined.

'Hello, Brian, love,' she said, reaching over and kissing his cheek. She sat down on a chair, holding her handbag in her knee so tightly that he wondered if she suspected someone of trying to steal it.

'I'm sorry,' he said. His throat felt constricted, but the doctors had explained that was because most of his muscles had wasted during his coma. 'I don't know who you are.'

'It's me. Marie. Remember?' She said it warily.

'Marie.' He tried the name out for size, but it meant nothing to him. He shook his head. 'No, sorry, I don't remember that name.'

'You will one day, Brian.' Her voice trembled as she spoke. 'The doctor said you can come home in a day or two. I've got us a nice little house from the council. One of the new ones.'

'Tell me about us, Marie. How did we meet?'

'We met in a pub, on the day war broke out. The Ship Inn. You were with your friend, Jack Daventry. The posh one.'

He started. 'Jack Daventry. I know that name.'

'Anyway, you walked me home.' Her words came out in a rush. 'Remember. I didn't think I'd see you again, but the following Wednesday you turned up at my bedsit late at night. I wasn't supposed to let men in, old Mrs. Cooper would have thrown me out, but you had a way about you, you did. We got married on the day you got called up.'

'I wish I could remember.' He did not have the heart to tell her that it was not their romance he struggled to remember. That was such a complete blank to him that he gave up immediately. It was Jack Daventry. He knew the name, and in his mind saw a shadowy figure without a face, but when he tried to remember sitting in a pub with Jack on the outbreak of war, the image went blank again.

'I'd better be going,' said Marie. She stood up, and leaned over to give him another kiss on the cheek. She barely made contact, and he supposed that it was the scarring below his lost eye that put her off. 'I'll come and see you tomorrow, shall I?'

'Yes, I'd like that.'

'Would you?' She looked mystified. 'Why?'

'Because . . . well, I suppose because you're my wife.'

She smiled, and he decided that she was quite pretty under the thick spectacles.

* * *

Annette sat at the kitchen table, surrounded by paperwork. In the centre of it all was a cold cup of tea that she had long since forgotten. Terry popped his head around the door. 'Annie, love, are you ever coming to bed? It is Saturday night.' He winked.

She looked up and smiled at their personal joke. 'Yes, of course. I'm just looking at the files about dad.'

338

Terry stopped short of rolling his eyes heavenward. He walked into the kitchen and sat opposite her. 'Isn't it time you gave this up, sweetheart?'

'I can't. I need to find out what happened that night. Don't you think my father's killer should be brought to justice?'

'Chances are he already has, sweetheart.'

'In the war, you mean?'

Terry nodded. 'He could have been killed.'

'Then again he might not be dead. I've been looking at the witness statements. A night watchman on his way to work said he saw two men near the scene. Then there's one witness — a woman called Marie Benson. She lived in the same boarding house as the student doctor who attended my father. She said she had seen nothing, but when our blokes went to question her again, she had suddenly upped and left the bank she'd been working in and disappeared without leaving a forwarding address. Isn't that odd?'

'Annie, please. I've heard all this, and it's not that I'm unsympathetic, but . . . ' He sighed. 'It's stopping us getting on with our lives. Don't you want a baby one day?'

She shook her head. 'I don't know if I do. What if I turn out like my mother?'

'And you think finding your father's killer is going to prevent that?'

'It might help with some of the anger I feel. I don't want to have a baby then find I'm bitter about the past, as mum was. It's not fair on any child.'

'You're not your mother, Annie.'

Annette sat back and sipped at the cold tea, before grimacing. 'I went to see her the other day.'

'Did you? You never said.'

'I thought I should, because she has no one. Especially not now my grandparents are dead.'

'She didn't have them before, from all accounts. And neither did you. But you've got a family now.'

'I made the mistake of going in my uniform,' Annette continued. 'She didn't even know it was me. She thought I'd gone to arrest her and went wild. Did I ever tell you how horrible the Women's Auxiliary Service was to her?'

Terry nodded. 'They were like that with a lot of, shall we say, fallen women? It's not surprising they were disbanded.'

'I should never have stayed away so long. I accepted her order not to visit anymore too easily, because it was better than going and seeing her in that state. I was a coward.'

'You're not a coward. You said yourself that she wasn't much of a mother to you.'

'No, but she's the only one I've got. And she tried, you know, for a while.'

'Annie,' Terry reached across to her. 'Let's have a family.'

'Give me a little while longer. I just want to talk to a couple more people.'

Terry withdrew his hand, and stood up. 'Six months. I'll give you six months, and then if you don't find anything by then, I want you to promise me you'll let this go.'

'I promise.'

Even as she said it, Annette was not sure if she could keep her promise. Part of her cried out to have a child. She supposed that was a biological response. But an even bigger part of her remembered how spectacularly her mother had failed. If not for Sam, Annette dreaded to think where she would have ended up. Could she risk becoming a mother only to find that she resented her child's intrusion on her life? She liked to think she would never harm a child, but what if the problem ran too deep? What if she was just like her mother, Clara?

At the same time, she knew she was hurting Terry. He longed for children, having seen all his friends with theirs. He wanted a son he could play football with or a little girl he could cherish and protect.

Annette did not know if she could ever give those things to him.

29

Jack looked up at the Priory. It had definitely seen better days. Despite the family making money during the war, they had been unable to obtain the materials needed to maintain it. There were slates missing from the roof, and the wooden doors and window frames were in dire need of repainting. It made Jack feel sad for reasons he did not understand. He had never really felt at home here. But he had never really felt at home anywhere. His regrets, he supposed, were for the awful boy he had been and how he had wasted so much time on bitterness whilst under the Priory roof.

His Uncle Charles opened the front door. 'Jack! Good to see you.' Jack searched his face to see if he spoke the truth. 'You'll have to forgive me opening the door myself. We lost old Stephens a few months ago. I'm sure he was waiting until your grandmother died.'

'Sorry to hear that.' Jack took the hand that Charles offered. 'I'm sorry about grandmother too. And Bobby.'

A cloud passed over Charles' eyes. 'Perhaps

you can tell me about the last time you saw him.'

That, thought Jack, explained the reason for his warm welcome. He was the last member of the family to see Bobby alive. He understood that. Bobby had saved his life. The least he owed him was to remember as much as he could about their time together.

'Never mind that for now. Come on in,' said Charles. 'We'll get your bags later. I'm sure I can rustle us up some coffee. I've become quite self-sufficient over the past few months. Tell me, how are Charlie and Ronnie?' He led Jack to the drawing-room. Like the outside of the house it was in dire need of redecoration. The cushions on the sofas were threadbare, and a cloudy pall hung over the air, suggesting that the chimney was well overdue its annual sweep.

'Last I heard they were skiing down the Alps. I didn't see them much. They consider me an old man.'

'Oh I know that feeling. They see me as ancient. How is your father?'

'Happy. Life in Switzerland seems to suit him.'

'And your mother?'

'The same as ever. She's got a new boyfriend.' They exchanged knowing glances. 'I hear that Aunt Rebecca isn't here anymore.'

'No, no. We separated. She's living in a flat up near the castle.'

'I'm sorry to hear that. I always thought you two were happy. In fact, when I was a child I used to wish my parents got on as well.'

'Coffee!' said Charles, clapping his hands together. It signalled the end of any conversation about Rebecca. 'Then we'll talk about your future with Harcourt's. We're very happy to have you joining us.'

* * *

Half a mile away, Rebecca was also receiving a visitor.

'Good God, darling, where have you buried yourself?' asked Clementine, looking around the flat. As far as Rebecca was concerned it was light and spacious. However, by Clementine's standards, it was tiny.

'I like it here. I've got a great view of Stony Newton,' said Rebecca.

Clementine looked at several paintings which were dotted around the floor. 'It seems to me you see rather too much of Stony Newton. Though I do like the way you've managed to completely ignore the presence of that awful new council estate.'

'Yes, I'm trying to capture Stony Newton

as it was, before the war. Not that I'm any good.'

'No, you're not.'

'Thank you, Clementine. I knew I could rely on you to give me an honest opinion.' Rebecca laughed. 'It's alright, I know I'm not. I'm just trying to find out what I'm good at. I wrote a novel last year.'

'Oh dear.'

'Yes, that's what I thought when I read it back to myself. Here's your coffee.' Rebecca handed over a chipped mug of coffee, which Clementine took with a wry grin on her face. She plonked herself on the corner of the bed. 'I'm working too. In the office at the pit.'

'But you're still on the board of Harcourt's, aren't you?'

Rebecca nodded. 'Yes, but I wanted to earn my own money. I've been reliant on Charles for too long. If I'm going to make a clean break . . . ' She stopped. Even though she had made the decision to make the break from Charles final, it was still hard to talk about.

'Darling, are you sure you're doing the right thing? You still love him, I can see that. And he still loves you.'

'No,' Rebecca shook her head. 'No, he doesn't. Something changed. I don't know what.'

'You don't think it might have something

345

to do with what you told me, do you? I've been wracking my brains and it seems to me that's the only explanation.'

'He doesn't know about it, and even if he did, I would hope he'd understand.'

'If you thought that, you'd have told him years ago, darling.'

'I was going to, but the more time passed, the less it seemed to matter. It's almost as if those things happened to a different girl. A girl called Becky, who I used to know.'

'She's still in there,' said Clementine, echoing what Jed had said. 'I can see her when you're in social situations. Almost as if you think you're there under false pretences.'

'That's all my life has been. A false pretence.'

'Why don't you come and spend some time with us in the States, darling. At least there's no rationing over there.'

'I can't leave. Ricky is home now. He's working at Stony Newton hospital.'

'And he still will be when you return.'

Rebecca leaned against the windowsill. 'He's going through a bad time, Clementine. He blames himself for Bobby's death. He's managed to convince himself that if he'd been there, Bobby wouldn't have died. It's ludicrous, but obviously I can't say that to him, because to him it isn't. The worst of it is that he thinks we hold him responsible.'

'No one is to blame. We've lost so many young men. And those who came back aren't what they were. Paul's son Mackenzie seems fine now, but even he's haunted by what they found when they reached the camps.' Clementine shuddered. 'To think all that was going on and no one did anything about it.'

'If Jack hadn't encouraged Bobby to escape from that POW camp, Bobby might still be alive. And now he's taking Bobby's place at Harcourt's.'

'Come on, darling. That's not fair. And it's not like you. It was expected of them to try and escape. And Bobby was a grown man.'

'Oh I know. And Jack lost his leg, so he's hardly come out of it unscathed. It's just that he was always so nasty to Ricky and Bobby when they were children. I keep thinking back to their birthday. Do you remember? The day of the riot. Jack smashed up their train set, simply because Charles spent more time with them than with him. Now he's supposed to be a changed man, and we're meant to accept him with open arms.' Rebecca's face broke into a sad smile. 'I've still got the picture of the boys.' She went to the dresser and took out a faded black and white photograph of the twins. 'Do you remember? Ricky was a cowboy and Bobby was a pirate. He wore that eye patch for a week afterwards.'

'I remember.'

'And now he's gone. It's not supposed to happen, Clementine. Your children aren't supposed to die before you. The worst of it is, I can't even turn to Charles. He's switched himself off from all of us.'

'What? Even Ricky and Charlie?'

'Yes. It's not that he doesn't have anything to do with them, but he's as distant with them now as his parents used to be with him. I sometimes wonder if it's because of me.'

'You wonder too much. You spend too much time alone here, with these awful paintings.'

'I'm not alone. Not all the time.'

'Oh yes, you did mention someone. When am I going to meet him?'

'It's complicated.'

'You mean he's married.'

'Yes.'

'Oh, do tell.'

'It's Jed. The boy I used to play with as a child.'

'Oh, I remember him. Handsome man. Didn't he have that awful wife?'

'Yes, Maggie. But . . . '

'But what?'

'Oh, he's sweet and he treats me like a china doll. But that's the problem. It's like he's afraid of breaking me. I'm used to a bit more passion.'

'So the earth doesn't move then?'

'It wobbles from time to time, which I suppose is all I can expect at my age,' Rebecca grinned. 'Oh, listen to me. I'm awful. He's a nice man. I should be grateful anyone is interested in me nowadays.'

'Rubbish!' Clementine scoffed. 'He's the one who should be grateful. You're a real catch, Rebecca. I don't know why you don't realize that yourself.'

When Clementine had gone back to her hotel to change for dinner, Rebecca went into the small cupboard in the corner of the studio and took out the portrait she had been working on before Clementine arrived. It was a rough sketch of the photograph she had shown Clementine, but Rebecca had added a third, taller figure. It was Charles. Had Clementine seen it, she might have reassessed her opinion of Rebecca's talent. The picture had a much bigger emotional impact than those of the castle and its surrounding fields. The outlines of the people in it had been sketched with love, as Rebecca struggled to recapture that day, before all the problems had begun. When she and Charles had been in love, and their family, with the imminent arrival of their daughter, was almost complete.

She sketched a few more lines, before sighing and putting it back in the cupboard. It was like an itch and she would only scratch it once a day. Any more than that and the emotional toll became too much.

As she shut the cupboard door, the bell rang. She went to look out of the window and saw him standing on the doorstep. 'Come on up,' she called through the open window.

Knowing it would take him a while to get up the stairs, she rushed around tidying up the room before looking in the mirror and patting down her hair. She was more aware than ever of the fact that she was not getting any younger. When she heard a quiet knock on the door, she came to the conclusion that she was not going to lose twenty years in those few seconds and gave up preening herself.

'It's open. Come in.'

When he arrived Jed looked as if he also wished he could lose twenty years. How silly they both were, she thought.

'Afternoon, Jed,' she said, turning and giving him her most attractive smile. 'If you're going to be visiting often, perhaps I ought to be moving to a flat on the ground floor.'

'I'd happily climb any amount of stairs for

you, Becky,' he said. He put his walking stick against the wall and pulled her into his arms.

★ ★ ★

After straightening her uniform, Esther knocked on the open office door. 'Ricky. Sorry, I mean Doctor Harcourt. Can I speak to you for a moment?' Around her the hospital bustled, with patients being rolled up the corridors to surgery or walking out under their own steam having been discharged.

'I've got more than a moment to spare for you, Esther,' said Ricky, getting up from behind his desk. He smiled warmly. To her surprise, he gave her a kiss on the check. 'And less of the Doctor Harcourt. We're family. How are you?'

'I'm good. Great.'

'Then what's the problem?'

'It's not actually me.' Esther looked around her and closed the door. 'If I tell you something will you promise not to say anything? I don't even know if it's true.'

'If what's true?' Ricky gestured to one of the chairs. 'Sit down. Do you want some coffee?' He went back to his own seat.

'No, thanks. I'm okay. It's about my friend, Gertie. She works on the geriatric ward with Mister Latimer. She was really enjoying it

351

there . . . rather her than me . . . after nursing dad I just don't have the patience anymore.'

'I was sorry to hear about his death,' said Ricky.

'Thanks. Well anyway, Gertie . . . Oh God, I hate saying this, because it sounds like gossip. But she and Mister Latimer were . . . together.'

'Together?' Ricky raised an eyebrow and grinned. 'Come on, Esther, I'm practically your brother. You don't have to be coy with me.'

Strange, thought Esther, but Ricky did not seem like a brother anymore. She had left the Priory a long time ago and that life seemed like a dream she had once had. He had grown very handsome, with the war giving him a maturity that was very different from the puppy-like boy he had been when they grew up. 'Okay, she was sleeping with him. Then one night he came to her, whilst they were on duty, and said he was exhausted. He was almost in tears, she said, and he admitted he had given a patient too much morphine. It killed him. Then he asked Gertie to help him falsify the records. She did as he asked, because she loved him, but he dumped her soon after.'

'And now she wants revenge?'

'No!' Esther frowned. 'Oh I don't know. Is

that what you think? That she made it up to get back at him?'

'It's obviously crossed your mind.'

'That's true.' Esther sighed. 'But I don't think Gertie is that vindictive. Also, she wouldn't implicate herself, would she? She'd just say he'd done it and put a veil over what she had done.'

Ricky nodded. 'Yes, that's true. It's funny, you coming to me with this. I'm not supposed to discuss it, but obviously you already know. There have been murmurs about Latimer for a while now. But nothing concrete. With all his patients being elderly and close to death anyway, it's hard to pin anything on him. In fact, I've been asked to go down and speak to the daughter of one of his former patients.'

'So you knew about this all along? Yet you thought Gertie was being vindictive?'

'I didn't know for certain, Esther. Latimer has left a lot of vindictive women in his wake. He supposedly had an affair with Lizzie Alsop by all accounts. Remember her?'

'Of course, I know Doctor Alsop very well. She's our local GP nowadays. Maybe we should speak to her.'

'We?'

'Yes, we. I want to get to the bottom of this as much as you do, Ricky.'

'Then it looks as if you'll be travelling to Portsmouth with me. How does this weekend sound?'

'Perfect!'

30

Annette read through the statements again. She was on her lunch break in the station canteen, trying to get excited over a plate of liver and onions.

From what she read, it seemed that the blackout way back in the first week of the war had made it nigh on impossible for anyone to see much of anything. Added to which, the fear of being caught in an air raid meant that people tended not to move around very much. They went to work — if they were not part of the armed forces — and then went home, staying as near to the shelters as possible.

She knew from personal experience that as the war progressed, and the worst of the Blitz had taken place, people became more complacent. They fell into living almost normal lives again, which included going out at nights, albeit in the dark and only until the curfew. They even treated the air raids as an adventure. It brought Londoners together in the subways, and the British spirit was indomitable. But in those first few uncertain weeks of the war, people were more frightened and convinced that Hitler would turn up in their living-rooms.

She read through the statements of the people in the boarding house, and the young medical student who had attended her father. Elizabeth Alsop. Her attempts to find the girl had failed so far. She knew that Miss Alsop had graduated from medical school, but she was not practicing in London anymore. Annette had applied to other counties, but information was slow in coming back to her. The implementation of the new health service was taking up most of the medical profession's time. With the creation of more paperwork they were not too pleased to have to search for information on their members.

Alsop's statement read:

I was just getting ready for bed, when someone knocked on my door and told me there was an injured man outside. I rushed outside and found the driver of the taxi. I tried to stem the flow of blood, but by the time the ambulance arrived, he was already dead. Despite that, I travelled in the ambulance with him and tried to revive him, but to no avail.

Annette read through all the other statements, her brow furrowed. Why had she not noticed it before? None of the other tenants at the boarding house mentioned being the one to wake Alsop, and she had not named the person. The investigating officer should have asked her, and she wondered why he did not. She put it down to a natural deference to doctors, even if they were medical students. No one would question Alsop's integrity. Not that Annette suspected Elizabeth Alsop. But reading through her statement again, Annette felt that it was remarkably low on facts.

'Annette, love?'

She looked up to see Terry. 'Hello. I was meant to be meeting you, wasn't I?'

'You were. But it doesn't matter. I've got some news for you. You know they took all those partial fingerprints from your father's taxi?'

'Yes. But they said that they were worse than useless, given how many people used the taxi.'

'Maybe so, but one of them has come back as a match to someone known as a crook.'

'Really?'

'His name's Brian Miller. He did a bit of time before the war. He was into all sorts. Drugs, the black market. There were a couple of charges of sexual assault which were dropped when the women involved became

357

too afraid to continue the case against him.'

'But just because he took dad's taxi doesn't mean he killed him. He may well be an evil bastard, but not necessarily the one I'm looking for.'

'Except that someone else reported a break-in, near to the boarding house, and say they saw Miller leaving it. The boarding house, that is. They recognised him as he was a regular in that area. The police couldn't question him at the time because he'd gone and enlisted. The army was a bit reluctant to risk losing anyone then, so they were a bit obstructive.'

'Where is he now? Please don't tell me he died during the war.'

'He's alive and living on the outskirts of London. Our blokes over there know he's there and are keeping an eye on him. But all evidence points to him having settled down and married.'

'Ah.'

When Terry grinned, Annette knew there was more to come. 'You'll never guess who he married.'

'The medical student? Elizabeth Alsop?'

'No, what made you say that?'

'She doesn't name the person who alerted her to dad's injuries. So I thought . . . '

Terry shook his head. 'No, not her.'

'Well tell me and put me out of my misery!'

'Marie Benson.'

Annette flicked through the files, even though she knew the name well enough. 'She was one of the tenants in the boarding house. The one who claimed to have seen nothing then upped and disappeared. Oh Terry. That's too much of a coincidence, isn't it?'

'I'd say so.'

'Added to which, a woman can't testify against her husband. Oh, it all makes sense now.' She leaned over and kissed him hard on the mouth, mindless of the other officers sitting at tables eating and drinking. 'You are the best husband any woman could have.'

'You can prove that to me later,' he said, winking.

'Oh, believe me, you're in for a huge vote of thanks.'

'I should warn you about Miller. According to the fellas in that district he lost his eye and his memory in the war.'

'That's bloody convenient. Not the eye. The memory.'

'You think he's shamming? It's possible but why? He doesn't know we're on to him.'

'But if he was involved with dad's death, that's not the only thing he was into. It's a good way to start a clean slate.'

'Nah, once a crook always a crook.'

'I'm not suggesting he isn't. But it's handy to be able to pretend you've forgotten everything that went before. How can a jury convict a man of a crime if he can't even remember doing it?'

'I think this might be genuine, Annie. He was in a coma for eighteen months. The doctor I spoke to at the army hospital said that Miller's lucky not to have come out of it with more serious brain damage. I think you have to proceed along the lines that he really won't remember, love.'

'Okay. I will.'

'And be careful, because if he hasn't really forgotten, he's still a nasty little creature.

*　*　*

'I think this is the place,' said Ricky, looking at his slip of paper then up at the boarding house in Portsmouth.

Esther climbed the steps and read the list of tenants. 'Yes, you're right. Irene Tucker.' She pointed to the list. 'She's on the first floor.'

She pressed the bell and they waited. The door was answered by a tired looking middle-aged woman.

'Miss Tucker?' asked Ricky.

'That's me. What do you want?'

'I'm Doctor Richard Harcourt and this is my associate Nurse Esther Linney.'

'I didn't call a doctor.'

'Actually we wanted to speak to you about your mother's death,' said Esther, gently.

Irene Tucker went to close the door. 'I'm not speaking to reporters. Especially those who turn up pretending to be doctors.'

'No!' Ricky held up his hand in supplication. 'I really am a doctor, Miss Tucker, and Esther really is a nurse. We're investigating Mister Simon Latimer. Do you remember him?'

'Yes, of course I remember him. He tended to my mother.'

Ricky thought the poor woman looked even more exhausted than she had before.

'Please can we come in and talk to you?' said Esther.

A few minutes later, Irene Tucker had reluctantly let them into her tiny bedsit. 'I have to go out to work soon,' she said. 'I work nights in a factory.'

'We won't keep you long,' said Ricky.

'I can't offer you any tea. I've used up my rations. But I can give you some water if you want.'

'We're fine,' said Esther, who perched on the edge of the bed.

Ricky sat on a chair near to the window. He

realized that if he craned his neck and stood on one foot, he might be able to see Southsea beach.

Irene Tucker stood by the room door, almost as if she would run at any moment.

'Can you tell us how long ago it was that Mister Latimer tended your mother?' asked Ricky. He already knew, but figured it was a way of easing Irene into the conversation.

'Mum died in nineteen-thirty.'

'Your mother can't have been very old,' said Esther. 'I gather you had younger brothers and sisters?'

'Yes, that's right. Mum was forty-five when she died. I was twenty-one. My brothers were fourteen and thirteen and my sister was ten. They're all grown up now, and spread all over the country.' There was something very sad about the way she said it.

'It's just that we know Mister Latimer as a specialist in geriatrics,' Ricky explained. 'How did he come to be attending your mother?'

Irene shrugged. 'I don't know. I think he was working as a locum at the time, helping out one of his friends. That was our regular doctor, Doctor Jones. Anyway, mum was very ill. She had breast cancer.'

'I'm so sorry,' said Esther.

'They'd operated,' said Irene, as if she had

not heard Esther, 'but the cancer had already spread.'

'At the inquest you said that you'd accidentally given her an overdose of morphine,' said Ricky. 'Is that true?'

'It's true that I said that at the inquest, yes.'

'You must have been exhausted looking after your mother and your younger siblings,' said Esther.

'I was. That's why when he offered . . . ' Irene put her hand to her mouth. 'She was going to die anyway, you see.' Tears filled her eyes. 'He said it was the humane thing to do. So I thought 'Why not?' She was in agony, and I was in agony watching her. Then they found out about the morphine during the post-mortem. He came to see me and said it could ruin his career. He was very handsome then.'

'He's still not too bad now,' said Esther, earning a sharp look from Ricky.

'I was flattered by him,' said Irene. 'And I did think it was sad that he'd lose his career after he'd been so kind. So I lied at the inquest and said it was me. They took my word for it. I stupidly thought we'd be together after that. Me and Simon Latimer. But I didn't see him for dust.'

'Would you be willing to give a statement to this effect?' asked Ricky. 'You see, your mother may not be the only one that Latimer has killed during the course of his work.'

Irene Tucker shook her head. 'No, I won't give a statement against him. Don't you see? He helped me put an end to it. Or so I thought.'

'What do you mean?' asked Esther.

'Well I've got it now, haven't I? I found a lump about a month ago. I suppose that's God's way of punishing me for letting my mother die.'

'No,' said Esther, getting up from the bed. She went to Irene and put her hand on her shoulder. 'You've no reason to be punished. Whatever Latimer's reasons for what he did, your mum was suffering and you helped put that to end.'

'Are you getting proper treatment, Miss Tucker?' asked Ricky. 'I've got a friend in London who is an oncologist. I could give you his name.'

'I can't afford London doctors,' said Irene.

'You don't need to with the National Health service,' said Esther.

'Actually . . . ' Ricky started to say. His friend worked in private practice. 'No, you shouldn't. I could have a word with your doctor about referring you.'

'What? In return for me turning Latimer in?' asked Irene.

'No, I would never use anyone's health as leverage,' said Ricky. 'This is quite outside what we were talking about.'

'I shan't ever speak up against him,' said Irene. 'Never.'

As Ricky and Esther walked along the seafront later, Esther sighed. 'She's got it really bad for him, hasn't she?'

'Yep. What is it about handsome homicidal maniacs that women are drawn too? I notice that you were a bit dreamy over him.' Ricky tried to stem a rising tide of jealousy. Where had that come from?

'Not dreamy at all! I just conceded he is a good-looking man, that's all.' Esther grinned and took his hand. She meant it to be a friendly act, just like when they grew up as children. It felt different though. She was more aware of Ricky than she had ever been. 'That was nice though, what you said about contacting your friend.'

'So there's hope for me yet? Can I assume you're over Bobby now?'

'Oh Ricky, that's a dreadful thing to ask. Bobby is dead. How can I say I'm over him when he's not even here to get over? It would be like denying his existence or denying that he ever had any meaning in my life.'

'No, I suppose not,' said Ricky, glumly. 'I miss him so much, Esther. I'd got tired of the twins thing, and I needed to get away and be an individual. Losing Bobby has been like losing a limb. So I do understand how you feel about him. We both lost him.'

'Ricky . . . '

'What?'

'Oh nothing. It doesn't matter.'

★ ★ ★

Mister Simon Latimer received the telephone call from Portsmouth at around five o'clock in the evening. He was just about to go into dinner with his wife and a few colleagues. He made a few more calls before dinner, and verified the information given to him.

Those who attended the dinner said that he seemed very happy. 'Almost at peace,' one attendee reported.

The next morning he went shooting alone, which was unusual. He was found several hours later in a wooded area. He had put the shotgun into his mouth and blown his brains out.

★ ★ ★

Most of the time he found Marie's precise little ways amusing. The way that towels on the rail had to be perfectly aligned, and tins in the cupboards with their labels facing outwards. As soon as he got up off a chair, she plumped up the cushion and straightened it, even though he might only be going to the loo. Today her little ways annoyed him.

'You shouldn't read at the table,' she said, sweeping his book out of his hands, and closing it to lose the page. She wiped some imaginary crumbs off the table, and went back to the kitchen to fetch the tray. 'I don't know, Brian. The police coming here. What will the neighbours think?'

'They might think you've drowned me in cleanliness,' he said.

'Don't be fac . . . face . . . silly.' That was another thing that amused him. When she tried to use big words, without knowing their meaning. It was not even that she was stupid. When it came to money, she was extremely clever. She kept a little book in which all outgoings and incomings were listed in neat rows. She knew to a penny how much they had coming in and going out. When he had requested a Spitfire model kit, it had taken days of her checking each list, to ensure they could afford it. He suspected that she hoped he would forget. When she ran out of excuses for him not to have it, she went with him to town to ensure he bought the cheapest he possibly could.

'You're so reckless with money, Brian,' she had said whilst they were in the shop. 'Anyone would think you'd never had to struggle to make ends meet.'

'I wish I could remember,' he had replied. When he said that, she changed her mind and insisted he buy the most expensive Spitfire model in the shop. It was only when they returned home and she realised he would be constructing it on the dining table that she had second thoughts again. So it had been moved to the shed, which he preferred, as it meant an excuse not to be around her fluttering and fussing.

'I found these plans in the bin,' she had said to him the next day, entering the shed holding sheets of paper.

'I prefer to work without them,' he said.

'So how do you know if you're doing it right? I don't want to spend all that money for you to end up with a heap of junk.'

'I know what I'm doing,' he said, then wondered where that came from. How did he know that he could build the kit without plans?

'I suppose that's from you being in the Royal Engineers,' she had said.

'Yes, that's probably it.'

She sometimes made him feel like a child, in need of care and guidance. He was never allowed to go for a walk on his own, and if he happened to nip out to the corner shop without telling her, he would return to find her waiting at the gate, tapping her feet and sighing heavily.

She had told him he spent some time in a prisoner of war camp, but somehow being with Marie made him feel more incarcerated. Yes, he could walk out of the door anytime he wanted, but he was tied by the fact that he did not know where he would go. She had told him he had no relatives living, and that most of his friends had died in the war.

'Surely someone survived,' he said.

She shook her head. 'No, none of your friends did. It's very sad, but that's what war does.'

Other times she looked at him with so much love in her eyes, that he felt guilty for not remembering how much he loved her. The doctors had told him his memory would return one day, but the longer he spent cooped up in the house with Marie, in an area of London where nothing seemed familiar, the less likely it seemed.

When she had received a telephone call saying that Constable Annette Parker wanted to see them, she went into overdrive, cleaning the house through the night and fretting constantly about the neighbours.

'She's here,' he said, when he saw an attractive woman getting out of a car. 'And she's in plain clothes, so you need not worry about the neighbours.'

'How do you know it's her?' Marie went to the window, and lifted up the lace curtain.

'Why else would she be looking at this house? We're not expecting anyone else, are we?'

'Doesn't she look a bit dark-skinned to you?' said Marie.

'What does that matter?'

'I just didn't think they were letting them into the police force.'

'Them?'

'You know. Coloureds.'

The hairs on the back of his neck bristled. Marie's bigotry was another thing that bothered him. They lived in a part of London with a large black community. He liked talking to the people who had come over from the West Indies and hearing the stories of how they had helped fight the war. He was saddened that they came to Britain with so much hope and found themselves working menial jobs.

He liked the aromas of the cooking. When faced with the plate of steamed fish, bullet-type peas and half-boiled potatoes that Marie served up, he longed for the spicy fried chicken and rice that his neighbours enjoyed.

'Please don't say anything about the colour of her skin when she's here,' he said.

'Why?'

'Because it's bad-mannered.'

'Why should I show manners to the likes of that?'

'Marie . . . '

She backed away. He did not get angry with her often. Or he did, but he did not show it. But the warning in his voice seemed to have been enough to tell her that on this point he would not be bullied into seeing or doing things her way.

Five minutes later, Annette Parker sat awkwardly on the edge of the sofa, clutching a cup and saucer in one hand. He could see her wondering where she might put it, so he drew the little coffee table closer to her.

'Brian . . . ' Marie said.

'What?' He waited for her to tell him that the coffee table did not belong that close to the sofa.

'Nothing.'

Annette Parker looked at him gratefully and put her cup down. 'The reason I've come to see you today, Mr. Miller is actually a personal matter. In the view of the police, my father's murder has remained unsolved, and with so much having happened since, they're not rushing to solve it. They have other concerns since the war.'

'What have we got to do with your father's murder?' said Marie. Her hands were in her lap. She tore at loose skin from around the nail on her index finger.

'Nothing, I hope. It's just that we found . . . the investigating officer at the time that is . . . found a partial fingerprint of Mr. Miller's. Now there were lots of partials, what with it being a taxi. But, I'm sorry to say Mr. Miller, after all you've been through, none of them were of a known criminal who was seen in the area that night.'

'He's not like that anymore,' said Marie. 'He's suffering from amnesia. He doesn't remember anything, and he's a good man now. He's got the love of a good woman, you see.'

'Yes, I understand that, Mrs. Miller. But murder is murder. Now you said on the night that you saw nothing.' WPC Parker was talking to Marie. 'And yet it took place right outside your boarding house. But someone saw Mr. Miller leaving the boarding house the following morning.'

'That's right,' said Marie. 'He was with me. All night.'

'You told the investigating officer that you were alone. You said . . . ' WPC Parker opened up a small notepad. 'You said that you washed your hair, and then went to bed at around nine because you had a busy day at the bank and you were tired. You say you slept soundly and didn't hear a thing. Are you telling me now that you lied back then?'

'I wasn't married then. I mean on that night. Our landlady had strict rules about men visiting and about rooms having single occup . . . rooms being just for single people. And after we married, I still had to live there for a while. So yes, I lied.'

'So can I hazard a guess that you weren't sleeping as soundly as you first said?' WPC Parker raised an eyebrow, and looked from Marie to him. There was something in her eyes that intrigued him. Perhaps she felt it too. The distance between him and his wife. The sense that they were strangers rather than lovers.

'I'm afraid I don't remember,' he said, trying to bring up the memory of a night in Marie's arms. It eluded him.

'Look,' said Marie. 'Whatever he was then, he's not that person anymore. He's a good man now.'

'But he's still a suspect. I'm sorry, Mrs. Miller. Mr. Miller. I don't think amnesia is a valid defence against murder.'

'It wasn't him,' said Marie, her eyes behind

her spectacles filling with tears. 'It was Jack.'

'Jack?'

'Yes, I can't remember his second name, but he came to see Lizzie.'

'Jack Daventry?' he said, looking at Marie. Her eyes widened and she nodded. He wondered why she had lied about not knowing the man's second name. She had mentioned it to him at the hospital.

'Lizzie Alsop was training to be a doctor.'

The name meant something to him. Something vague and shadowy, but like Jack Daventry, it was a name that sparked something in his mind. 'I don't know why,' Marie continued, 'she was only a working-class girl, like me. But she was one of those with ideas above her station. We were sort of friends. I thought she was a bit stuck-up, myself. But anyway, I heard something on the landing, and went out. He was there. Jack Daventry. And he was saying to Lizzie, 'You've got to help me. I've stabbed him.' Then they went downstairs and I went back into my room, not wanting to get caught up in any funny business. Brian said to me, 'Keep out of it, love', so I did. He understood that I had a reputation to consider.'

'I've heard that story before,' he said. He tried to remember Marie's bedsit, and the conversation they had no doubt had, but his mind went blank again.

'There, so it must be true,' said Marie.

'I wonder if I could take your fingerprints, Mr. Miller,' said WPC Parker. She was giving him a strange look. 'I'd like to compare it with the partial.'

'Yes, of course. If I do have anything to do with this, I'd like to know,' he said.

'I wish you'd told the truth at the time, Mrs. Miller,' said WPC Parker. 'It would have saved us . . . me . . . a lot of anguish. Perhaps you could see me out after I've taken your fingerprints, Mr. Miller. I'd like to speak to you in private.'

'Anything you say to my husband, you can say to me,' said Marie.

'Nevertheless, I'd rather talk to him alone.' Her tone said that WPC Parker was not to be argued with.

He agreed, and saw her to the door, leaving Marie sitting in the armchair, still pulling skin from around her fingernails. He went all the way out to her car with the policewoman, and was acutely aware of Marie watching from behind the net curtains.

'Mr. Miller, I hope you don't mind me saying this but you're not what I expected from reading your file.'

'War changes a man. Or perhaps amnesia does.'

375

'For your sake Mr. Miller, I hope you never remember who you were.'

'I was pretty bad then?'

She nodded. 'Yes. You were into some very dark stuff.'

'Including, you think, killing your father?'

He saw a flicker of pain in her eyes. He liked this woman, and would have enjoyed getting to know her under different circumstances. 'If your wife is telling the truth, then this Jack Daventry had something to do with it.'

'And if she's lying?'

'Think yourself lucky that a woman cannot testify against her husband in court. The fact of you being in the boarding house at the time my father died, and that your partial fingerprint was on the taxi door, does not prove that you were involved in his death.'

'But from what you say, I probably was. If that's the case, it's no use me telling you how sorry I am. Nevertheless, I am. Deeply sorry. I hope that if I do ever remember, I'm still able to feel that sorrow.'

She looked at him for a long time, before saying, 'I'm going to get these fingerprints checked and then track down this Jack Daventry. If you do remember anything, let me know.'

He stood waving goodbye to her as she

drove away, feeling that somehow she was a link to him recovering his memory. There had been something about Marie's story that felt familiar to him, but there was also something else. Some niggle in his mind about the story.

Eventually he turned around and went back to the house. Marie was in the sitting-room, rubbing furiously at the coffee table. 'She got ink on it,' she said. 'You should have refused to do it. I think you can, you know.'

He looked at the coffee table but could not see any ink. He suspected Marie was wiping away the memory of the dark-skinned policewoman. 'Marie, if I killed her father, I want to know.'

'And be hanged for it? Of course you don't think of me, left alone with no money and with no one to take care of me.'

'What are you afraid of, Marie? If you don't think I did it, and your alibi is valid, what does it matter if they have my fingerprints?'

'Because you didn't do it! I know you didn't. You were different then, so even if you were involved, it's not fair that you should be arrested for it now. And anyway, why does she need your fingerprints if she knows you were there? Aren't the ones they've got good enough?'

'They need to double-check, I suppose.'

The next few hours were difficult. Marie walked around in a state of controlled fury, cleaning all the things she had cleaned that morning. He was glad when bedtime finally limped around. At least for eight hours he could escape.

He lay awake, as he always did in the dark, enjoying the solitude. He could hear her breathing next to him, on her side of the bed, and knew she was awake too. But she never expected him to talk to her in bed, and seemed to prefer it if he did not, so he had a reprieve from all the tension and fussiness.

So it came as quite a shock to him when she did speak. 'You want to go away, don't you?' she whined. 'You'd prefer to be executed rather than stay with me.'

'Don't be ridiculous.'

'You should be in love with me by now. Why aren't you? I'm your wife.'

How could he explain to her that her saying it did not make it so? He had to feel she was his wife. Unfortunately, as kind as she tried to be in her less fussy moments, he could not for the life of him work out why he had married her. There was no sexual attraction — on either side, as far as he could tell — and no tenderness. It was understandable, he thought, in his case. He could not remember. Her distant behaviour was a mystery to him. He put it down to her natural reserve. But there must have been a time, he thought, when they were in love. When they kissed. When they made love. When they called each other silly names. He had once dated one of the girls in the women's corps and . . .

The thought stopped him dead. It was a memory! A vague one, but a memory all the same. And a feeling that even if that girl had not been the love of his life, nor he hers, there had been an understanding, a connection, an affection. When had that been? As always when he remembered something, the more he tried to grasp at it, the faster it slipped away from him.

He sat up in bed. One thing he did remember was that Marie told him they married before he enlisted. So if he did see a girl in the women's corps, then he must have been having an illicit affair with her. Maybe Marie had found out. That would explain the distance. How to broach the subject though? If she did not know, then he might be storing more trouble for himself.

It was all part, he thought, of the man he used to be. An adulterer, a criminal, and at the very worst, a murderer.

'What's wrong, Brian? Why are you sitting up?'

'I just remembered something.'

She sat up too, and in a voice filled with panic, asked, 'What? What did you remember? Tell me.'

31

Jack saw Lizzie enter Stony Newton hospital as he was leaving. She passed him by in a flash of efficiency, dressed in a brown skirt suit. Even its drab colour could not hide her loveliness. Whether she saw him, he did not know. He waited in the grounds, keeping his eye on the main door and Lizzie's car, whilst he chain-smoked. She was in the hospital for an hour and he had been just about to give up and go home when she finally came out.

'Lizzie . . . ' He walked up to her in the rolling gait he hated so much. At first it seemed she would get in her car and ignore him, but she waited, with her hand resting on the open driver's door.

'Jack.'

'I saw you go in and thought I'd wait.'

'Did you come about your leg?'

'Hmm, they still haven't found it, but they think it might be in France somewhere.' It was a lame joke, but he felt it suited his own lameness. He stopped to wonder why he was even talking to her. No doubt she was still with her handsome married consultant.

'How . . . erm . . . how are you? Doing

okay?' The question was brisk, professional.

'Yes, not bad. It's better since I've had the second op. The Germans made a bit of a mess of it. I suppose it didn't matter to them if I died or not.'

'So you've had another amputation?' Again her interest sounded professional rather than caring.

He nodded. 'They took it off above the knee over a year ago.'

'You're doing well on the prosthetic.'

'Yes, I bet you hardly noticed the way I walked.'

'You're not the only one around here.'

'Is that a comment on my self-pity?'

'No.' Lizzie sighed. 'It's meant to put you at ease, and let you know you're not as noticeable as you think.'

'Thanks for that. It's true that I've become invisible. At least with women.'

'Poor you.' Her mouth turned up at the corners. 'At least you're alive.'

'Yes, let's be thankful for small mercies,' he said, darkly.

'Did you want anything, Jack?'

'Just to say hello to an old friend. I'm living in Stony Newton now, you know. Working at Harcourt's. I hear you're a GP in the new health service.'

'That's right. I've just been to see one of

my patients. She's due to give birth.'

'Are you happy?'

'That's a strange question.' She frowned.

'Is it? I'd just like you to be happy, Lizzie. You know I did a lot of bad things before the war, and I hurt people. It was only when I was in the camp with my cousin, Bobby, that I realised the importance of family.'

'We're not family.'

'No, I know, but . . . well, we're friends, and I let you down, like I've let others down. So I'd like you to be happy. I daresay you're married to some handsome doctor.'

'I'm not married to anyone.' Her eyebrow arched. 'This new contrite Jack Daventry is a wonder to behold. What are you after?'

'I'm not after anything, Lizzie. I just wanted to apologise and wish you well.' He turned to leave her.

'Jack.'

'What?'

'You've nothing to apologise for. We've all done things we regret.'

'I don't believe that of you.'

She laughed briefly, but it was humourless. 'You'd be surprised. Jack . . . '

'What?'

'I hope you're happy too. Or I hope you will be one day, when you've come to terms with losing your leg.'

He nodded and pursed his lips. 'Yeah, well at the moment that looks like being a cold day in hell.'

'There are people you can talk to, you know. Psychologists.'

'Been there, done that. I think the best thing I can do is get on with my life and try not to mess anyone else's up. See you, Lizzie.'

He walked away from her feeling happier than he had for a while. In reality he wanted to stay with her, to ask her out. But he felt he would be pushing his luck. He had caused Lizzie Alsop enough problems. The best thing he could do was not bother her anymore. He did not deserve a girl like her.

'Jack!' she called, when he was about twenty yards away. He turned back. 'Have you got a lift home?'

'I was going to get a taxi.'

'Come on, I'm going that way. I'll give you a lift.'

'You already have,' he said, smiling. Nevertheless, he made his way back to her.

* * *

'Thank you for seeing us, Doctor Alsop,' said Esther. They sat in Lizzie's small consultation room at the new health centre. 'Ricky and I. I mean, Doctor Harcourt and I, have been

. . . Oh it's hard to explain but, you see, I got this idea that Mister Latimer was killing off patients. I mean, it seemed stupid even to me. But the thing is we've found out a lot in the last few weeks.'

Lizzie Alsop looked at her watch. 'Is this going to take long?' Despite her apparent ennui, Esther could see that Doctor Alsop had become watchful. 'I do have patients to see.'

'Yes, sorry. Ricky says I always go the long way around things. The thing is that there are some questions over the deaths of some of Mister Latimer's patients. There's a woman in Brighton who says she was talked into saying that she had mistakenly given her mother an overdose of morphine, when she knows it was Mister Latimer.'

'Knows or suspects?' said Lizzie.

'What do you mean?'

'You see, I can imagine the poor girl must have been overwrought, and full of guilt when she made the mistake. It's perhaps natural that some twenty years after the event, she's trying to convince herself it wasn't her fault.'

'How do you know it was about twenty years ago?' asked Ricky.

'What?'

'We haven't said that. I just wondered how you knew.'

'Well, of course, Mister Latimer and I worked together for a long time. He told me about his cases. That one in particular, as it was such a dreadful thing to happen to that poor girl. And her mother, of course.'

'And what about my grandfather?' asked Ricky. 'Frank Wilson. Do you remember that case?'

'Of course, I knew Mr. Wilson well, having grown up in Stony End. And your mother. How is she, by the way?'

'She's well. You signed Granddad Wilson's death certificate, didn't you?'

'That's right.'

'Myocardial infarction.

'Yes. I'm sure I don't have to tell you that if a patient has a stroke, it can often be followed by an even bigger stroke.'

'Yes, I know that. But his medical records for that day show an improvement. His BP was close to normal. He had woken in the evening and taken on liquids.'

'But he was far from being out of the danger zone. Look, Ricky, I'm really sorry about your granddad, but he was an obvious candidate for a stroke or a heart attack. It was only a matter of time.'

'You had an affair with Mister Latimer, didn't you?' said Esther. Ricky grimaced at her.

'I don't see that's anyone's business but mine,' said Lizzie.

'I think it's important if he got you to lie for him.'

'That is quite enough, Esther Linney,' said Lizzie, her temper flaring. 'Just remember who you're talking to here. I am a General Practitioner with a good reputation. I won't risk that reputation because you've decided Mister Latimer is the bogeyman. And might I remind you, the man is now dead. What good can it do to upset the families of deceased patients by having them question whether their loved ones were murdered?'

'You don't think people have the right to know the truth?'

'Not if the truth won't do them any good. And what about the medical staff that Latimer has worked with? If you're right and he has persuaded people to lie for him, or even if he hasn't, do you think it fair to ruin the reputations of the innocent for a guilty man who will never have to face justice?'

'You know as well as I do,' said Ricky, 'that we have a sacred trust. We are devoted to saving lives, not taking them. Even if someone is close to death's door, we do not hurry it along.'

'I've heard that somewhere before,' said Esther, her lips curling slightly.

'And,' said Ricky, warming to his theme, 'that trust is placed, by the public, in all medical staff. For God's sake, Lizzie, if we don't police each other, and we keep secrets from patients, who the hell do we answer to?'

'What do you intend to do?' asked Lizzie.

'I . . . we . . . ' Ricky gestured to Esther, 'intend to present our findings to the General Medical Council. It will be in their hands then.'

Lizzie smiled, sadly. 'They won't do anything. Believe me, I tried.'

'Oh . . . ' Esther nodded, finally beginning to understand.

'To really understand, you'd have to have known Latimer,' said Lizzie. 'The force of his personality. I was terrified of him, we all were. But we also admired him. He had it in him to command great love and respect. It took me a long time to realise that he was a master manipulator. I tried to get your mum to ask questions about your grandfather's death, Ricky. I was a coward, I admit it. I was ready to be pushed. I just didn't have it in me to jump. But I'm a good doctor, despite one mistake, and we need good doctors, especially now. I'll let you two decide what to do. Now, I'm sorry, but I really do have to get on.'

32

Jack reached across Lizzie and picked up the packet of cigarettes from the bedside table. She lay on her belly, smiling.

'Okay?' he said, stroking her naked spine as he brought the cigarettes across the bed.

'Better than okay. You don't do too badly for a one-legged man.'

'Thanks.' He lit two cigarettes and passed one to her.

'Hmm, just like in the films,' she said. She rolled over onto her back and the sight of her bare breasts almost drove him crazy again.

'Am I forgiven now?'

'For what?'

'For what happened before the war.'

'I'd have thought that was pretty obvious.'

'Oh, I don't know. You might use me then throw me away.'

'You should be so lucky, Jack Daventry. I've no intentions of letting you go. Not after tonight. Unless . . . ' Her voice became a little less certain. It touched him to hear it. She was the epitome of efficiency in her professional life. Calm, cool and collected. It was comforting to know that beneath that lay a woman who could still be vulnerable.

'Unless you think I'm going to dump you. No chance.' He leaned over and kissed her lips, trailing the kisses down her throat and to her nipple. 'God, I want you so much.' He stubbed his cigarette out and started to kiss and caress her again, slipping his fingers between her thighs.

'Jack, stop it for a moment.'

'You don't want this?' He stopped immediately, despite sounding disappointed.

'More than anything. But I don't want there to be any secrets between us. I want to tell you something. About why I've forgiven you. Only I'm afraid you won't forgive me so easily. People don't, you see. They're always more forgiving of their own mistakes than other people's.'

'If it's about your affair with Latimer, I know. You told me, remember. Darling, I don't care that you had an affair with a married man. I slept with a married woman. So we're even.'

'More than you think,' said Lizzie. She told him then about Frank Wilson and her part in hiding his cause of death. 'If Esther and Ricky decide to go to the authorities, I'll be struck off. But I can live with that if I know that you can forgive me for it.'

'You only did for Latimer what you did for

me,' Jack said. She had started to cry, so he held her in his arms. 'I suppose you loved him.'

'No, it wasn't that. Not by then. I was afraid of him. He had more power than me. But . . . well when you came to me for help, I hadn't taken the oath. I was only just starting out. By the time Frank Wilson died, I had. It was my duty to ensure he had the proper care. I let him down. I let myself down. I keep thinking that one day it's going to come crashing down around me, just as you do with the taxi driver's death. That's why I was more able to forgive you. Because I made the same mistake, and when I did I understood how much pressure you must have been under that night. You were a bad boy back then, but you weren't evil. However much you tell yourself you were. And besides all that, if we're going to work as a couple, there can be no secrets. We have to lay everything out on the table, and deal with it.'

Jack nodded, feeling her hair tickle his chin as he did so. 'I was going to kill him, you know?'

'What? The taxi driver?'

'No, Miller. He was in the prisoner of war camp with me. So was my cousin Bobby. You remember Bobby?'

'Of course. I practically grew up with your cousins.'

'It was Bobby who taught me I couldn't go on the way I was. I was a swine to him and Ricky when we were children. Yet despite that, he was willing to risk everything to get me out of that camp. Even his own life. I was family you see, and family matters to Bobby. It took him to show me that it mattered to me too. I've always felt . . . I don't know . . . as if I didn't belong in the Harcourts. It wasn't that they made me feel that way. God knows my Uncle Charles tried with me, and I think Aunt Rebecca would have if I hadn't been such an evil little swine to her. But there's something not right. Or at least there was until Bobby was willing to risk his life for me. I wish I'd known him better. He was a strange one, Bobby. Some people thought he was stupid and a bit slow, because he was so quiet. But he was smart. He just knew when to talk and when to listen.' Jack laughed awkwardly. 'Listen to me, waxing lyrical about my cousin. You wouldn't have thought it possible if you'd known how gladly I destroyed the twins' train set.'

'Stop punishing yourself for the things you did as a child. Did I tell you that I once stole a bar of chocolate? Dad went mental.'

'You stole a bar of chocolate. Oh my God,

Lizzie. How could you? Of all the things a person could have done. I'm so shocked. I can't believe I've just made love to a woman who stole a bar of chocolate.'

She giggled, and playfully slapped him. 'You are still a swine.' She stretched up and kissed him. 'But you're my swine and I love you. Is that alright? Am I allowed to love you?'

'Well, I have so many other offers.'

She made a playful attempt at getting up in a huff, but he pulled her back down to him. 'I love you, Lizzie Alsop. And don't you ever forget it.'

★　★　★

'Mum!' Lizzie entered through the back door, pulling Jack after her. 'Mum!'

'I'm up here.'

They heard Maggie coming down the stairs, and stood holding hands, waiting for her to reach the living-room. Jack whispered something in her ear, and Lizzie replied with a kiss. 'She won't bite,' said Lizzie.

Then she turned her head and saw her mother looking at them. Maggie's face was filled with horror. 'What's going on?' she snapped.

'Mum, I want to tell you something.' Lizzie

laughed, elated. 'Me and Jack are getting married.'

'No!' Maggie screamed, bringing her hands up to her face. 'Have you slept together? Tell me you haven't slept together.'

'I'm not pregnant, if that's what you think,' said Lizzie, the smile disappearing from her face. 'I'm far too sensible for that.'

'Well, let's be thankful for small mercies,' said Maggie. 'You can't marry him, you can't.'

'I assure you, Mrs. Alsop, my prospects are very good. I'm a director of Harcourt's and . . . '

'That's got nothing to do with it. Have you slept with him, Lizzie? I demand you tell me now.'

'And I say it's none of your business, mum.'

'Yes it is. For God's sake, you little idiot. He's your brother.'

'What?' Lizzie thought her legs were going to collapse under her. Jack went to catch her but she jerked away from him. What had they done?

'Your father told me,' said Maggie. 'He said that he and Rebecca had a baby boy and left him on the Priory steps. Jack was that baby.'

'How long have you known all this?' asked Lizzie. 'And how do you know Jack is the baby?'

'I've known since before you were born. I didn't realise till I saw Jack later that he was Rebecca's son.' It was strange how Maggie did not refer to Jack as Jed's son. 'She lied to everyone. Even her husband.'

'So my Uncle Charles knows all this,' said Jack.

That was when Maggie hesitated. 'Probably.'

'So why hasn't he said anything?'

'Because he wanted to protect your mother and Rebecca, of course.'

'So why haven't you said anything till now?' asked Lizzie. 'Let's face it, mum, keeping secrets is not your forte. Especially one like this. You'd have done anything to turn me against dad.'

'I didn't want to hurt you, sweetheart.'

Lizzie looked at her mother, and bit her lip. 'Don't you think this has hurt me even more? Finding out the man I want to marry is my half-brother?'

At that point, Jed came in. 'Hello, Lizzie, love. I didn't realise you were home. What's going on here?'

'Mum has just told me and Jack the truth. About us being brother and sister.'

Jed's face turned ashen. 'That's not true,' he said.

'Oh yes, it is,' said Maggie. 'You told me

yourself. He's Rebecca's brat.'

'And yours, dad,' said Lizzie.

'He always was an idiot where she was concerned,' said Maggie.

'But he was never found . . . I mean . . . ' Jed stared at Jack. 'Oh God. What a mess. Whatever Maggie has told you, you're not my son, Jack.'

'Yes, he is, Jed! You're just saying that to make them feel better. But they're planning to get married. Brother and sister. Are you going to stand by and let that happen? It's unnatural. Their children will be deformed. You've got to tell the truth.'

'We'll go to Rebecca and ask her,' said Jed.

'No!' Maggie shrieked.

'Why not, mum?' Lizzie folded her arms.

'Because you can't. Let sleeping dogs lie, that's what I say.'

'I'll ask again,' said Jack. 'Does Uncle Charles know about this?' A flash of something in Maggie's eyes hinted at the truth.

'You've been blackmailing him,' said Jed. He sat down in a chair and sighed, before looking around the room. 'That's how we got this house, and you put Lizzie through school. And now you're afraid that if it all comes out, you'll lose your cash cow.'

'I resent that accusation,' said Maggie. The tips of her ears had turned pink.

'Then let's go and see Rebecca to find out the truth, shall we?'

'There's no need to involve anyone else. All that has to happen is that Lizzie and Jack stop seeing each other.'

'Maggie, you heartless cow.' Jed looked at his wife with more hatred in his eyes than Lizzie had ever seen. She had always sensed her parents were not in love, and that on some level they didn't even like each other very much. But she had never seen it so clearly or realised how deep the loathing ran. 'They're two kids in love. Let them find out the truth, so they can be happy.'

Maggie refused to go, but five minutes after Jed, Lizzie and Jack left the house, en route to Rebecca's flat, they saw her following them. When they got to the block of flats, a neighbour informed them that Rebecca had gone to the Priory to do some paperwork, so they turned back down the hill, passing Maggie as they did so, but not offering to walk with her. She waited a few moments then followed on. It occurred to Lizzie to feel sorry for her mother, but she had her own concerns to deal with. Her mother would have to come later.

'Do you think it's true, dad?' asked Lizzie in a low voice. 'About mum blackmailing Mr. Harcourt.'

'I'm afraid so. I've had my suspicions. I know . . . ' Jed stopped.

'What?'

'They spend a lot of time together.' He did not elaborate. 'But he doesn't like your mother. She's stolen off the company so many times, and the Harcourts know it, but she's never been sacked. So I guessed she had something over him. Are you alright, Jack?'

Jack took a deep breath. 'Not really. I was only telling Lizzie recently that I've always felt like an outsider in the Harcourt family. But if I'm Rebecca's, I shouldn't feel that way.'

'She won't know,' said Jack. 'You see, we thought . . . well I don't know what we thought. We were kids at the time, and when we didn't get news of you, we couldn't ask. We were terrified of getting into trouble. Then I think we tried to put it out of our minds. But she still thinks of you, you know. She was only talking about you the other day. About how she wished things had been different.'

'So do you know the truth? If you're not my father, who is?'

'I don't know that much. I have my suspicions.'

'But Rebecca is definitely my mother.'

'I think you'd be best letting her tell you.

You see, it's not really my story to tell and I might get things wrong. It's best if you hear it from her.' Jed stopped and turned to Jack. 'Whatever happens, try not to judge her too harshly, Jack. She's not a bad person. She's just a victim of circumstances.'

'She's lied to my Uncle Charles . . . ' Jack paused. 'I keep forgetting, he's not my uncle Charles. He'd be my stepfather, I suppose.'

'Don't make up your mind about anything, until you've heard what she has to say.'

When they reached the Priory, with Maggie following on behind them, Ricky and Esther were visiting, talking something over with Charles in the drawing-room. Rebecca, they were told, was in the dining-room, signing some papers.

'You'd better come through,' Jack told Charles, Esther and Ricky. 'You'll want to hear this.'

Rebecca looked up from her paperwork when the posse of people arrived. 'What's happened?'

Jack asked her outright. 'Is it true you're my mother?'

'I'm sorry, I don't . . . '

'Jack is the baby we left on the doorstep,' said Jed. 'He's little Charlie.'

She dropped her pen on the dining table with a clatter. 'But I thought . . . ' Her cheeks turned very pink, then very pale.

'Is it true that you're my mother?' Jack asked again.

'I don't understand,' said Rebecca. 'You weren't found. I wanted you to be found, but . . . little Charlie . . . ' Her eyes filled with tears, and she stood to reach out for him, but Jack was in no mood for an emotional reunion.

'I'm afraid I lied,' said Charles. 'When you asked me about foundling children on the doorstep. You see, Patty told me — which was obviously a lie — that she couldn't have any more children and that Jack was her only chance to save her marriage. So I helped her to get him to London.'

'You know?' said Rebecca, looking at her husband. 'About me leaving him there? You know?'

'Yes. Maggie told me. Then proceeded to blackmail me about it for years.'

'But why didn't you ask me?' said Rebecca, her voice overwrought with emotion. 'If you'd asked me, I'd have told you the truth. Is this why you've turned away from me? Because you believe I abandoned my baby?'

'You've just admitted yourself that you left him on the doorstep, Rebecca. You surely don't expect me to believe you dumped someone else's child there. Why on Earth would you?'

'I need to think' said Rebecca, putting her hands to her head.

'What? Of more lies?' said Jack.

'No, no, Jack, not that. You deserve the truth, even if you won't like it very much. Sit down everyone. I'll tell you all about it.'

★　★　★

He noticed that Marie's hands were trembling as she poured Annette Parker's cup of tea. 'So,' she said, 'what you're saying is that my Brian couldn't have done it.'

'No, not quite,' said Annette. 'What I'm saying is that the fingerprints we have on file for Brian Miller don't match your husband's.'

'Perhaps you've got the wrong fingerprints on file,' he said. 'Or the files got mixed up. Or maybe it was a different Brian Miller.'

'No.' Annette shook her head. 'They're the right fingerprints. You say you lost your memory?'

'Yes.'

'We checked with the hospital and you're telling the truth about that.' She looked at Maria accusingly. 'Perhaps Mrs. Miller could explain to us why her husband's fingerprints have changed in the nine years since the war started.'

'He didn't do it,' said Marie, perching on

the edge of her chair. She cocked her head towards him. 'It was Brian who killed the taxi driver.'

'But I'm Brian,' he said. 'Aren't I?'

'When I told you about that night, I lied,' said Marie. She was talking to Annette, and refused to look at him at all. 'Brian was with me. He turned up just before Jack Daventry did, and he was hiding in my flat when Daventry turned up. He . . . Brian . . . said there'd been some trouble, and that he would be blamed for something he hadn't done. At the time I suppose I thought it was romantic, hiding a fugitive. When we heard Daventry's voice in the hall, Brian whispered to me to go out and see what was going on. I saw Daventry knocking on Lizzie's door, just like I told you. But I lied about what he said. He didn't tell her he'd killed the taxi driver. He said it was Brian. He begged her to help him. Said he didn't want the man to die. I went back into my bedsit and told Brian what I'd heard. He knew though. He was playing with his knife. I thought he was going to stab me. So when he started kissing me, I went along with it. I let him do anything he wanted to me, because I was so afraid of dying.'

'He raped you?'

'I don't know. I suppose so. But I didn't want to be that sort of girl, so when he'd finished doing . . . it . . . I asked him to marry me. To make it legal. He was against it at first. He laughed in my face. Said he'd never marry a plain cow like me. Until I told him that a woman couldn't give evidence against her husband. I suppose I blackmailed him. The idea was that we would get married, but not live together. I didn't want him near me ever again. I just wanted to be respectable. So we got married and he went off to war.'

'Then what happened?' he asked. He was trying hard to recapture that night. To try to think himself into the role of a man who would murder a taxi driver, then rape a frightened girl. All he knew was that he did not want to be that man.

'I got a letter after the war, saying that Brian had been found, but was in a coma. He was abroad at first, so I didn't see him. But I got money you see. From the army. Then they told me they'd brought him home and did I want to see him. I didn't really, but I didn't like to tell them. So I went to see him. Only . . . '

'What?'

'I was getting money, you see.'

'Yes, you've told me that,' he said.

'And they carried on paying me, so I thought, who was it hurting? You were in a coma, so you didn't know any different.'

'He's not Brian Miller,' said Annette. 'Is he?'

Marie shook her head. 'No, he isn't. I don't know who you are. I'm sorry.'

His first feeling was of immense relief. He was not a cold-blooded murderer and rapist. He also understood the strangeness he experienced in Marie's company. It had nothing to do with his amnesia. It was because they did not really belong together.

The relief was soon replaced by anger. She had known that, and let him go on thinking he was some criminal.

'What you've done is really serious,' said Annette to Marie. 'It's fraud.'

'Will I go to prison?'

'I don't know.'

'Brian?' Marie appealed to him.

'I'm not Brian,' he said. 'You said you weren't hurting anyone, but somewhere I've got a family, and they probably think I'm dead. For God's sake, Marie, I might even have a wife! Children! Did that never occur to you?'

'I'm sorry. I really am. If I could take it back I would. But it's not just about the money. Not anymore. You've been kinder to me than he ever was. I love you now.'

'I'd better go,' said Annette, standing up. 'I've got the answers I want. Chances are the real Brian Miller is dead, and it sounds to me as though Jack Daventry did his best to save my father, though I would like to speak to him about it one day. As for your fraud, Mrs. Miller, I'm sorry but I'm going to have to report it.' She picked up her handbag.

'I'll show you to the door,' he said.

When they reached the front door, he asked, 'Do you have an address for Daventry? The thing is, I do know that name, and if I know him, the chances are he knows me too.'

'Yes, of course. He's living at a place called the Priory in Stony Newton. Do you know it?'

He started to shake his head. 'No . . . yes. I mean, it sounds familiar.'

'I hope you find your answers. I would like to speak to him one day — to finish this story altogether — so if you do see him, point him in my direction.'

'I will. I'm very sorry about your father.'

'It's time I let him rest. And it's time I went home to my husband.' She smiled wryly. 'The funny thing is that the minute I saw you, I couldn't believe you were a killer. Call it a copper's instinct.'

'I don't know who or what I am yet,' he said, darkly.

'She does love you, you know.'

'She has even less idea who I am than I do.'

'Good luck Mr. . . . Good luck.'

Marie had not moved from her chair. She sat staring into space. 'I'll go to prison,' she said.

'Just offer to pay the money back.'

'How can I? I don't have all that money.'

'I'm sorry, Marie, but that really is your problem. Not mine.' He was about to turn away, but something deep within him — pity perhaps — stopped him. 'Tell them you were confused and because you'd hardly seen him, and nine years had passed, you made a mistake.'

'She knows the truth. The policewoman.'

'Somehow I don't think Annette Parker is your enemy. Besides, you didn't make a confession under caution. I'm not big on the law, but I don't think it would be admissible in court.'

'Will you be here when they come to arrest me?'

'You lied to me, Marie.'

'I know, and I'm sorry.'

'I could forgive you if not for the fact that you didn't give a moment's thought to who else might be looking for me. You just wanted the money.'

'At first, yes. I know, and I did wrong. But not when we'd been together a while. I love you.'

'If you loved me, you'd have told me the truth and let me find my family. We, you and I, don't belong to each other. That's something I've felt all along. I need to find out where I do belong and I can't do that with you pulling me back.'

'Don't I mean anything to you?'

'How can I answer that when I don't even know who I am?'

33

They sat around the table in the Priory dining-room. Maggie leant back with her arms folded, and a satisfied look on her face. Rebecca suspected Maggie had waited a long time for this. Charles was at the far end of the table, his head bowed. Ricky and Esther looked toward Rebecca with concern in their eyes. It seemed to her that they were the only ones with any sympathy for her. Jack and Lizzie sat on opposite sides of the table, hardly daring to look at each other. Jed stood near the window, avoiding Rebecca's glances.

'The most important thing you need to know,' said Rebecca, speaking to Jack and Lizzie, 'is that you're not brother and sister. Jed lied.' She cast him an angry glance. 'And he's not the only one.' Her angriest glare was for Charles, who sat with his head still bowed. 'And yes, I've probably lied too, but not in the way you think I have, and not for the reasons you think. That night, when I left Jack on the doorstep here, was one of the most painful nights of my life. So painful that I've spent years putting it out of my mind.' She sighed. 'I'm getting ahead of myself. I need to go back to the beginning.'

*　*　*

When Becky's mother first met Frank Wilson, he seemed the answer to a single mother's prayers. He was young and good-looking. And at first, he adored them both, spoiling them with treats and laughter. But Myra was something of a flirt. She never meant anything by it. At least not at first. Nevertheless, Frank, young and unsure of himself, increasingly became more possessive of them. Then he started hitting Myra, until she learned not to cross him.

Their lives, when he was at home, were dark and miserable. But not always. In between his fits of anger, he would be kind and caring, but more often than not he would sit in the rocking chair near the fire, mulling over things Myra had said, or what she had failed to do, such as keep the house clean. It did not help that she fell into a depression from which it was impossible for her to recover under the circumstances in which she lived with Frank.

Becky, though young, soon learned to protect her mother, by helping around the house, keeping it clean for when Frank returned home from the pit. She got to know when he was due home. Not by the time on the clock, but by the knot that constricted her stomach.

Then something wonderful happened. At least for Myra and Becky. The war started, and Frank decided he would go and be a hero. For three years, they lived without the shadow of his arrival home, and on the few occasions he did come home on leave, he was there such a short time, they could cope with it.

It was whilst Frank was away in the war that Sam started calling around. He was sixteen years old, and not what anyone would call handsome, but he paid attention to Myra, and was kind to her. Something she had not known for some time.

They hid the truth of their relationship from Becky for a long time. Even when her mother started putting on weight, Becky had no idea. Nor did she realise when she found her sobbing mother lying in a boiling hot bath with an empty bottle of gin and a knitting needle. She only learned on the night Frank returned home from the hospital, having been injured. As bad luck would have it that was also the night Myra went into labour.

Myra tried, in between contractions, to convince Frank it was his, but he was not that stupid. He had been home on leave ten months earlier, and, he said, had counted the days.

He did nothing at first, other than sit in the rocking chair, grinding his teeth, whilst Becky followed her mother's instructions. He refused to call a doctor. 'She's not bringing shame on me,' he muttered to Becky, when she suggested it.

It was only when Jack was born that Frank jumped into action. As soon as the baby uttered his first weak cry, Frank dashed up the stairs, and said under his voice, so the neighbours would not hear, 'I'm going to smother the little bastard.'

Jack, wrapped in Harcourt's bandages, lay next to Myra, whimpering. Frank picked up a pillow and pressed it down on the baby's head, whilst Myra and Becky screamed in terror. Becky, though small, managed to pull Frank off. She snatched up the baby and ran off into the night with him. She had no idea where she was going. All she knew was that she had to stop Frank killing the baby.

'I met Jed on the way,' said Rebecca, swallowing back the sobs that threatened to engulf her. 'He said he'd help me. We left the baby — Jack — on the steps of the Priory. Then,' she said, looking at Charles accusingly, 'we never heard anything else. I tried to find out, but I was afraid. I didn't know if I'd broken the law, or whether my mother would get into trouble. And I was so afraid of what Frank would do to her if the truth got out.' A tear rolled down her cheek. 'Frank never even asked what I'd done with the baby. As soon as it wasn't his problem anymore, he thought we could all get back to normal. But she couldn't. Every day she would ask me 'Have you heard anything yet?' and every day I had to tell her no. In the end she couldn't live with the not knowing.' She looked at Charles. 'And I know what we did was wrong, but I was fourteen years old and completely out of my depth. It was the only way I could think of to save his life, and even then it seemed I'd failed.'

Jed turned from the window. 'I'm sorry I lied.' He spoke to Rebecca and Charles rather than Maggie. 'She was taunting me about not giving her a baby and I just said the first thing that came into my head. My only excuse is that I was young and stupid.' He looked at Maggie. 'I hope you're bloody satisfied!'

Maggie glared back at him. 'It's not my fault you lied to me!'

'No, but it's your fault you've been blackmailing Charles all these years.'

'Is that true?' asked Lizzie.

Maggie had the grace to look ashamed. 'I

412

only wanted the best for you, darling. And anyway, you don't know what it's like, being married to a man who's in love with someone else. She's been there, all our lives, like a shadow over us.'

'That's not an excuse,' said Lizzie. 'Not for what you've done. I . . . Rebecca, Charles. I'm so sorry.' She got up and left the room.

Jack seemed about to follow her, but he waited for a moment. 'You're my sister?'

Rebecca nodded. 'Yes, but I didn't know that. I'm sorry, Jack.'

'That's my fault. And your mother's,' said Charles. 'I only paid Maggie because I was trying to protect both of them.'

'You could have asked me,' said Rebecca. She was tempted to ask if he did it to protect himself and the Harcourt name, but the presence of others stopped her. There was so much unsaid between them.

'Yes. I know. I should have.'

Jack spoke again. 'You said my father's name was Sam. What else can you tell me about him? I'd like to find him.'

'He moved to London to be a taxi driver,' said Rebecca. 'His full name is Sam, or Samuel, Jenkins.'

'What?' Jack visibly paled, and sat back in his chair.

'Sam Jenkins. He had a sister, though

413

rumour has it she was his mother really. Her name was Hilda but she died a while ago.'

'Sam Jenkins.' Jack croaked the name out. 'Dear God.' He got up from the table and followed Lizzie out.

Jed moved from the window. 'I'd better go. Come on, Maggie, we've taken up enough of their time.'

For a change, Maggie meekly followed him out. Esther and Ricky also stood up. Esther walked over to Rebecca and reached down and kissed her. 'We love you,' she whispered.

Ricky winked at Rebecca. 'We'll talk later, mum. But Esther is right. We love you.'

As they left, Esther gave Charles a shy smile and Ricky patted him on the shoulder. They were doing their best not to take sides, and it broke Rebecca's heart to see them in such a quandary.

★ ★ ★

Maggie all but chased Jed down the path to the Priory gates.

'You needn't think you're divorcing me, Jed Alsop,' she said, catching up with him and grabbing his arm. 'If you think I'm going to let you go to her now . . . '

'You fool, Maggie,' he sneered. 'She doesn't want me. She loves Charles. She always has

414

and for as long as I can remember.' He snatched his arm away and limped out of the gates, turning onto Factory Road with no idea where he was going.

'All this is your fault. You lied to me.' Maggie walked along side him.

'And that excuses you breaking up Rebecca's marriage? That excuses you blackmailing Charles all these years? What I said was wrong, I admit that, but you were goading me. Even so, even if what I'd said was the truth, it was still no excuse for what you've done. Our daughter has to deal with the knowledge that her education was paid for by your extortion.'

'And how do you think you got to be made manager, Jed? How do you think we got the house we live in?'

He stopped and stared at her, as the horrible truth dawned on him. 'And you think I should be what? Grateful?'

'Yes.'

Jed shook his head. 'I'm not, because I know I'm a good manager. I know that even if you did blackmail Charles Harcourt into giving me the post, I've earned it since. The same with our Lizzie, and I'll tell her that when I next see her. You might have found a way to pay for her education, but she got her medical degree by her own efforts. And you know what, Maggie? Whether you believe it or not, we'd have both made it without your intervention.'

'I know that. You're smart and so is she. I love you, Jed. I've always loved you, even when I knew you loved Rebecca. Don't leave me. You can't leave me.' Her voice became hysterical.

'Did you love me whilst you were sleeping with Charles Harcourt? What? You thought I didn't know about that?'

'He made me do it. He said that if I didn't, he'd tell you he was blackmailing me.'

Jed threw back his head and laughed. 'So he blackmailed you over you blackmailing him? Your lies don't get any better, Maggie.'

'I won't let you leave me. I'll tell everyone about how you got your post. I'll tell them you made me sleep with Charles.'

'Okay.' Jed started walking again. He called over his shoulder, 'When they ask me, I'll tell them the truth. That's if one of the other six people in that dining-room don't tell everyone first.'

'Jed, don't go. Jed!' Maggie screamed after him. She followed him all the way back to the top of the hill, crying, 'You won't get rid of me, Jed. You won't.'

★ ★ ★

'Do you still want to speak to me, even though my mother is a blackmailer?' asked Lizzie, trying to make a joke of it. She blew her nose into her hanky, and then noticed Jack's stricken face. He had found her in the copse behind the Priory. 'What? What is it? What did I miss?'

'Sam Jenkins was my father.'

'What? No. How?'

'He told us he was from Stony Newton.' Jack sat down in the grass. 'Before Brian stabbed him. He told us he was from around here. He even told me he knew Aunt . . . Oh I've forgotten. She's not my aunty is she? She's my sister. He told me he knew Rebecca. She's just confirmed his name. I killed my own father, Lizzie.'

'No, no you didn't. It was Brian Miller who killed him.'

'Yeah, but if I hadn't been there, doing that deal, it might not have happened. He seemed a nice bloke and now I'll never know him.'

'We have to put this behind us, Jack.' Lizzie took his hand and squeezed it. 'All the lies, all the secrets. If we're to survive, we have to let it all go. We are starting from the truth. Aren't we?'

'Yes.' Jack nodded dumbly, wondering if he could ever let it go. 'Yes, even though that truth is so painful.'

'But at least we won't be like Rebecca and Charles in thirty years' time, having our worlds torn apart by other peoples' secrets.'

'He was my father, Lizzie.' Jack's eyes filled with tears. She pulled him into her arms.

'I know, darling. I know, but you tried to save him. That has to count for something.'

Jack pulled back a bit and wiped his eyes on his sleeve. 'I'm being selfish again. You've got enough to contend with, what with your mother and the Latimer thing.'

'There's not much I can do to change my mother, but it's time I told the truth about Latimer. Esther is right. The families deserve to know the truth.'

'Will you be struck off?'

'Who knows? Maybe I can convince them I thought it was a genuine mistake on his part. But obviously falsifying a death certificate is pretty serious.'

Jack kissed her long and hard. 'I'll be holding your hand every step of the way. I promise.'

★ ★ ★

'I feel sorry for them both,' said Esther. She and Ricky were in the flat above the garage. Ricky had made coffee. 'Poor Aunt Rebecca, living with that. And Uncle Charles, torn

418

between loyalty to his sister. And loyalty to your mum, I think.'

Ricky took a deep, calming breath. 'Who knows what any of us would do in that situation?'

'Do you think they'll get back together?'

'I don't know. I hope so. They're not right apart. Everyone can see that. But I wonder if too much water has gone under the bridge.'

'All that time, wasted on a misunderstanding. I'd hate for that to happen with someone I loved.' She gazed across at Ricky. 'Ricky . . . '

'Hmm.' He took a sip of his coffee.

'I've been thinking about what Lizzie said. About Latimer being dead. I think she's right, you know. If we take this to the authorities, all it will do is cause anguish for the families.'

'I thought you were devoted to the truth. If today has taught us anything, it's what happens when the truth is buried.'

'I agree, but not when the person who's really responsible isn't around to take the flak. Just like Frank Wilson, trying to smother Jack as a baby, Latimer has escaped from it all. It will be Lizzie who gets it. She may be struck off. Then there are the others he's duped into covering his tracks.'

'But if we don't reveal the truth, what's to stop other doctors having the same power trip? I know what you mean about Lizzie. She's a good doctor and a good person who made a mistake in trusting him. But doctors also have a duty to save lives, not take them, Esther. If you don't want to go any further, I'll respect your decision. I'll tell my bosses that the results of our investigation were inconclusive.'

'I need to think about it for a while. It would help if I wasn't so churned up about other things.'

'What other things?'

'You've got this idea that I'm still in love with Bobby.'

'Aren't you?'

Esther shook her head. 'I had a huge crush on Bobby when I was younger. I think it was almost masochistic, because whilst everyone else in the family loved me and accepted me, he never did. But I don't have feelings for him anymore. I haven't since long before he died. Only you thought I did, and at first I didn't want to hurt you by not seeming to care about him. I keep remembering what I said that day, and it churns me up to think I wished him dead. I didn't, not really. But the point of all this is that you don't have to worry that I'm still in love with him.'

'Why are you telling me this now?' Ricky's eyes were bright with hope.

'Oh why do you think, you idiot? I love you. I've tried not to, but I just do.'

He smiled and vaulted across the room to sit at her side on the sofa. He stroked her cheek and then kissed her. 'You're just what I've always wanted,' he said.

★　★　★

They had not said a word since the others left the dining-room. Both locked in their own thoughts and memories, neither knew where to begin. They sat at either end of the table, separated by twelve feet of walnut wood that might just as well have been twelve miles.

'Patty told me she couldn't have any more children,' said Charles, finally. 'That it was her only chance to keep John. I drove her down to London that night and she registered the birth several weeks later. Then when she had Ronnie I found out she'd lied about that. But I never guessed about Jack. Not until Maggie Alsop told me. Then I wondered why I hadn't seen it all along. He has your eyes.'

'We both have my mother's eyes,' said Rebecca.

'Yes, yes, I see that now. I mean, I don't because I didn't know your mother very well. But I can see why he would look like you. I wish you'd trusted me with the truth.'

'I could say the same about you.'

'I know.'

'I didn't con you into marrying me so I could become respectable. Yes, I did pursue you, but it was because I loved you. Not because I was after your money or the Priory. Not that I wasn't happy here. To start with. Why the hell did you sleep with Maggie, Charles? Paying the money to keep her quiet, I could understand. But sleeping with her?'

'I wish I could give you an answer, but I don't have one. I won't insult your intelligence by saying that she ensnared me. I was lonely, I think, and I like sex as much as the next man.'

'It's not like I ever refused you. Not even when I sensed you'd stopped loving me.'

'No! I never stopped loving you, Rebecca. I suppose I had this ideal of you. You were pure when we met. Then to find that you might not have been. That Jed had made love to you before I did.'

'Except he didn't. No one did.'

'Well, I know that now.'

'What if I had turned out to be Jack's mother, Charles? What would you be saying to me now?'

'I don't know, Rebecca. All I know is that my life is miserable without you. Do you love Jed?'

'No. Jed just understood. Or at least I thought he did. I had no idea he'd told Maggie those lies. I still love you.'

'Despite everything?'

'Despite everything.'

He stood up and walked to her end of the table, sitting down in the chair nearest to her. He reached out his hand and stroked her cheek. She caught it with her own, as the tears began to fall. 'Will you forgive me? Not just for Maggie but for lying about Jack?'

'I was thinking the other day,' she said. 'How it's always easier to forgive our own mistakes than other people's. I never forgave Frank, even though when I look back I understand that he had every reason to be angry his wife had become pregnant by another man. Not that it excused what he did, but it must have been a blow to him. But then I remembered how many times she forgave him for the beatings. That was as much a betrayal as her sleeping with Sam Jenkins. Even more so, because he was her husband and he should have treated her kindly. He should have forgiven her for her one lapse just as she forgave him for his many mistakes. What I'm saying is that of course I forgive you. That doesn't mean it doesn't hurt, but I can see you've been hurt too. If I'd been honest with you from the beginning . . . '

'Darling, don't. You were a child then, and I remember how sad you always seemed at that time. You must have been terrified for Jack. And even if Jack had been yours, I should have been more understanding. You're right. We are apt to forgive our own mistakes before we forgive others. But in your case, there's nothing to forgive. Rebecca.' He leaned across the table to her. 'Becky,' he said, smiling. 'My Becky.'

* * *

Rebecca had made drinks for everyone who remained at the Priory. Ricky, Esther, Jack and Lizzie. They sat out on the terrace drinking them. She smiled to see Esther and Ricky together. Esther was always meant to be a part of their family and now it seemed it would be official. Things were strained with Jack, but he had changed so much since he was a child. He was more mature and not as hot-headed. The only thing that would make the scene complete was if Charlotte was there. And Bobby, said a quiet voice inside her.

She sensed that there were unseen problems with Jack and Lizzie, but nothing that affected their love. Then she heard Esther murmur to Lizzie, 'It's all over now. We're not going to say anything.'

'Thank you,' Lizzie whispered. At that, Jack leaned over and kissed her head, before giving a thumbs up to Ricky and Esther. One day, thought Rebecca, I may know what that's all about. But there had been enough revelations for one day.

'Who's that?' said Charles, looking out towards the Priory gates.

A man was walking towards them. He was some distance off, but Rebecca thought he was wearing an eye patch. It spoke to something deep inside of her. She stood up unsteadily. It could not be. Could it?

'Oh my God,' said Ricky. He stood up, knocking his chair over as he did so. He ran down the path, ahead of Rebecca, who lurched after him, still unable to keep a steady grip on her emotions. She sensed rather than saw Charles just behind her. They had all realized together.

The man stopped when he saw them, seeming to falter.

'Do I know you?' he asked when they drew nearer. 'Please tell me that I know you.'

★ ★ ★

He recognized the house the moment he arrived at the gates, but most of his memories were still murky. He recalled a funfair and men screaming and shouting. Alarmed, he almost turned and ran. But common sense told him that these memories were years old. All was calm now and he had nothing to fear from this place.

He saw a young man with his face running towards him, followed by a pretty middle-aged woman with lovely blue eyes. His blue eyes. A man with a scarred face was close behind her. Up on the terrace other people stood and watched him as he made his approach.

The woman was the first to answer his question. 'Bobby,' she said as tears ran down her cheeks. 'My Bobby.'

She threw her arms around him. The young man who looked like him and the man with scars did the same. Even though he could not remember everything clearly he knew without a doubt that he had found the people who belonged to him.